Books I and II
of the Arthur Series

Harper Fox

FoxTales

FoxTales Publications
www.harperfox.net

Books I and II of the Arthur Series
Copyright © 2017 by Harper Fox
ISBN 978-1-910224-06-9

Cover art by Harper Fox
Cover image licensed through Shutterstock

Book I

When First I Met My King

Harper Fox

Chapter One

Once upon a time there was a king.

Once upon a time there was a king, and his kingdom was an abandoned fort and twenty bare acres of moorland, far and away in the north of Britannia, shadowed by Hadrian's great Wall. *Vindolanda*, the Romans had called it. *The fair meadows*.

Once upon a time there was a king, and the king's name was Tertius, which means *third*. His mother, who believed in the ancient magic of threes, had rejoiced at his birth. Three fine sons!

The year before, the king had been a prince, just like Primus and Secundus, his brothers. Their father—a tribal chieftain named Ban, who'd served with the army, learned Latin, earned honours and been let keep his land—had named his boys with numbers in this dispassionate Roman way, but he hadn't loved them any the less for that.

Tertius had inherited his kingdom one wild spring night, when a gale had blown back from Ban's fair meadows the sounds and scents of a raiding party of Picts, ferocious hunters no longer held in check by Roman swords. Tertius had been away, hunting on the ridge beyond the Wall. He'd become so adept with his father's army spear that he'd earned the nickname Lance.

In the chamber Ban had shared with Elena, three surviving deerhounds lay in a heap on the bed. Lance set the spear aside and clapped his hands, and they got down reluctantly, tucking their tails. He reached into the still-warm pile of clothes beneath them and extracted one of Ban's woollen tunics. He unfastened his jerkin, shrugged out of it and quickly pulled the tunic over his head.

No, not Ban's. This garment smelled of dogs and better days. Lance stared through the moonlit weave. Elena, happier with a spear than a spindle in her hand herself, had nevertheless made each of her three fine sons his own tartan to wear, and this one belonged to Secundus, who'd beaten Lance into the world by the barest half hour.

Secundus, his brother and twin. *Like Romulus and Remus*, Ban had declared, proudly showing them off in the temple of Mithras, whose destruction was not nearly as complete as poor Tomas thought. *Like Holly and Oak*, Elena had cried out in the depths of her sacred cave. Lance, who veered from boyhood to manhood and back six times at least in a day, sat down on the edge of the bed and wept.

He tried, anyway. But his heart was like a dead coal. His sobs tore at him like sickness. He should have given all the clothes away, if he'd really cared for the souls who lived on at Vindolanda. Ban's Roman togas and cloaks could have been sold, and Elena's fine robes, because she'd been a queen indeed, a Votadini noble from the tribe beyond the Wall. But he hadn't. He'd left it all here to be slept on by dogs. He didn't care, even if every breath he drew through tunic's fabric put his brother back in his arms. On cold nights they too had slept tangled like deerhounds, unaware of where one of them stopped and the other began.

Lance fell silent and sat up. The dogs were watching him. When he got to his feet, they tried to follow him, but he stopped them at the door. He was the king of Vindolanda, after all. "No," he said. "Not you last ones. You stay here and mind my fort."

Chapter Two

The night wasn't fit for a dog. Lance's deerskin boots tracked firmly over the turf, but he understood that his body was obeying him from habit and willpower alone. The air was cold in a way he'd never experienced before. His chest made a hollow sound when he breathed in. He climbed the slope to the main street as quickly as his stiffening limbs would allow.

The road lay like a frozen moonbeam. Just within Lance's earliest memories, chariots had bowled along it, and its stones had rung to the beat of gleaming horses. The beasts and the men astride them had been mythical heroes to the boy, from hooves to scarlet crests. Not all the soldiers had vanished, of course—many were locals, like Ban, or tough souls from Gaul, or Batavia over the northern sea, used to the climate and fond of their native-born wives. They had merged into the landscape like rain. Only now, ten winters later, were green cracks appearing in the finely laid stone.

Two women were running down the moonbeam. The elder was covering ground with long, efficient strides, but the girl beside her was stumbling, sobs breaking out of her in clouds of steam.

The baker's wife, Cerys—one of Elena's cave-sisters, up to her elbows in dough by day, on nights like this a priestess—and her daughter, Lance recognised, raising a hand to hail them.

They came to a ragged halt in front of him. "Lance," Cerys said. Ice had formed around her lips and in the pleats of her long braid. "You can't go up there tonight."

The cold had entered Lance's skull. On some full-moon nights, his mother had allowed him, alone of all his brothers, to accompany her to the cave. On others, he'd been smilingly ordered to stay clear. "Is it... Is it because of the dragon?"

"What? No. But the wild things are beginning to die out in the open. A deer without a mark on her, just lying by the lough. We'd have brought her down with us, but the girl began to choke on the very air."

They were both dressed for the rites, in long dark woollen robes. Sheepskin capes too, but none of it was doing Dara any good. She was doubled up, clutching her mother's arm. Like most children of the settlement, she'd been hanging on by a thread, waiting for springtime, sunshine and good food. Lance took off his cloak. "Why did you go up?"

"Why does Father Tomas drag us to his miserable hut of a church in all weathers and winds?"

"Because he thinks his god gets angry and sends punishments. Is that what the dragon does too?"

Cerys looked disgusted. "Of course not. But she misses your mother. And she sees so little of the rest of us these days, she's beginning to fear we're dead."

"She's very nearly right." Lance bundled Dara into the cloak. "Take her down. Tomas is bringing everyone into the praetorium overnight—look, I can see their lights. Go there."

"What about you? Take back your cloak, stupid boy!"

13

"Make her breathe through the wool. I'm only going far enough to fetch that deer. We need meat."

He watched them retreat down the hill. Then he turned to face north, where the Herdsman stretched out starry limbs across the sky. At the Herdsman's foot, the star the Romans called Arcturus glowed like a tawny coal, comforting somehow amongst all the bitter diamonds. In his right hand the Herdsman bore an upturned crescent, hard to see against the shimmer of the full moon. *Corona borealis*, Tomas had called it: the crown of the north, but Elena had said it was a cup, a cauldron of rich, hot broth you could lift to your mouth, drink deeply and survive...

Lance's head spun. His empty belly clenched so hard that pain rang through him like a bell. He could move faster without the cloak, which had never been his anyway. He set out for the line of the great Wall.

This had always been his favourite route. He had often pursued it alone, through the fort's north gate and down the treacherous cliff-face steps to the burn. The stream's course had worn, over unimaginable time, a V-shaped gap in the ridge Elena called the Dragon's Spine, the tilted outcrop of black, enduring rock where the emperor Hadrian had set up and held his frontier. Holes in their natural barricade had not pleased the Romans, but the stream supplied water for all the fort's needs, and they had straddled it with a turreted tower built into the line of the Wall. This, too, was falling into disrepair, or being aided to it by Picts and villagers in need of stone for their sheep enclosures. Lance had always found it easy to scramble under its archway and into the moorland beyond. He did so now, forgetting his weariness and pain.

He had never understood the differences he felt when he entered the world to the north side of the ridge. He knew that the

soon, but she felt the stubborn force of cohesion that burned deep inside him. The spear flashed. He made his move.

Spring and run. They were one, the boy and the hare, in the first instant of the chase: he was upright and off as quick as she. Then they ran and ran.

***

She was exhausted. How had she failed to shake off her pursuer? He had no dog, and when his first cast with his wooden spear had missed, he should have given up. Nothing on two legs could challenge the pace of the hare. And yet, whenever she slowed, over the thrum of her heart she heard him, feet light on the turf, drawing ever closer. He had coursed her from the lough almost all the way to the base of the cliffs on the north side of the ridge. They shot up, black and threatening, cutting off the moor. Her game was up. She released it with reluctance. The hare-form ate little: could thrive, it seemed, on freezing fog and moss. It had been useful. Now there would be pain.

Lance dropped to a panting halt in the cliff shadows. He could barely remember why he'd been running. It made no sense to have chased so skinny a creature this far—even caught, cooked and eaten, it wouldn't repay him the energy he'd expended. He glanced around hopelessly. The moor was empty, not a flicker of movement from the black crags to the places where the horizon melted coldly into sky.

Shivering, he picked his way through frozen tussocks towards the foot of the cliff. Something—an angle of the moonlight, maybe—had thrown into sudden view the entrance to a cave. He stumbled in blindly, past caring if a wolf-pack had claimed it first.

The cave wasn't deep. Its earth floor was dry. As well as his meal, Lance had lost all chance of getting back to the village tonight. Dropping onto his backside, drawing his knees to his chest, he decided not to care that he'd probably die before morning. There were other things to think about: that voice, the sound of sunlight, still resounding in the chambers of his skull, and…

And the paintings. There were outlines on the cave's far wall, vivid in the moonlight.

Lance stared. Once, long ago, he'd eaten a mushroom of the wrong sort, and except that mushrooms of any kind had vanished from the fields at the beginning of this eternal winter, he wondered if he could have done it again.

He could see horses. Not tall ones like those the Romans had brought: more akin to his own old pony, whose unquestioning, warm-breathed friendship he'd pushed far to the back of his mind after the famine had claimed her. Even smaller, though, by contrast with the stick-like human figures, their bellies round, black-tipped legs vigorous, bodies just here and there daubed with a vivid ochre.

There were cattle, too, some recognisable to him, and one vast ox, which surely must have been someone's hungry fantasy. Even more bizarre, a fur-covered elephant, drifting as if through an unending dream, a little deeper into the shadows of the cave… Lance had heard of these beasts in the Roman books from which Father Tomas had tried to teach him Latin, had smiled at stories of the Carthaginian general who had gone into battle perched on the back of one. Reaching out frost-cracked fingertips, Lance touched the painting and smiled.

A little of the black pigmentation came off on his skin. Surprised, he eased back. It was just a few grains, but he didn't want to damage the finely drawn thing. How had it survived, if it dissolved so easily?

He looked around. Something had changed in this ancient shelter, something recent. Perhaps a prevailing wind had altered, some shielding outcrop fallen. Yes, the wall was damp. The endless winter was reaching its erasing touch even into this last refuge. The next time some outcast found his way to the wrong side of the ridge, the paintings would be gone.

He wished it wasn't so.

Then something scraped and moved in the depths of the cave, and Lance forgot everything in terror. He jolted back. His nerves were raw with starvation, and he stood for a moment in rigid silence, pressing his breath deep into his lungs. The scraping came again. The lights of pity and love which had briefly flared in his mind flickered out. He was a rigid knot of self-preservation once more.

There was just the outside chance that the sound could be his hare. Hunger sank its claws into his gut, so sharp that he couldn't bear to remain still an instant longer, and he edged into the shadows of the cave.

Chapter Three

There was a bundle of rags, with sticks poking awkwardly out of it.

The bundle breathed. It twitched, issued a rasping cry, and used its sticks to try to scrabble away from him. The movement allowed him to distinguish a head, a frail skull patched with strands of dead-white hair.

It was a woman, or the skeletal remains of one. Once she was as far away from him as the confines of the cave would allow, she pushed herself up into a sitting position. Lance thought he heard the scrape of her spine on the rock. She was panting hard, as if she'd run and run, and the cracked black hole of her mouth was flecked with foam. Then, to Lance's bemusement and horror, she began to grin, and after catching a few more wheezing breaths, she spoke.

"Well, boy? You've hounded me to earth. Don't you have the nerve to finish me?"

Lance stared at her. The voice was surprisingly clear and strong, not the rasp her toothless mouth had threatened. "What?"

he said, and his own sounded weaker—dry and thin with starvation. "I was chasing a hare. But I lost it."

"Hah. Not for want of trying. Come on, what's it to be? The knife? Or are you bold enough to snap my neck?"

"I'm not going to hurt you," Lance said, perplexed. "Who are you?"

She seemed to give it thought. She crouched herself together, drawing her knees to her chest. In the depth of her milky eyes, Lance saw a glimmer of amusement, and he dared a step closer to her, tugged by an indefinable curiosity. "I am," she murmured, as if to herself, barely audible, drawing the boy a little closer still. "I am… the *witch*!"

Lance leapt back. She had unfolded with a shout, arms and legs thrust out at him like spikes. He caught his heel on a stone, and landed with a thump on his back.

Immediately he scrambled up, tears of pain and fright stinging his eyes. Through their distorting veil he watched her resume her woodlouse curl against the wall. It took him a while to realise that she was wheezing with laughter. It shook her bony body like a storm. When she managed to draw breath, it exploded from her in a wild cackle that bounced off the walls of the cave and startled a handful of bats from their roost. Her eyes became slits and streamed with water. *"Witch!"* she rasped again, and rocked under another shrieking convulsion.

The word meant little to Lance. It was her movement that had scared him, triggering the reflex that would have saved him from a lunging boar or the strike of an adder. *Witch* was a name Father Tomas used for any elderly woman of the village who had met with his disapproval. *Send your children to me for their stories, my lord Ban, not to that old witch.* Gathering himself together, he saw that she was still laughing at him, and for an instant considered finishing her off with a knife or a stone in very fact.

But the shock she had given him had shaken some frozen part of him loose. Whoever she was—whatever her odd sense of humour—she was a creature even weaker and poorer than himself. And Ban, although his concern for his children's education had been patchy, had always insisted on one thing: you never raised your hand, nor if you could help it so much as your voice, to a woman, an elder or a child. *You display them perfect courtesy, boy. Because I am a king, and you are my son.*

The memory sent a thread of gold through Lance's mind. It was the first link, between the father he had loved and the one who had deserted him by vanishing into death. Only when it was forged did Lance realise what an abyss of black rage it had crossed. He swallowed hard, and brushed dry earth off his clothes. "Ma'am," he said. "My name is Lance. I am the son of Ban, the king of Vindolanda. If you are in want, I will help you, if I can."

It took a few seconds, but the shrieking cackle stopped. Wiping her eyes, the old woman scrutinised him. "You will help me?" she said. "What will *you* do for me, prince of Vindolanda?"

Prince of Nowhere. The voice in his head had been a man's, and young as green oaks in springtime. He'd have pointed out to her that now, in the wake of slaughter and grief, he was king, but he didn't want to set her off laughing again. "Well," he replied cautiously, "you do seem hungry. Maybe I can catch you something to eat."

"Hmm. And maybe I'd let you, if you wouldn't faint and die of the cold three steps outside of this cave."

Lance opened his mouth to protest. But when he thought about setting off once more across the marsh, a weariness dropped on him, so massive and terrible that it sent him to his hands and knees, head spinning, a veil of red descending over his eyes.

"Here," said the old woman, softly. "Here, child."

She was sitting beside him. Lance couldn't recall her leaving her spot by the cave wall, nor being aided to sit there himself. He watched, dizzy and passive, while she ferreted about in the folds of her torn black robes, and to his surprise, produced a handful of hazelnuts. Looking at them in her dirt-creased palm, he felt a wash of sickness: she smelled appalling, or one of them did. Either way, his manners pricked him again, and he said, weakly, "Thank you," and took them from her hand.

She must have managed to roast them somewhere. They were dry, and crumbled deliciously in his mouth. His spit gave a long-starved squirt, and he put a hand to his lips in embarrassment. The old woman cackled softly at him, nodding her head back and forth. "There," she said. "When you feel better, go and fetch me my supper."

The hazelnuts did him a disproportionate amount of good. He sat for a little while in the light from the setting moon, feeling strength creep back into his limbs. Then he set out, spear in hand.

He couldn't hope to stalk anything at this hour, but his feet took him unerringly down through the bracken and the marsh towards the burn. The air felt no warmer around him, but something had shifted or changed: under a frozen skin, the stream was now running fiercely with meltwater from the hills. Here and there it had carved out pools for itself, where it glimmered with a crystalline light.

In the first pool Lance came to, shining grey and brown, belly dappled with pale rainbows, a massive trout was circling beneath the ice. Instinctively Lance dropped low so as not to shadow the pool, but the fish was spiralling with such calm intent that he thought it wouldn't have noticed him anyway. It barely flinched when Lance struck with the spear: quivered on the end of it like a strange flag when he raised it triumphantly high above his head.

When he got back, the cave was full of firelight, a flickering beacon across the moor. He didn't know where the old woman had found the kindling, or the strength to gather it, but she was sitting between the rocks in the entrance, poking contentedly at the flames. She took the fish from him wordlessly, jerking it off the spear with her bare hands and spiking it through with a bronze cooking spit she had also procured from somewhere. She balanced the spit on two stones, nodded in satisfaction, and began to turn it, apparently oblivious to the heat.

Lance wondered if he'd fallen asleep. Barely a moment seemed to have passed, but a wonderful fragrance was filling the cave, and the trout's skin had turned golden brown. Hunger racked him. He tried not to look or breathe. He watched the painted wall determinedly while she ate, pulling the fish apart with her fingers and attacking it indiscriminately, guts, bones and all.

She wasn't the quietest eater. Lance kept his face politely expressionless, focussing his mind on the dance of the giant ox, the horses and hunters, reborn in the flames. Perhaps they were meant to be seen by firelight. He tried to lose himself in wondering what their makers had been like, what their loves and their wants must have been, and he almost succeeded...

"Well," the old woman said to him, holding him out a big piece of trout on the spit, "what do *you* think they wanted?"

Lance stared at her. "The same things that I do," he said without thinking, and waited for her to laugh at him.

But she only nodded. "That's right," she said. "A warm fire, company, and most importantly a full belly. Matters of the spirit should come first, I'm sure, but they seldom do. So eat this, before your britches slide off you entirely."

He couldn't believe there was anything left of the trout to be had. At his last glance, the old woman had reduced it to fins and tail. But here was a fair rich slice, dripping with grease from the fire. Lance, who had not yet learned to question gift horses, took the food and the mind-reading at face value, and began to eat.

He fell asleep almost immediately afterwards, hardly taking the trouble to wipe his mouth and lie down. It was a deep and dream-filled sleep, in which he turned into a hare and ran and ran after Elena and Ban's departing spirits, but still could not catch up. Transforming back into his own flesh, he wept and mourned as he had never done while waking; lay down by the grass-covered Wall and howled, until a strange, low-pitched singing joined with his own sounds of grief, and he lifted his head.

A dragon was floating over the ridge. Enthralled, tears forgotten, Lance staggered to his feet and tried to run toward the dancing, glittering beast. But she opened her great jaws and sang to him that the time for their joining had not yet come, and then, absurdly, she placed the end of her tail in her mouth as if to end the discussion, and Lance woke smiling.

***

He was alone in the cave. He felt strangely bereft until he heard the old woman scuffling about outside. He got up stiffly, stretched, and went out into the weak daylight, noting to his astonishment that despite its shroud of misty clouds, the sun was nearing zenith. "Why did you let me sleep so long?"

She stopped pulling handfuls of greenery out of the rivulet that ran past the cave, and fixed him with a brightly sarcastic gaze. "Forgive me, Your Highness. I forgot all about your schedule of public engagements. Here, take these—we'll have watercress soup for our breakfast. Boiling it should take the fluke-worm out."

She looked much better this morning. Now she was just a grubby old woman, not an insect-puppet jerked around by unseen strings. Lance was bemused by the changes in her. She had put on weight overnight, disproportionate to the meal he'd been able to give her. Somehow she'd contrived to stitch the cobweb tatters of her robe back into one garment. It wasn't overly clean and nor was she, but both had acquired a dignity. More mysteriously, her balding pate was now covered with steel-grey hair, which she had braided into a plait as thick as a tow rope.

She watched him alertly as they ate their soup, which was almost too bitter even for a courteous prince to swallow without pulling a face. "Disgusting, isn't it?" she said cheerfully. "That's its power—to cure you of dark thoughts. Tell me what such a fine young sprig of the White Fields aristocracy is doing out here, starving in the marshes."

"We ran out of food in the village last night. I came out to hunt, and to bring back a deer that had frozen to death by the lough."

"Is that all?"

"Yes, ma'am. Except that I saw a hare, or I thought I did, and I chased her out here, or..." He hesitated at the golden gleam in the old woman's eyes. "Or I thought I did."

"And is *that* all?"

What more did she want? "I dreamed about a dragon," he said suddenly, not knowing why. "And I keep hearing a voice. He calls me *Prince of Nowhere*, and he says he's on his way."

She sat up alertly. "Ah. Pass me my scrying glass, boy."

"Your..."

"My glass! Well, whatever I have these days—the cauldron will do. Let me see."

Lance unhooked the bowl and handed it to her. She stared into the murky remains of their breakfast, swirled the liquid around, thrice to the right, thrice to the left, then uttered a raven-like squawk. "Aha! It is so. And so soon!"

"What is so, ma'am?"

"You'll know soon enough. We must stir our shanks. No wonder the morning is brighter, the streams running clear." She squinted into the cauldron. "Oh, this bowl's a good one for scry. There's Vindolanda, burning down. And there's good King Ban, running for his life while Elena stayed and swung a sword and then a kitchen knife, and then a pan, to try and save her bairns."

Lance recoiled. She was insane. He had to act accordingly. Instead of jumping the fire to strangle her, he said, tightly, "My father's dead. Don't dare to speak of him so."

"It's not the time to speak of him at all. We have important matters in hand."

"I said don't *speak* of him so!"

He lurched to his feet, overturning the cauldron. The last of the watercress splashed across the floor of the cave. The old woman didn't move. "You had better go," she said. "My bones ache with fever, and in return for this outrage, you must fetch me the herb that grows in the ferns to the east of the lough. It looks like a daisy, but its leaves smell clean and sweet."

"You don't look as if you have a fever." Temper dying, Lance hung his head. "I am sorry. I could have burned you."

"Never mind about it now. Hurry, boy," she added harshly, as he hesitated to leave her. "I am very ill, and the plant will cure me."

Lance was back before the shadows of the crags had retreated far on the moor. He knelt before the old woman, and watched in dismay as she snatched the handful of flowers and leaves he had brought, glanced through them once and hurled the lot into the fire. "Stupid boy," she said. "Did your mother teach you nothing? Those are weeds, noxious rubbish. Go back and search again."

Lance sat back on his heels and looked at her, confused. Elena had certainly taught him to recognise feverfew, and that was what he had picked. There was little point in arguing with her—his evidence was sizzling wetly on the fire.

Perhaps she was delirious. Obediently therefore he got up and went to fetch more. He checked every stem he gathered to make sure he wasn't confusing it with camomile. This time his offerings met with a worse reception still: she dashed them from his hand, swearing at him again in a strange language he was quite grateful not to understand.

He wanted to be offended, but under the rage in her eyes he could see a terrible anxiety. Pity stirred in him. Was she scared of dying? She had seemed so fierce: he wouldn't have thought she'd fear her own end in this way. Then, how little he knew of the world! *Good King Ban, fleeing for his life...* Impossible, but his life was full of uncertainty, even where he had thought it most fixed. "Please, my lady," he said, mindful of her age and his own ignorance. "Describe it to me once more."

Her hand flew out and caught him a painful crack on the mouth. Lance gasped. No-one outside of his family had dared to strike him. Ban, for all he had freely chastised his sons himself, would never have permitted an outsider to lay hands on them. Carefully, tasting his own blood, he got to his feet and walked away.

He gathered the feverfew again. *The same*, he breathed to himself: it was the same. If she turned it down this time, he would tie her up, infuse it for her himself and feed it to her. Remembering how Elena had grasped his nose to make him open his mouth for medicine, he grinned. What would the old monster do if he tried that?

For the first time it occurred to him that he didn't know her name, and he wondered why he hadn't asked her. Why she hadn't told him. Never mind. He could think of enough things to call her. The same—these damned plants were the exact same as before. Nevertheless Lance made his way further and further round the edge of the lough, in the hope of finding some that were fresher. Perhaps that was what she had meant.

His mouth hurt where she'd hit him. Although the terrible cold of the night before had let go its grip on the land, all was still grey, the noon light a dead glare behind clouds. Since the raid on the village, Lance had hardly noticed how little sunlight he'd seen. He remembered the boisterous springs that had once swept White Meadows, the crystalline windblown light that made the coltsfoot dance and sent the lambs scattering wildly over the fields. Blackthorn blossoms would open and shine before the leaves came, bright on the dark thorny wood. Celandines would gape and give back the sun in the oily sheen of their petals, and between one day and the next the marshes would turn pink in a delicate flush of bogbean. Now it was as if his eyes had forgotten how to recognise any colours but grey, sedge green and mud brown. Suddenly, acutely, Lance missed the sun.

As if in response to his longing, the clouds parted a little over the shore. A thin light, faint but very clear, picked out a glimmer of gold at the lough's edge. Its beauty passed through Lance like a blade, but, determined not to lose track of his intentions, he lowered his head and made his way stolidly toward it. Perhaps the pale gleam was that of young feverfew leaves. Perhaps he'd find what he needed there.

Yes, fresh leaves. That was what they were when Lance crouched down to gather them. He was ankle deep in the lough, but had lately spent so much of his time with wet, cold feet that he had barely noticed. He put his hand into the water and reached out.

Shock jolted through him. Another hand was there in the water with his—a long, pale hand with a tracery of scales. It grasped his wrist for an instant, as if in recognition or greeting, then vanished.

And then, instead of leaves, he was looking at a sword.

Chapter Four

He sank to his knees in the shallows. He was chilled, his reflexes slow. He raised his hand, shaking water from it. Fear tried to lurch up out of his gut: what had touched him?

But he wasn't afraid, only depthlessly surprised. He looked at his wrist. The only part of him not freezing cold was the place where that shining hand had touched him. He was warm there as if kissed by Bride herself, by the blazing goddess of springtime and fire Elena welcomed at Imbolg, for all Father Tomas reproved her and told her that Bride was Maria, the mother of Christ. He felt as if he would be warm there forever, and for a moment that meant more to him than the beautiful sword still shining at him up out of the reeds.

He watched it blindly, his breath coming shallow and fast in his throat. Then it shifted, as if it would slide back into the depths of the lough, and Lance surged forward to grasp it.

He got clumsily to his feet, taken off-balance by the weight. Water sheeted off the blade, and what he'd thought to be rust fell away, only a layer of mud and silt over bronze so fresh and bright it could have been forged yesterday. But Lance, the soldier's son, knew weaponry, and this was nothing created by a Roman of his father's generation, or even many generations before.

It didn't look Roman at all. Unconscious of the sunlight now streaming down around him—one shaft of it, in all the shadowed marshland—he turned over the sword from the lough. It was plain, heavy, but so beautifully balanced that he had no difficulty wielding it. Its wooden hilt—bog oak, he thought, or yew, perhaps—was delicately inlaid with spirals of copper and gold.

A stone had been set into the hilt, a flattish disk with some kind of spiral marking upon it. The bands that held it together were streaked with verdigris. When Lance tried to make out its pattern, he couldn't.

His head spun and ached with the effort of failure. As a child, he'd have run with this wonderful thing to the village, to show anyone who'd listen what he'd found. But the weight of the sword in his hand, and some solemnity of light in the air all around him, told him in silence that such times were past for him. He had to go back, and straight away, but as a guardian and provider, not a foolish boy.

Then his brow cleared, and he lifted his head. He was child enough still to be wildly excited. The gap in the clouds closed above him unnoticed, and he splashed his way out of the lough: began running, as soon as his feet hit dry land, as fast as he could for the cave.

Only when he was slowing up, breathless, in the shadow of the crag, did he remember the old woman's herbs. She was standing on the turf outside the cave as if waiting for him, and he braced up. He no longer minded what she said to him or even what she did, but he was sorry to have forgotten her needs.

"Did you find it?" she called out to him eagerly. Her robes and her long grey hair were drifting on the wind, and from this distance it almost seemed to Lance that she was smiling.

"Yes," he called back. "It grows fresh at the top of the lough. But then I found this, and I forgot about it. I'm sorry, ma'am. I'll go back straight away."

But the old woman didn't look sick anymore. She crossed the space between them in long, loping strides, and she held out her arms for him. Lance, astonished, walked into her embrace. "Dear Lance," she said. "My dear good boy."

***

She wouldn't, or couldn't, tell him anything about the sword. She laughed at his solemn determination to go home, told him they'd survive a while longer without him, and sent him off once more to hunt.

That night by the fire, however, a spirit of festivity seemed to come over her. The sword was set out carefully on the floor of the cave between them, where they could both see and admire it. She produced from somewhere a tiny flask and offered it to Lance, her face creasing up like a horseshoe bat's with merriment. Lance drank and obligingly choked, and she burst into cackles and finished off the potion herself without turning a hair. All she would say about his find was that he should keep it—consider it his own, until time and event told him otherwise. His other questions she deflected with a vacant, senile smile Lance knew by now was entirely feigned.

She did, however, at last tell him her name. It was late, the fire dying, the boy almost asleep on the cloak she'd laid out for him. *Viviana*, she whispered, and the word fell like rain into his mind, like a cool round stone into a well. Then, when his eyelids were

33

flickering: *Viviana. The word-shapes change. The stream divides, but not the source. Viviana. Viviana.*

She watched over him that night. He was almost restored to himself, and she could not push on events any further. It no longer lay in the power of Viviana and her kind to awaken or summon the land's buried dragon. That task now lay in hands that held swords, and all she could do was try to ensure that those hands were the right ones.

In the ancient darkness left behind when the flaring Roman lights had gone—in the new darkness cast by the shadow of Christ—she and her sisters had reached out for one another, and had done what they could. When she threw her knucklebone dice across the floor of the cave, or sang to the fire until its flames turned blue and danced for her, she thought they had succeeded.

She thought all would be well. She was sorry she'd told him about his father, but perhaps he'd disbelieved her, or forgotten her words in the thrill of discovery: he was sleeping with one hand on the hilt of the sword. He knew the use of one already, thank heaven—she was much too old now for that kind of teaching— and a king was coming, a warrior with dragon blood in his veins.

Then, like all the mothers who had come before her, she knew that she mustn't sit and watch over what she'd sown. In the grey dawn, while he was still curled in his dreams, she got up silently and stretched, relieved at the prospect of her own rest. She thought about the hare, and the freedom of that wild running, but she was done with it for now, and the boy had behaved so well by her that she didn't need it. Didn't need anything further from this world, and so she bent over the sleeping boy, allowing herself one regretful caress of his hair.

On her way out of the cave she paused, and wiped off with her thumb one of the few remaining traces of the painted, dancing beasts. The wall was empty now, a rainwashed blank. Then Viviana returned to the lough.

Chapter Five

Lance traced the old woman's footprints to the water's edge, and stood there calling her name. Fear stirred in his stomach. Anyone less likely to drown herself he couldn't imagine, but maybe she'd come to harm by accident. He waded a little way out and searched the reedy shallows. No sign. He waited, thigh-deep in water, beginning to shiver. Then he stripped off his tunic, breeches and boots, threw them to the shore and dived in.

Nothing. She was gone. The moors felt empty, emptier by far than before he'd met her. Loss went through him, keen as a knife. His bare two nights with her had felt in some way like time with his mother, redeemed from the jaws of death. She'd taken him in, and he in his turn had saved her.

He staggered out of the water, gasping for breath. He picked his clothes out of the reeds and put them on, becoming aware of the changes in the world around him. Last night he'd have frozen to death in the water. The night before, he'd have had to crack its surface to get in. He was cold now, but only as he would have been on any spring morning, coming up here with brothers and sisters to bathe.

He had to go. He'd promised Tomas he'd bring food to the survivors in the praetor's house. The deer would have thawed by now, and he was strong again and could carry it easily. Perhaps the old woman had set off before him and he'd find her alive and well down there, outraging the priest with her herbs and incantations.

Lance ran back to the cave. He had no scabbard for the sword and so pushed it through the slack in his belt. The weapon bumped awkwardly against his thigh as he began to retrace his route through the marsh. He could see the deer in the distance, sprawled where he'd left it. The flesh would still be good, and every scrap would be gratefully consumed, but foolish sorrow filled him at the sight of the carcase. Nothing should be dead on such a morning as this, not a beast or an old woman, not Elena, not brothers and sisters or...

The deer leapt upright. Pale by moonlight, here in the sudden sun the creature shone out brighter than hawthorn. A white hart! Lance stared in astonishment. No beast more magical roamed the loughs and moors. In Elena's stories, its appearance meant sovereignty, sacrifice, nobility. Lance's regrets about supper vanished. He watched, immobile, while the hart shook itself and trotted off, head high, towards the ridge.

On instinct Lance followed, not in the spirit of a hunter now but as a worshipper. How his mother and sisters would have exclaimed at such rare news! His father would have called together the men of the village and forbidden them to harm the beast.

For the first time since the raid, Lance felt no backwash of grief at these unstoppable *would-have* thoughts. Even his new disbelief and rage about Ban faded off into the distance. Maybe the old woman really had cured him of his sorrows with her throat-stripping watercress soup. Elena's myths of the white hart might be prophecies, joy returning to Vindolanda with the spring.

He stumbled up the last few steps of the crag. The Wall was falling into disrepair here, and it didn't take him long to reach its crest. He halted, one hand poised on the hilt of the sword.

The white hart had vanished. Instead, making their way boldly along the valley road to Vindolanda, a dozen men were riding.

Saxons! The thought flashed like lightning through Lance's mind. His only evidence was the colour of their hair, shining gold and red in the sun. Danes, perhaps... It didn't matter. Saxons and Vikings seizing land here, Goths and Vandals descending on Rome in such brutal hordes that the army had abandoned towns like Vindolanda and left them to burn... Every loss Lance had endured was the fault of raiders like these, a small-scale invasion he would stop with his own hands right now.

With his own sword. He unhitched the weapon and it seemed to leap to his grasp, no longer a burden but a living extension of himself and his rage. Yes, he would stop them, if his own blood had to be the price.

The riders came to a halt on the road. Had they seen him? Lance almost hoped so. He felt ten foot tall, a vengeful giant on the dragon's spine. But as he watched, one of the men pointed in the direction of the V-shaped notch in the ridge to the east, to the place where the burn poured through.

The turret, magical gateway guarding the moor. Lady Viviana's moor, Lance's sole refuge... Fury swept like a blizzard through his mind, whiting out all thought, all sense of self-preservation, all sanity. He dropped back down the north side of the Wall, landed lightly as a cat, and began to run.

***

It was Bear who had spotted the water. His guardian, a straight-spined old soldier of Roman descent named Ectorius, nodded in approval. The boy must learn to be aware of the needs of horses and troops, and become adept in meeting them. Their journey had been long, and the animals were thirsty. Ectorius nodded, giving permission for him to lead off toward the glittering burn.

They had almost reached the ruined turret when Bear reined in his horse and stood listening. Ectorius exchanged a glance with his own son, Gaius. Neither of them could hear anything but skylarks, and the long-billed water birds called curlew which sang so joyously up on these moors when the sun came out.

It was shining brilliantly now. The locals all the way from Pons Aelius in the east had complained of an endless winter, and although Ectorius had seen signs of it—barely the beginnings of growth in the fields, the people thin and weary, lambs few—all around them, this spring day was perfect. The good weather seemed to be following them. Gaius, a big, raw-boned lad, with a face as kind and ugly as his father's own, had teased Bear that the sun had started to shine from his regal backside, and the boy had begun to take such nonsense good-naturedly, instead of trying to engage his foster brother in mortal combat every time they quarrelled. Now, as often, Bear had seen or heard something imperceptible to other senses, and Ectorius had learned to take him seriously. "What is it?" he softly asked.

"I'm not sure. Someone coming, I think. But he moves like a cat, or the wind."

Ectorius drew his sword. He motioned to the armed grooms travelling with them to take up defensive positions. Their journey had been safe so far, but up here in the borders, so the tales said, little Pictish hunters could emerge from the very hills to seek their prey. Their reputation was uncanny. Blue ghosts who sailed in on the wind and snatched up lambs and babies from cradles... It was nonsense, of course, Celtic twilight, but nevertheless he made ready.

Yes. He could hear it now, too. Light, running footsteps. Bear had trotted his horse forward to meet the sound, almost into the shadow of the turret's arch. Ectorius didn't think there was much to worry about, and he knew that from now on he had to let the boy fight his own battles. Reining back his horse, gesturing to the others to do the same, he kept a discreet watch.

It was just a lad, and a skinny one at that. But he leapt with such force from the reeds behind the arch that Bear did not stand a chance: in an instant he was dragged from his mount and down into the stream. His thin, dirty assailant crashed into the water with him. "Saxon!" the newcomer bellowed, shoving Bear under the surface, sending rainbows flying. "Danish pig! This land will never be yours. I defy you!"

Bear was startled into passivity. He was winded, too, and shocked by the water's cold sting. It was an instant only. Ectorius watched in approval as he twisted out from under and sprang to his feet. His sword had never left his hand. "Saxon?" he demanded in his turn. "Dane? How dare you, you savage? I am prince of Cerniw, and my father was the son of the Dragon of the South, as good a Briton as ever lived!"

The blade flashed. The dark-haired lad staggered up out of the water and jumped back, but only far enough to draw his own weapon.

Ectorius leaned forward in his saddle. This stranger bore a sword such as the old Roman had never seen, and he wielded it well. Too well for his protégé? Ectorius tensed. If the boy fell, all was lost…

Then, suddenly, the very air changed. The flaring rage between Bear and his opponent seemed to fall out of it like scales. Bear had been schooled in the rules of combat, and apparently so had his opponent, although God alone knew where. Engagement with a worthy foe must be fair. Soldiers on the battlefield could hack at one another like butchers, but this boy had offered himself one-on-one. Bear found his balance, waited till the other was firm on his feet too, and made his move.

Blade hit blade, and sparks flew.

Ectorius watched the fight progress. Bear was putting into practice all he had been taught, and keeping his head, too, which could not always be counted on. The other, after his initial burst of rage, had settled into a combat stance that was almost cool, and heaven only knew where he had got that astounding sword. Bear was actually smiling—had breath and poise to ask, between parries, "Well, what are you, moorland warrior? A long-legged Pict?"

"*Pict?*" the other demanded, accurately mimicking Bear's outraged echo of *Saxon*. "I am Lance, son of King Ban of Vindolanda…" He paused, long enough to spring up the stream bank, obliging Bear to move after him, fighting uphill. "As good a Roman as ever drew breath."

"Oh? I am Roman, too, by upbringing."

The boy called Lance seemed to consider this, although he didn't ease the ferocity of his attack. "In that case we probably have no fight."

"Probably not," Bear admitted. He was getting the worst of it. Childishly he added, "But you started it!", and lunged in with an uncontrolled thrust whose force Lance effortlessly caught and turned against him, dumping him backover into the water once more.

The splash was considerable. Gaius roared with laughter. Lance put up his sword at once and waded in, one hand extended to help.

And Cerniw's heir lost his temper. He scrambled to his feet, evading the other boy's grasp. His hair swung round his face like a wet lion's mane, and he seemed from somewhere to gain a foot in height. "Peasant!" he snarled. "You have no idea who I am! How dare you block my way, here or anywhere in this land?"

Ectorius frowned in an effort to keep his face straight. It felt like only yesterday he had watched the child being chased by its nurse around his courtyard for a change of undergarments, but he held his tongue: like the fighting, within certain bounds he must let the budding regality have sway. Lance only looked disgusted. What a change came over that handsome face, when his smile was replaced by disdain! He turned his back and began to walk away.

A mistake. In this state of mind, Bear would not be ignored. And he was a good boy, Pendragon's heir, but he had the hot blood of both his parents—the warrior king, and the bride he had stolen, starting a war in the process, and she just as much of a spitting wildcat as her new lord could handle—running through his veins. He could only take so much, Ectorius knew, for all the lessons in courteous defeat he had tried so patiently to learn. He might have been gracious, had Gaius not laughed. Instead, he grabbed Lance by the shoulder, spun him round and knocked him down with a flying punch.

Ectorius jumped off his horse. "Arthur!" he barked. "Stop that at once. How dare you treat a brave warrior so shabbily?" He strode across the stream. A time would soon come when he would not be able to clout his ward over the head to restore his manners, but until then, Ectorius retained full parental privilege. Bear took the blow without flinching, as he had been taught, his eyes wide and fearless on his guardian's.

Then Ectorius glanced down. The lad lay motionless and pale on the turf. His eyes were closed. "By Our Lady, Art. What have you done?"

Arthur's mouth fell open. His face suffused with shame and horror. "He was defending his father's land, as you would have done yours," Ectorius said sternly. "And he has not the benefit of all your training, you spoiled child."

Arthur tore out of his grip. He crouched down beside Lance. He shook him, then collected himself and began to search for the injury. It didn't take long: tenderly he raised his head, reached beneath it and sat back with bloodstained fingers. "He fell onto a rock. I have killed him. Oh, Father Ector—the shame to me, that I should have served a noble enemy thus!"

Once more Ectorius repressed a smile. Round and rough-tongued enough in his daily speech, the boy did tend to poetry when he was upset. Somehow it sat well on him. Taking pity, Ectorius knelt down stiffly on the turf himself. He felt for Lance's pulse beneath his jaw. "Well," he said. "Perhaps we need not bury him *just* yet. Don't sit there gawping, child! Fetch me some water from the stream."

Chapter Six

Lance sat up gasping at the splash of ice-cold water into his face. He stared at the old man, then at the elder of his two companions, who was standing with his hands on his hips, clearly amused by this small drama. Then his attention was caught by his opponent, disarmed now and kneeling a few feet away, eyes fixed on the turf.

"What's wrong with you?" Lance asked mildly, dabbing at his split lip. "I'm all right."

Arthur jerked his head up. "Oh! Thanks be to Tamara, goddess of Cerniw's river," he said fervently. Then, when the old man cleared his throat: "To Iesus and his blessed mother, I mean. I ask your forgiveness, Lance of Vindolanda."

"Granted," Lance said unsteadily. "Forgive my calling you a pig. I thought you were..." The elder knight had hoisted him effortlessly to his feet and was dusting him down: embarrassed, Lance stepped away and tugged his clothes straight for himself. He tried to remember what he *had* been thinking, while he ran down from the top of the ridge. Very little. His mind seemed to have been caught in one long dream, from the time of the hunt in the snow until this very moment. What had woken him? He frowned at the sight of the bright-haired boy still kneeling on the grass. "I thought you were invaders. Where did you say you came from?"

"Cerniw—as far southwest as you can go without riding into the sea. Farmland, tin mines, not much else, but… it is very big, at least, the land I will inherit. Isn't it, Father Ector?"

"At present," Ectorius responded with feigned gravity. "Whether it stays that way will be up to you." He shook his head. "At the moment we seem set on tackling our enemies one by one. And you, young man—does all this territory belong to your father?"

Heat touched Lance's face. He'd made a large claim, hadn't he, when he'd declared he was King Ban's son? "No, sir," he said honestly. He pointed to the patch of grey stone in the distance that marked Vindolanda. "Just that settlement there."

"Valuable to us, nonetheless. We've travelled a long way, and don't want to risk the moors at night. Will your father make us welcome?"

Lance hesitated. The cobwebs of the dream were still all about him. There had been a running hare, some paintings on the inside of a cave, a strange old woman. She had told him things—some marvellous, some almost impossible to bear. "My father is gone," he said at last. He looked toward the village. "*I* will make you welcome."

"May heaven reward your hospitality," Ector formally replied. "I must introduce myself. I am Ectorius, of Londinium and the Forest Wild. That tall, ill-favoured gentleman there is my son, Gaius, and the scapegrace child still rightly on his knees at your feet is Artorius. Arthur, in his own rude Kernowek tongue."

There was something infinitely distressing to Lance in the sight of the young man's abasement. Nobody like that should ever

45

have to kneel. "Please get up," he said. "If there was ever cause of offence between us, it's forgiven."

This time Arthur took the hand extended to him graciously. "That's very noble of you, Prince of... What did you say it was called?"

"Vindolanda. It means *fair meadows*. Nowhere."

Arthur's grip tightened warmly. He surged to his feet like water-weighted barley after rain. "Then, as Father Ector says— heaven reward you, Prince of Nowhere. Oh, wait—I'm forgetting something."

Ector watched in satisfaction while his ward went to fetch the sword with his own hands. Having been pardoned for his crimes by his new friend, he was shining again, although Ector could see the experience had changed him: that, outside battle, he'd never attack an unready man again.

He picked the weapon up in a casual soldier's grip. Ector had taught him swordsmanship since he was tall enough to lift a wooden facsimile, on his feet and from horseback, carefully pitting him against the older, bigger Gaius, whose infuriating calm in victory and defeat had also taught him something. To the old man's surprise, he suddenly let the blade drop from his grasp. "What ails you now?" Ector demanded, striding over to help him. "Don't throw that about. It's a good one."

"Yes, I... I know. Father Ector," he whispered, going pale. "Do you hear that?"

Ector could hear nothing but the purr of the wind. He shook his head. "What do you hear, boy?"

"A kind of drumming, like the sound your heart makes in your ears at night. But deeper than that, slower..." Gently Art hefted the blade, turned it in the sunlight. "The hilt seems to warm in my hand. I don't feel as if there's any difference anymore, between..."

"Between what?" Ector glanced apprehensively at Gaius, who was giving Lance a leg-up onto a lead-rein horse. Ever since Arthur had been placed into his care, the boy had been subject to headaches and visions, sometimes so extreme that he would fall into a kind of seizure, an empty-eyed waking dream. It definitely wasn't convenient for him to start one now. Ector shook his shoulder. "Bear!"

"Between my insides and my outsides. If I close my eyes, I could merge with the earth and the air and disappear."

"Keep them open, then," Ector brusquely advised. "This young prince has offered us shelter. It's for you to lead our party there and honour his trust."

Arthur returned to himself with an effort. He stepped forward, reached up and placed the sword reverently back into Lance's hands. "It's a fine thing," he said. "Did you have it from your father?"

Lance drew a breath. Ector, after raising two sons, knew very well the look of a child considering a story, and a tall one, usually to cover a stranger truth. Then the boy's expression cleared. "No," he said frankly. "I found it in a lake."

Arthur smiled, as if this absurdity was just what he'd expected to hear. Now it was Ector's turn to shiver in the wing-shadow of a vision, and he looked away, pretending to wonder at the beautiful sweep of the land, the ridge where the legendary Hadrian had built his wall.

Gaius left Lance and came to stand beside him, concerned. "What's wrong, Father?"

"By God, Gaius! The sword from the lake!"

Chapter Seven

Arthur and Lance rode side by side down the track. Lance was speechless. He was twice as high off the ground as his old pony had ever carried him, and the beast beneath him now was a long-boned, fine-skinned chestnut dream by contrast. His knee bumped off the prince of Cerniw's, and he gasped and flinched away, for all he'd willingly tried to kill him not half an hour before.

Arthur shot him an amused glance. "All right, Your Majesty?"

"Don't call me that. My father ruled a village, not a nation. My boast was a vain one, made in anger—I'd be grateful if you would forget it."

"All right, then, Lance?"

He swallowed hard. The sound of his name—the simple question—from this stranger's mouth... His head was full of echoes from a past he'd never had. His bruised skull throbbed and his empty belly reminded him that half a fish in the wilderness, however magical, didn't make up for months of starvation. "I am fine," he said stoutly. "I've never ridden a horse like this, that's all."

"Really? What do you ride at home?"

"A pony. Or I did, at any rate. There was a famine, and..."

Arthur's jaw dropped. "You didn't."

"Of course we did. There's no room for petty affections when children are starving."

"I meant, did you personally..."

Lance wanted to lie. But some mix of horror and sympathy in the grey gaze fixed on him drew the truth out of his mouth, like a thorn from a wound. "Actually I hid in a barn and wept. But I was just a boy then."

"I see." Arthur rode on for a few paces. Once more his knee bumped against Lance's, this time deliberate, companionable. "This horse belongs to my foster father. She's served him well for ten years or so now, so he brings her as a spare, not his battle mount. Her name is Balana. Do you like her?"

"More than I can possibly say."

Arthur broke into laughter. "Come for a gallop, then! She might be past her prime, but she'll carry you like the wind."

"Won't Sir Ectorius mind?"

"Maybe. I'm expected to be young and foolish at present, though, and we can say I egged you on." He put a hand back to clap the rump of his sturdy black stallion, which capered and snorted in response. "Hengroen wants a run, too. Hold on—you can ride, can't you?"

"Of course. What do you mean?"

"Just that you don't seem too steady in your seat. Ector will skin me if you fall off and get hurt again."

Lance did his best to find purchase on the slippery leather beneath him. He was used to a broad, hairy back, mud and burrs providing traction. Once again, honesty broke through his pride. "It's this Roman saddle. I can't get a grip."

"Ah. You have to ease down into it. Let the horns at the front hold you in, and lean back against the cantle. That's it." Arthur watched in approval while Lance did his best to obey. "Don't be concerned. Father Ector says a man who learned to ride bareback will always be a better soldier than a spoiled brat like me. Saddles can get lost or stolen, but a horse will always have a spine. Are you settled?"

Lance could hardly breathe for excitement. "Yes!"

"Come along, then. Away!"

Gaius watched his foster brother and the ragged prince tear off down the valley. "That lad's giving ours a run for his money," he observed.

Ector grunted. "About time somebody did."

"Either that, or Bear will break his neck for him."

"Hah. Our moorland prince die happy, if so."

Gaius glanced at him in surprise. Ector was perceptive, but usually quite blind to this one trait in his ward. "Aye," he said cautiously. "It's a dangerous gift, though, isn't it—to make men love you?"

"What?"

"Er... nothing. Only the wind."

"I'll wager he's never sat a horse like my Balana. Look at the two idiots go!"

Well-hidden fear behind the smile in the old man's voice. Gaius sought to reassure him. A prosaic soul, he had found his place in life as his father's firm right hand, his practical support when the demands of caring for the prophesied king had worn him down. For himself, Gaius was still not convinced they were raising anything other than dangerous old Pendragon's unwanted brat. He had married again since poor Ygraine, Gaius had heard, and had sons whose claims were based on something better than their mother's abduction and rape. "I wouldn't worry about this sword. He's supposed to find it for himself, isn't he? In a stone, too, if I remember aright."

Ectorius scratched his head, still habitually short-cropped from his years in the Roman army. "Well, he has. The sword *from* the lake, remember—not *in* it. In a stone, from a lake... The old sorcerer spoke in riddles. And look at the thing, Gaius! It has to be the one."

"But it belongs to this boy Lance," Gaius said thoughtfully. "That's an inconvenience, isn't it? Unless…"

He shot a sideways glance at his father, and saw that Ectorius was half amused, half appalled by what he read there. "No, son," he said. "You're my good lad always. But there'll be no forcing of events, and we're this boy's guests now. Let's watch and let things happen as they will."

Gaius followed on obediently. *The sword from the lake*—words heard so long ago that they had merged with the background of the firelit kitchen in which first he'd heard the story. He had been five, and still frightened by the old man who had emerged from the storm a few hours before. His father, too kindly a soul to turn away a wanderer on such a night, had bidden him welcome. Then the old man had stepped close, opened his robes and revealed a baby nestled in the crook of one skinny arm, and he'd spoken words to poor Ectorius that had made that worthy Roman noble pale to grey, and follow the old man down to the kitchen as if usurped in his own stronghold.

Once there, installed by the fire, the visitor had refused all offers of food and drink, and had begun to tell a story of the dragon of the south, and a mighty king whose lust for a woman had started a war so terrible that the land was not safe for his heir. Gaius hadn't understood the half of it. Surely a baby—beside all the annoyance his adoption would cause Gaius, his father's only son—could not be the means of saving the whole realm of Britannia.

Saving it from what, Gaius had failed to gather, watching jealously from beside Ector's knee, aware that his father's hand on his head was distracted, oblivious to whether he was petting his son or a dog. The child must be protected, and brought up to be a king. Certain things must happen. He must find something called a *graal*. He must discover a weapon that would be a sign of his reign's beginning and its ending, his power and his death.

Nonsense, perhaps. An old man's ramblings, a baby stolen from some poor cottager's cradle. Ector had never spoken of the strange visitation again, nor complained of the burden laid upon him. Gaius's mother was dead, and Ector had simply stepped into the breach once again, clucking over the bundle in his arms as it began to wail from hunger. And the night had turned cold, in the swish of the departing sorcerer's robes, and words had hung in the air like snowflakes to Gaius's dazzled vision: *the sword from the lake...*

***

And so it was that Lance, Prince of Nowhere, returned to Vindolanda at the head of a troop of Roman dignitaries, mounted on a horse fit for a king. His pulse was still thumping from his race with Arthur across the flats: what a creature Balana was! He'd watched the cavalry beasts wheeling and stamping about when he'd been barely tall enough to touch their shining bellies, but never thought to ride one, let alone in the company of a future king, before whom it was somehow all right to let his joy at this new experience show.

He's generous, Lance thought suddenly, reining Balana back to a trot on the outskirts of the village. *He likes to make people happy.*

This conviction too filled Lance with a depthless, incomprehensible joy, like seeing white swans take off from the surface of Broomlee Lough. It shouldn't have mattered to him. Arthur would be here for one night only, gone in the morning, his kindness or otherwise no more to Lance than a passing gleam of the sun.

But Arthur flashed him a conspiratorial grin as he drew level on the flagstone road outside the praetor's house. Lance's throat tightened in a mix of pleasure and pain. "Here we are," he said, glad he had the excuse of their recent gallop for the unsteady rasp in his voice. "We don't have much after this long winter, but my people will shelter and feed you."

"That's nice." Arthur trotted a few paces at his side, then to Lance's surprise put out a hand and pulled Balana's rein to draw her to a halt. The clatter of iron on stone died away to utter silence. "But where are these people of yours? This place is deserted."

Lance sprang to the ground. Riding proved to have been easier than standing and he staggered, clutching at Balana's mane for support. "Oh, no. This can't be. It was only two nights—just two nights."

"What was?"

"That I was away. We were starving. I promised I'd hunt, and bring back something to eat."

"Things were as desperate as that?"

"You've no idea. Summer didn't come this year. It only arrived..." Lance choked faintly, and once more told the impossible truth. "It only arrived with you. They can't all be dead, Art. They can't be gone."

Arthur swung easily down from the saddle. If he noticed that his new friend had cut short his name and dispensed with honorifics, he gave no sign. "Of course they're not dead." He looked around. "We'll find them. Tell me—if there was no food here, and you've been gone for two nights, have you had nothing to eat yourself in all that time?"

"No. I chased a hare, but she turned into an old woman and gave me a fish and the sword."

"Oh, Gods." Arthur took a firm grip on his arm and glanced anxiously back up the track. "Father Ector! Guy! Hurry up, will you? This poor prince has gone mad for want of food."

The rest of the party clattered up behind them. Lance drew a breath to try and explain himself, then lost it at the sight of a ragged figure in robes bursting forth from the praetorium.

He braced up. Any sign of life was a relief, but he was surely in deadly trouble with Father Tomas now. "I'm sorry," he began, and tried to put together in his mind the story he'd just offered Arthur, the one about the fish and the witch and the hare. "I'm sorry, Father. I only meant to go up and fetch the frozen deer Cerys and Dana found dead on the path. Oh, there you are, Dana," he added distractedly, as the girl emerged from behind Tomas, overtook him, dashed across the courtyard and flung her arms around Lance's waist. She was still coughing, and wrapped in Elena's cloak. He patted her hair. "But it came back to life and ran away. I must tell the men not to hunt the white hart, Tomas. Where are all the men?"

Tomas stumbled to a halt. His eyes were red-rimmed with sleeplessness. "Where do you think they are?" he demanded in a croak. "Every able-bodied man—and woman, for that matter—is out on the moortops, looking for you." At last the old man noticed the visitors. "You see," he offered helplessly, spreading his hands, "once upon a time we had a king. A queen too, and although an unrepenting heathen, she doctored and cared for us, brought babies into the world with her own hands. We had this boy's brothers and sisters too, a horde of them, barely tamed puppies, but good. All gone, all gone. And these two long nights past, we thought our Lance was lost to us too. He's all we have left, you see."

Ector and Gaius dismounted. "You are priest of this village?" Ector asked gruffly, surveying the dilapidated house and outbuildings, the various infants who had crept out of unknown hiding-places and followed Dana's lead in attaching themselves to Lance however they could. "A priest of Christ?"

"Alas for me! I came from the shrine at Brocolitia. I have known better days. If you be heathen sons of Mithras, slay me if you will."

"Good grief, no." Stiffly Ector went down on his knees. "My name is Ectorius, a stranger here, but a Christian like yourself, and no cause for fear. These are my sons, Gaius and Arthur, just as..." He tugged sharply at Guy's swordbelt. Arthur was out of reach of anything more than a ferocious look, but both he and his foster-brother guiltily knelt too. "Just as devout as I am. God be with you, Father Tomas."

"And also with you." The old man's response was reflexive. His face was a blank of astonishment. Lance had gone down at Arthur's side, not in an access of humility but under the weight of children. He felt extremely strange. *We thought we'd lost our Lance. All the men and women out looking for you. All we have left, you see.* The shepherd's little boy, fat somehow despite the endless winter, tried to climb into his arms. Lance tried to help, and instead went down sideways, making the infant shriek and the flagstones change place with the blessed sun reborn.

Arthur stared up in horror at his guardian. "None of your doing, Bearcub," Ector said, taking pity. "The boy's half dead of hunger, that's all. Gaius, carry him indoors—but take that sword from him first, before he runs himself through."

"Should I keep it safe for him, Father?"

"No, you weasel. Take it with him and set it by his bed." Ector turned to the nearest of his grooms and lowered his voice: the skin-and-bones priest and all the wide-eyed children of the settlement were gazing at him and his party as if they'd tumbled from heaven. "Take gold and ride back to the last decent-sized town we came through—Corstopitum, was it, the place by the river? Buy grain and meat, and tell them to have a dozen ewes and a tup sent up here to replenish these flocks. Oh, and bring wine. Damned if I'm drinking whatever goat's piss these poor bastards have been living on. Well, what are you waiting for? Go!"

Chapter Eight

"You shouldn't have let him. I said we'd provide for you tonight."

"Well, we've quartered ourselves upon you. Sir Ector is an old Roman. If you garrison your troops upon a town, unless there's some political point to be made, you don't expect them to feed you. It's not just for tonight, you see. We're badly in need of rest, and we hope to stay longer." Arthur tucked his foot up onto a bar of the high stool against the wall near Lance's bed. He'd made himself very comfortable there, while visitors came and went.

Far more of them than Lance could have anticipated. Figures from his childhood: the blacksmith, the farmers who worked Ban's fields, the butcher, enduring presences to whom Lance and his siblings had been little more than a nuisance in their younger years, children underfoot—all of them had come, singly or in groups, as they arrived back from their search on the moors. They'd stood awkwardly at the foot of the bed or sat boldly upon it, each according to his nature. None of them had said much. Lance, who would have expected a clout around the ear for causing false alarms and uproar, was confounded. "Have you been given chambers? Stabling and feed for your horses?"

"Yes, and your housekeeper—Edern, is it?—is busy at this moment preparing an evening meal. Which you may or may not be allowed to attend, so carry on eating your broth."

He had a nerve, Lance thought. Lance could hear running feet, scufflings and banging doors as Ban's household rushed to do this imperious newcomer's bidding. He also had a way of making nobody mind, just as Lance didn't mind being ordered to eat, or threatened with exclusion from dinner as if he'd been a five year old. He was feeling stronger by the minute, and would soon show this grey-eyed invader who was master in the praetor's house.

Meanwhile, it was a bone-melting relief to lie here. He'd been laid down carefully in Ban and Elena's bed, not his own, and Edern's wife had come clucking and crying to help him out of his clothes. Someone—Gaius, he thought—had placed the marvellous sword in an empty rack, on the wall opposite the bed where he could see it. The earthenware soup bowl was warm in his hands, the deerhound sprawled across his lap a pungent, flea-scratching comfort. "I didn't faint, you know. Your brother didn't have to carry me in."

"Oh, don't mind Gaius. He's so much older and uglier than I am, whenever I used to annoy him, he'd hoist me up like a sack of barley and cart me away."

"Does he still do that now?"

"I'd like to see him try. Just to be correct, he's my foster brother. Ectorius is my guardian." Arthur paused delicately. "There's quite a story there."

Lance blushed. Did his guest think he wished to pry? "I didn't ask for it."

"No, I know. I'm hoping to get yours, though, and I don't think the diplomatic wiles I've recently learned will work on you. I was thinking to trade."

Lance set the bowl aside. He tugged at the sleeping dog's ears. One good tale did deserve another, and he was longing to hear what had brought this prince to the tumbledown barns of Vindolanda. He was far from sure, however, that he was ready to reply in kind. "I don't know," he said cautiously. "Part of mine is dull, part sad and shameful. And the rest—the last two days—sound like a fantasy, something you'd dream after eating ergot wheat."

Arthur took this in quietly. "All right," he said at length. "I'll start, then you can decide if I've earned a return, or if my ergot dreams are wilder than yours."

So Arthur told the story of the storm in the Forest Wild, of the night sixteen years ago when he'd been given into Sir Ector's keeping—a child out of nowhere, allegedly the heir of Cerniw's dragon king. Lance's eyes grew obligingly wide, and his hand ceased its movement on the deerhound's head. He was a perfect audience. Only when Arthur had finished, and was watching him in amusement, did he even visibly draw breath.

"But did you know? When you were younger, I mean—who you were?"

"Who I *might* be," Arthur gently corrected. "Not for many years. The old man told Ector to bring me up as his own son, and so he did, if cleaning the stables and pigsties and getting my backside whipped if I did wrong was any measure. But a time came when I thought I should learn to be Guy's squire, since Ector isn't rich and couldn't afford to make noble young soldiers of both of us." He shook his head. "Believe me, I didn't *want* to lug saddles and swords about for the great lump. I had to do something, though, and so I asked them about it one day."

"What happened?"

"Well, Guy went the colour of that beautiful sunset out there and stared at his boots, and Ector... Ector wept, the first and only time I ever knew him do it. And they both knelt in front of me, though Ector had to pull Guy down to make him, just as he had to with your priest out there. And Ector begged my pardon for lying to me all these years, and said he wasn't my father at all. And so I found out that I was to be..."

He spread his hands helplessly. "A king," Lance finished for him, sitting up in bed. "How did it feel?"

"Horrible. I wanted to drop through the floor. I couldn't stand to see Ector and Guy kneeling there. I made them stand up, and then I ran off into the kennels to hide with the bloodhound's new pups." He snorted. "*Very* royal."

"I'd have done the same," Lance averred, brow knotted with sincerity. "You must have felt... *orphaned*. To lose the idea of a father like Ector, even if your real one *is* Pendragon... I couldn't have borne it, not calmly."

Arthur examined him with interest. Dark-eyed Celtic handsome, quite unaware of it, proud as the devil nonetheless. It was time to call in the debt on the exchange of stories. "I'm certain you've borne worse."

"No. Only different."

"Your priest said your whole family is gone."

"Yes, in a Pictish raid. It was over a year ago. My grief is done."

No, Arthur thought, and managed to keep it to himself. *Not by half. You almost wept over* my *poor sorrows not half a minute ago.* He got down off the stool and shoved the deerhound aside far enough to sit on the edge of Lance's bed. "If that's all you've got to say, you have to listen to me some more."

"I'd be happy to do so. No more stables and pigsties for you, I'd guess."

"And you'd be wrong. Well, not about the pigsties. But the first rule of Ector's household is—no man rests or eats until the horses are fed."

"Quite right, too."

"Oh, you're another like him, aren't you? No wonder he's taken to you. I'll be lucky if he doesn't adopt another son, and leave me here. I bet you'd make a better job of it than I will."

"Of what?"

Arthur sighed. The sun was setting in emerald bands to the west, the strange light filtering through the fort's Roman glass. He lifted his face to it yearningly. "Of becoming the future king of the Britons, of course."

Lance sat up. "Of the *Britons*? Not just Cerniw?"

"Since Ector told me my origins, I have had to behave like Pendragon's heir in more than name. The old sorcerer swore him to secrecy, but he promised to return and never did, and a time came when we couldn't wait. Saxon raiders are making deeper inroads every day in the south, just as the Danes are here. The Cerniw chieftains can't tackle them alone, or won't—sometimes it's easier to yield and make terms than to fight. So I have set off on what I believe is called a diplomatic mission."

"All the way from—what did Sir Ector call it? The Forest Wild?"

"That's right. Ector's name for his stronghold, deep in the woods to the northeast of Cerniw. Dumnonia is the Roman name for it. A long, hard journey, but we have friends in the north, it seems. I've spent the last month making myself pleasant with old Pendragon's relatives among the Votadini on the east coast. We were on our way west to Caer Lir when you crossed our path. I have another distant great-uncle there, the ruler of Rheged. If I can make friends and promises enough, we'll have allies at both ends of Hadrian's old wall—good strategy, I'm sure you'll agree."

"What about the Romans? Don't you believe they'll return?"

"I don't think so. They've got too many problems of their own. Ector still gets news from Gaul, but less and less often now. It seems to me that the battle everywhere is being painfully lost."

"My mother was a Votadini queen."

Arthur stopped short. More an avowal than a piece of information, that. Sudden intense focus in the brown eyes. "What was her name?"

"Elena. I am your ally by birth. My fight is your fight."

I offer you my services and sword? Arthur waited for it. This was the effect he had on men, from rusty old knights to striplings like this. Ector had told him the power was a good thing, when managed with humility and grace, but sometimes he had neither, and the responsibility scared him.

He wouldn't have minded it from this boy, though. He'd seen how he could fight. When half-dead from hunger, at that: what a force he'd be, after a few good meals and some lessons in swordsmanship from Guy! His new friend had nothing here in this godsforsaken village, not even family to defend. Arthur waited expectantly. For once he could accept with a good heart.

Nothing happened. Lance remained silent and still. The sudden fires died, replaced by something sterner, older. "Do you like it?" he asked. "Making yourself pleasant, I mean—all the diplomacy?"

"No. Bores me to tears. But I'll have nothing left to rule if I don't, so I have to find and meet the rulers in the north, and hope that they'll support me in my cause."

"You make me understand that my father was a king in name only."

"Oh. I didn't mean to—"

"You've travelled the whole island. You've met with these fierce chieftains, men of resources. You could raise an army if you wished."

"Not quite yet. But... yes, that's the general idea."

"While I tend Ban's farmyard and fields."

Then leave them. Ride into battle with me. Once more the words died on Arthur's lips. This skinny prince had a dignity unconnected to the insignificance of his father's realm. "Not tonight, you don't," Arthur said, almost shyly. "You've got to rest, Ector says. I know you don't approve, but he's having a meat-cow the size of three wagons brought up for tonight. If you sleep, you might be well enough to come down and do the honours of your house later on."

"Wait," Lance said, as Arthur stood up to leave. "I know I haven't earned answers—not under the terms of our agreement—but there's so much I want to ask you."

"Try me. I have to be kind to defaulting allies, Ector says, if their reasons are good enough."

"And if they aren't..."

"Why, make a hideous example of them, of course."

Lance hitched a half-smile. "Of course. What is it like in the Forest Wild, then? Why are you sometimes called Bear? And..." He paused, attention noticeably caught by a gleam at Arthur's chest, between the laces of his jerkin. "Sir Ector and Gaius knelt to my village's priest. They're Christians, then?"

"Yes." Arthur gave a tiny shrug. "Isn't everyone these days? Aren't you?"

"Er... yes, of course. You wear the solar disc, though. Forgive me if I wasn't meant to see."

"Oh, damn." Clumsily Arthur fished the pendant out. It was heavy and old, and on its reverse bore the signs of moon and dragon too, worse still in these days of the gentle, humble new god. "It was on a longer chain, but that got broken. This strip of hide's too short to keep it properly..."

"Concealed?"

Arthur met his gaze, amused and resentful. "I do believe that answering questions from you might be harder than I'd bargained for. You can just wait for the rest."

Lance settled back. He tucked his hands behind his head. "I'll see you at dinner, then. I tell you what—go down to my blacksmith, Garva. Say I sent you, and he'll make you a longer chain."

Chapter Nine

Early next morning, Lance was up and about, Father Tomas hobbling at his side. He filtered out the old man's chatter and fuss as they made the rounds of the settlement. He wanted to see for himself all the blessed signs of life he had heard upon waking at dawn: the clatter from the forge, the mewing of gulls coming in from the coast for new-broken plough, their voices skeining with the village children's cries. To his surprise, the prince of Cerniw joined them, emerging from an alley as if he'd lived here all his life and falling into pace at Lance's side. Although he looked fresh as the morning itself in dove-grey tunic and cloak, Lance sensed a change in him—that, this morning, he wished to be ordinary— and kept his remaining questions from the night before to himself.

He guessed that the stop in this wild place might serve as a welcome hiatus from Arthur's duties as well as his travels. There was no-one here to appease, no need to establish a diplomatic rapport with any of the shepherds or farmworkers he met. He went with Lance and Tomas through the vicus, admiring the smithy, talking to the bakers about their ovens and their grain, while Lance counted heads among the children to make sure that the last bitter nights—unreal as a dream to him now that he too was freshly clothed and fed—hadn't borne anyone away, and sought out the men and women who'd searched the moors for him to say shy thanks.

No-one questioned him overmuch. The child he'd been before his absence would not have escaped interrogation, but the young man who'd returned with royalty in tow was allowed his reserve, his new dignity. By the time he reached the outskirts of the town, he found to his amusement that rumour had raced ahead of him. He'd gone off into the night, it seemed, not to hunt but to answer a summons from Arthur himself, to bring him home for who knew what future splendours and promotions. After an exchanged glance with the prince of Cerniw to check that that he too was enjoying the joke, he let the story lie.

Later, when Tomas had grown tired and shambled off to his chapel, Lance rode out with Arthur to the fields. Sir Ector had loaned him Balana again, and he was entranced. He tried desperately not to get used to her powerful stride underneath him, but she was such an old hand that she had rocked him into a state of submission before they were clear of the village. All he had to do was sit down into her canter and keep the lightest touch on her reins, and allow the sunny morning to blossom out around him.

White Meadows had transformed overnight from barren silence to a rich mosaic of life. As well as Ector's generous gift of ewes and tups, every sheep the farmsteads possessed seemed to have given birth overnight, and the lambs were everywhere, scattering like snowflakes. Wind and hawthorn blossom whipped and flew in the crystalline air.

Arthur caught the joyous infection of the day and sent his black stallion bounding past Balana. "Where are you going?" Lance called after him, laughing.

"Not the least idea. Up to the top of that hill there, where the old road runs through."

That was the route Lance had taken in the bitter night, in a different world than this one, surely. He glanced up at the turret with a flicker of unease: his memories of Viviana and the moonlit lough were still too fresh for him to share the strange realm beyond the Wall with this new friend. Arthur sailed blithely past, however, only reining in when he reached the first crest of the road. "Look at that!" he cried, as if the sweet gape of the landscape beyond could somehow be new to Lance too, and somehow he made it so, with the flash of his smile and his broad, encompassing gesture. "The moors sweep from the tops of those escarpments like waves rushing onto the shore."

Lance drew Balana to a halt at his side. "I've only once seen the sea," he said breathlessly. "I travelled with my father to Caer Lir. It didn't look much like that, though—quite flat and grey."

"Ah, you should see Cerniw's beaches. The rollers come in like thunder."

"Are there many beaches there?"

"Dozens. Cerniw is nothing but coast—that, and strange circles of stone left by men who vanished so long ago, even the Druids have no name for them. Do you have those here?"

"Yes," Lance said, oddly pleased to be able to give him something in return for the vision of the great waves. "In the far north, a circle that looks like arrows fired into the earth from the clouds. And nearer to here, within a day's ride, four stones with little hollow cups in them. A fierce goblin's supposed to sleep under those, guarding a wonderful treasure." He paused, embarrassed. "A children's tale. Father Tomas says he knows who made these things—your stones and mine."

"Ah, of course. The devil."

Balana gave a great snort. The sound and the timing of it cracked helpless laughter from Lance, and he let her surge onwards to hide his response. "I'll take you to see the goblin stones. Other places too, if you have time."

"Please. Ector says we should stay until the moon gets full again, if you can bear us. We'll feed ourselves, of course." Arthur drew level and held out a hand to silence Lance's objection. "You really must accept this. It's just what soldiers do."

Lance shut his mouth. *Soldiers* had included him. As the son of a military man, the idea wasn't new to him, but for a long time now he'd felt like anything but. The army Ban had served was long gone. Once the moon was full, he'd be nothing but a farmhand again, and had no right to be making a Roman charger dance and clatter on the sunny road, which might yet be treacherous with ice. He made the smallest sign to Balana, who dropped into a sober walk. "All right," he said, sounding ungracious to himself. "I'm sorry. I mean that you and your people are truly welcome here, and I'm only ashamed that the vicus can't support you."

"Well, you've had a bad..." Arthur looked around him at the glittering, glorious day. "A bad winter. Why do you think the spring didn't come?"

"Oh, our sins, no doubt. Tell me more about Cerniw, or the Forest Wild. I bet it's never like this down there."

"The winters in Cerniw are seldom severe. It's a gentle land, if you don't mind being knocked off your feet by the gales nine days out of ten. The forest, though, where I grew up... We were often snowbound there for months, though we never suffered hardship in Ector's stronghold. And then there were the summers."

The faint catch of yearning in his voice transferred itself to Lance, who yearned suddenly too. "I can't imagine."

"Think of a deep land, sheltered. None of your great barren stretches, bare rock and thin sheep-nibbled soil like this. Deep earth, and time for the trees to grow three times as tall as the praetor's house."

"Ah. Even the tallest birches here scarcely reach past my shoulder."

"Think of stately oak and ash, miles and miles of it, unbroken but for sunshine, the meadow land of little farms, a few clearings where the deer and new fawns come to gather in the spring. It's easy to get lost. You can wander for days on the mossy tracks and never meet another human soul."

"You must love it there."

"You know, as a child growing up, I didn't. I didn't really *see* it. The glades, the tumbled rocks with half a dozen different kinds of ferns growing out from the cracks—all that was just the world. I see it now. Does that seem ungrateful, or strange?"

"To see with the mind what the eye has lost—to see properly then for the first time? No, not strange at all."

They rode on in silence. For Lance, the quiet between them was fraught: he'd gone too far, surely. This visitor was perceptive, and would perhaps ask next what Lance had lost, and seen properly for the first time only when it was gone. "Why do they call you Bear?" he demanded abruptly to forestall him, and was relieved to hear him laugh. "That was my other question—the one you wouldn't let me ask last night."

"Because we were trading, and you hadn't given me half enough. Still haven't, for that matter. I'm willing to bet your village priest never dipped you in the font and named you *Lance*."

"No," Lance agreed calmly. "I'm Tertius, just like most other Roman third sons. And I will explain, but..." He shielded his eyes and looked out across the gorse bushes, whose butter-gold flowers in the distance were being shaken by more than the wind. "You go first."

"Very well. My Latin name's Artorius, as you know. But I may have been... just a bit of a handful in my younger days, and Ector said it was like having a wild beast in the house, upending the furniture and rolling down the stairs. So, given my origins, he called me by the older word from my mother's language, Art or Urt—a little bear."

"I see," Lance said, smiling. From habit he'd brought out with him Ban's army spear, secured through a hoop on the saddle. "I'm sure you're far too dignified and well behaved to deserve the name now."

"Sometimes. Why? What did you have in mind?"

"Boar for your dinner, if you'd like it." He unhitched the spear. "Come for the gallop, but keep well in the rear of me—he's an old one, and mean. Gored a bairn to death two summers gone."

"Wait. It's your turn to tell me why they call you Lance."

"I'm about to do that very thing."

***

After that, Lance and the prince rode out almost every day. Lance still had his duties around the village, long hours to be spent in farmyards and fields in a game of frantic catch-up with the spring, but Father Tomas, still oddly frail and uncertain, wasn't enforcing this work with his usual vigour. He had befriended Sir Ector, who in his turn and for his own reasons was allowing his boy a long leash during these windswept days on the hills, and the two old men were often to be seen on the steps outside the little chapel, heads together in discussion.

Freed from sword-practice, battle drills and Latin reading lessons, Arthur followed Lance to the places he'd described—the standing stones and cup-marked outcrops, the crag-top where the goblin was meant to crouch, guarding treasure in the earth. Lance had a hundred half-forgotten stories about the land, and if these always stopped short of the lake and the wonderful sword, which remained on its rack in the praetorium—if the journeys themselves would stop short of the moors to the north of the Wall—Arthur on instinct held his tongue. The days were too sweet to him, the sun too bright.

Except on the shortest trips, Gaius accompanied them. He was slower, and much less enthralled by the sights and the myths, but Arthur was scrupulous about his inclusion. He knew that Guy was obliged to look after him, whether either of them liked it or not, and was determined not to make his foster brother's duties unpleasant to him. Arthur, growing up in a family not his own, had lived through the grief of not belonging—often, indeed, inflicted on him by Guy himself, whose jealousy had at times been bitter. But they had long since made their peace and were fast friends. So Guy made a third in their party, not just on guard duty, a participant in their chatter and jokes, although he tried his best not to show himself amused. Rich with companionship and action, time began to rush by like the beat of the curlews' wings.

Chapter Ten

When the moon was once more growing large, Ectorius told his ward that it was time they resumed their journey. He did so reluctantly: Art was tanned, and premature shadows of responsibility were fading from his eyes. It had been good for him, Ector thought, to have such a companion as King Ban's son. After giving his confession to Father Tomas, Ector had talked with the old priest long into the night, hearing with wonder and compassion what had befallen the village and Ban's one surviving child. Ector thought there could not be much wrong with a young man who had wrought himself so cleanly from such grief.

That night, when they had taken supper together and Lance had gone off, as he always did, to walk around the bounds of the vicus and see that all was secure, Ector broached the subject with Art.

"This Lance," he began. "He is of noble blood, and a good brave lad in his own right. He would make a suitable companion, and the time is coming when you should be looking about you for such friends. If you like it, I would be willing to have him travel on with us."

Art, sitting opposite him at the table, chin propped on one hand, smiled wryly. "Don't you think we'd better find out if *he* likes it?"

Ector had the grace to look embarrassed. He did sometimes forget, in his anxiety to fulfil his mission, that other people were more than adjuncts to it. "Well, why wouldn't he?" he demanded gruffly, and tossed the future king a torn saddlebag to mend. "Shall I ask him?"

"Leave it to me," Arthur said, with very transparent solemnity. "Such a request should come from the throne, not a... faithful servant."

For a moment Ectorius looked at him from beneath his eyebrows like a hawk. "Why, you little..." Then he sat back, with an inward smile of satisfaction at the heir he had raised. *If you could see him now, Uther.* "Very well, Your Highness," he said. "Quite so."

***

Yet it wasn't so easy to ask. Lance was not someone you picked up like a new horse at the mart. Despite their short acquaintance, he had impressed Arthur deeply with his strength in the face of loss, his lack of fuss. He seemed to have come to terms with himself, creating his world from the materials at hand: Art, who was painfully full of ambition, admired it greatly. Was it not appalling arrogance on his part, to ask such a person to uproot himself and follow him? And what if he said no? Following him up onto a steep, glorious stretch of the ridge, Arthur shook his head: that would be a blow to the royal ego, and probably a salutary one.

He was quiet, as they made their way east along the path of the Wall on their last ride. This was such an unusual state of affairs that after a while Lance looked at him and enquired gravely if some merciful god had struck him mute.

Arthur laughed, shook off his worries and immersed himself gladly in the present. The matter did not have to be settled immediately: they would spend tonight at Vindolanda, and not set off west until the next morning. As if in honour of the day before departure, Lance had at last taken down the sword from the lake from its rack and brought it out with him instead of his usual spear.

He had also finally offered to show Art the mysterious terrain beyond the gap in the ridge, the moors beyond that turreted gateway where he had dreamed his strange dream. Art was honoured to be invited there, onto the land Lance had been ready to defend with his life. For once Guy's presence was onerous to him. Art had entered all too easily into Lance's half-hypnotised recall of the place. To Guy it would be just another ride.

But this was the very type of distinction he had sworn not to make between himself and his brother. Art and Lance were picking their way down the slopes to the turret and the burn now, a long way ahead of Guy, who'd stopped—ever mindful of the rearguard, his duty of vigilance—to make sure a distant group of horsemen were only local farmers on their way home from market.

Art halted to let him catch up. Lance, riding at his side, stopped too. A thought leapt between them, like sun off a blade, not the first time each had known the other's intentions without so much as an exchanged glance. Both simultaneously reined their horses back, gesturing Guy ahead of them, and Guy splashed under the arch smiling broadly, indefinably pleased to be first into a new world.

Lance barely recognised the place in sunlight. It had been like this long ago, when he'd come here as a child, with no thought in his head but the prospect of adventure and enjoyment. The lough had cast off its cold grey skin and turned into a million points of light. Coltsfoot and harebells shook in the breeze, and even the deep marsh was illumined by flowering rushes, opening their feathery heads to the warmth. Art exclaimed and pointed at the family of swans serenely emerging from the banks, then shot a warning look at Guy, who had reflexively drawn his bow. *No killing here, not today.* The two followed Lance quietly westward along the foot of the cliff.

The cave was so small! For a moment Lance thought he must have mistaken the place. Art and Guy stopped with him outside it, gazing silently into the gap in the rock, barely visible in the strong light. "I sheltered here with Viviana," Lance said, wonderingly. "When I first arrived, there were… paintings on the walls, animals and dancing people. But the wind changed. The rain blew in, and they faded."

He'd spoken calmly enough. It came as a surprise to all of them when he suddenly turned upon Art a look of scorching intensity and said, "All things disappear. I must have dreamed Viviana: how could she have survived out here? Even dreams do not last. And tomorrow, you too will be gone."

Arthur stared at him. Lance had told him in plain terms the story of his nights on the moor, never once revealing pain or loss. Nor had he shown more than friendly regard for his guests. And Art, mindful that their visit would be short, had tried not to enjoy too much the undemanding friendship of a companion of his own age. He hadn't expected Ector's suggestion that Lance journey on with them, and he'd honestly believed that Lance could take him or leave him.

Perhaps it wasn't so. He opened his mouth to ask—and then shut it again, unaccountably reluctant to speak in front of Guy. "Well," he said awkwardly instead, "will you show me where you found this sword? Father Ector is very anxious about it—some prophecy he thinks I don't know about, given him by the old man who brought me to his court." As a ploy of distraction, it hadn't worked. Lance remained still, eyes blank and miserable, as if he hadn't heard.

Guy, looking on, took pity. "What, do you think I'm going to ride my clean horse into that swamp?" he demanded, dismounting and settling on the warm turf outside the cave. "Lance, take him and show him if he insists. Just for God's sake, don't let him drown in the lake."

Art turned his horse's head and followed Lance, who had already set off downhill. The track was narrow, but he edged Hengroen as close to Balana as he could. "Listen," he began, as soon as they were out of Guy's earshot. "As far as my being gone is concerned…"

"Forget it!" Lance said fiercely. Arthur flinched: it sounded less like irritation than an order that he actually cast the incident from his mind. "I've shamed myself. Please don't speak of it again."

Why are you angry with me because you think you've made a mistake? Arthur wanted to ask aloud, but it would have come out like a challenge, and in fact Lance's anger made him smile. It was hot, honest, utterly devoid of malice, a fire that would burn swift and clean. Fewer and fewer people these days dared to be angry with Arthur, and he knew that in future there would be fewer still. "All right," he said eventually. "I'll get someone *else* to tell you, shall I?"

"Tell me what?"

"That Ector wants you to leave with us tomorrow, and join us as part of our—"

"Of your retinue?"

"No, you stiff-necked monster. As one of our household, I was going to say, although that was a stupid word too, and what he means—what *I* mean—is that you should come with me as my companion and friend."

He paused. He could only see Lance in profile and a little from behind. The path wasn't quite wide enough, despite Hengroen's manoeuvring, and it seldom seemed to occur to the prince of Vindolanda to let the prince of Cerniw precede him anywhere. Still, Art could tell his jaw had dropped. He smiled. "You've the makings of a fine warrior, Ector says. And… we are recruiting, in a small way. Would you like to come?"

Lance closed his eyes. They'd left the track, but Ector's beautiful mare was picking her way through the rushes so surely that she needed little attention. And he wanted an instant of blindness, of seeing nothing but blood-filtered sunlight. When he opened them again, the world was still there. But Lance hardly knew it—hardly recognised his own self within it. The sky, the very turf beneath his horse's hooves, the long-familiar swell of the land that would conceal the lough for a few minutes more, until they broached the crest… All were different to him; he perceived them with a mind transfigured.

Arthur, who had mistaken his silence for hesitation, was awkwardly assuring him he need not find his board or expenses, that Ector would consider him his ward, just as he did Arthur, until he was old enough to wield a sword for his wage.

Lance let him run on. The voice was pleasant to him, as if he'd been hearing it all his life, like the sound of the wind through the gorse. Lance had been abandoned here. He'd had enough time now to accept that Viviana had told him the truth about Ban. He had been a lost child. But Viviana had taught him that he was a child no more, and must not behave as such. And now he was no longer lost.

No longer lost, but chosen. Found and chosen by the one soul in the world whose choosing could matter to him, by whom he would allow it. It had taken Lance very little time to understand that he would follow Arthur into battle, death and beyond, but that quiet certainty had belonged only to himself, and he had stilled his mouth and his heart from its expression.

He couldn't do better even now. He was smiling, and he wondered if Art would take that as his acceptance. They rode on in silence for a short while longer, and then they reached the hillcrest.

The lough lay glittering before them, giving back the sky its brilliant blue. A year had passed since Lance had seen it shine, had seen it anything other than half-frozen beneath leaden skies. He remembered how he had used to come up here in summer and stand in this very spot, to watch it dance in light.

He stopped, and felt rather than saw Arthur rein to a halt beside him. "It might seem strange to you," he said, "but for a while, this place was more a home to me than any I've ever known."

"No, it doesn't seem strange. I could make a kingdom here— these moors, and this beautiful lake."

"It's called a lough," Lance corrected. "To rhyme with..." He glanced across at Arthur's wrists, fine-made but already scarred, muscular with horsemanship and work. "To rhyme with *tough*."

"Well, Lance o' the lough, you must consider finding your home elsewhere. You don't have to decide at once—you can meet us at Caer Lir, if you wish. But tell me at least that you'll think about it."

Lance nodded. He knew he should speak, after such an offer, and he tried to find the words. But Arthur seemed quite satisfied, and after a moment turned back to his contemplation of the water. "Was it here that you found the sword?"

Lance looked down briefly at the weapon in its scabbard. "No, a short way further east. Come on and I'll show you."

The place was so ordinary that Lance was surprised he could find it again. Viviana's herb was growing in abundance all along the fringe of the lough now. How he had searched, to find her a few fresh strands! He could have cured all Vindolanda of its fevers now. Nevertheless he directed the horse with unerring certainty to the very spot where he'd first caught sight of the spiralling gold. "There, Art," he said, the short name coming easily to his lips now. "I found it just there, in the shallows."

"Just there," Arthur echoed. "Tell me the whole story of its finding."

Lance frowned. Why would Art assume there was more to it than Lance had already told him—that he'd gone out as bidden to fetch herbs for the old woman, and come back instead with the sword? Lance wasn't sure himself why he'd held back part of the truth. Possibly, he told himself wryly, because he didn't want his new friend to think him a lunatic. Well, that was too bad.

He drew breath, but Arthur gently interrupted him. "Never mind," he said. "I will tell *you* the story. You came here, and you saw the sword. But it was given to you by a hand, a pale beautiful hand that came out of the water and disappeared under it once more."

Lance stared at him. "She touched me, too," he said, although his heart was so high in his throat that he could barely speak. "Just once, on the wrist. I thought she would be cold, but she was warm as blood."

Arthur turned to look at him. "Was she?" he said, almost wistfully. "I never heard that part."

"Where… Where did you hear the rest?"

Arthur swung himself down from the saddle, landing in ankle-deep water. Lance's first, prosaic, thought was that he himself would not have been so cavalier about such fine boots. He'd observed that, while Arthur was never profligate with clothes—the party were travelling light, and anyway he doubted Ector ever allowed much extravagance—the things he had were of the best, and their spoiling wasn't the disaster it would have been to a child of Ban's household.

Lance realised he was seeking distraction because he was frightened. It was not so much that Arthur had known his story as seeing the change coming over his friend now. He'd lost his air of poise, and most of his colour, too. He had turned from the lough, and was staring off over the marshland to the east. He looked weary and lost. "The old man told how it would be. The one who brought me to Ector."

Forgetting concern for his own boots, Lance dismounted to stand beside him. "How do you remember?"

"Ah—I was a disobedient, sharp-eared brat, always hearing what I shouldn't. Poor Ector. He used to interrogate every passing guest to see if they were part of the prophecy. It isn't just that though. All my life I've seen him. I… I see him now."

"Who?"

Art smiled shakily. "Aren't you paying attention? The old man. He comes to me to tell me things I don't want to know. He sends me visions. He comes when I'm happiest, when I'm thinking of nothing but the sunlight and the pleasure of being alive. And all my life, I've been alone when he came. Now, though… Lance, turn now, and tell me that you see him too."

Lance obeyed. He *did* see something. Was he only flash-blind with sunlight on water? No—for a moment, a tall gaunt figure in black robes. Joy rose in him. Surely it was Viviana! She would answer Arthur's fears, solve his mysteries. He drew a breath to call her name, but the light shifted, and she was gone. "I thought I saw..." he began, and tailed off. "Nothing now. Do you see it still?"

"No," Art said miserably. "I wish I did. If he talks to me, it isn't so bad. But if he comes and goes like that, he means me to see something. And I guarantee I won't like it." He paused, swallowed hard. "You saw him, too, for an instant. Didn't you?"

Lance didn't want to lie to him. Even the thought of doing so burned him with shame. But if it distressed him, was it kind of Lance to feed the vision? "Perhaps," he said carefully, "you have heard him spoken of so often that he has come to be real to you."

"*Lance.*"

"All right. I'm sorry. Yes, I did."

"Thank you. Tell me the truth always, no matter how bad. Do you see the darkening of the lough?"

Arthur was stock-still in the shallow water, attention now fixed on the glittering horizon. "No," Lance said, and watching him go paler still, he put a hand to his shoulder, bony and warm beneath his jerkin and shirt. "I see only bright day."

"Then this is the vision. I wonder why he showed himself to you, even for an instant? I regret it, Lance. I would not have you caught up in these terrors." Then, to Lance's dismay, the proud prince hid his face in his hands and shivered like a child.

Chapter Eleven

"Once upon a time, the skin of the earth was so thin that it barely hid the fires below."

Arthur raised his head. He was sitting curled up on the bank of the lough, Lance's cloak wrapped around him. His brow had been pressed to his knees, but Lance had caught his attention. Lance recognised his look, remembered it from the faces of his brothers and sisters around the fire on long cold nights. He was sure his own had been the same. *Tell me a story...* "The skin of the earth was so thin that a dragon could sink through it, when she came home tired from hunting among the stars."

One quirk of the handsome mouth. "A dragon?"

"Don't tell me *you* don't believe in them, Uther's son. Anyway, it's only a tale."

"Yes, of course. Go on."

Lance looked around. The horses were peaceably cropping the turf a few yards away. Gaius was nowhere to be seen. "The dragon fell asleep in the warm, soft rock. They sleep for hundreds of our lifetimes, her kind, but they live forever, too. She was a very fine dragon, very big, as long as..." Lance pointed off towards the west, then swept a gesture round across the moorlands to the east. "As long as the space from horizon to horizon. All along her spine she bore a crest of upright scales. Many summers and winters passed, and when at last she shifted in her sleep, her scales slipped sideways, all unseen beneath the earth."

"What happened then?"

Lance got up and extended a hand, just as he had on the first day of their meeting. "Stand up and you'll see."

This time the grip on his was confiding and friendly. Art surged upright. He looked in the direction Lance was indicating. "Oh," he said. "The hills that look like breaking waves."

"Yes. Ice came, then rain, my story says. Great walls of ice, and a flood big enough to carve out the whole river valley. The dragon's scales had turned to stone, the black, hard rock the Roman army quarried to build their roads. Then the softer rocks underneath them, the mudstones and clays, all wore away..."

"And so we can see them. The dragon's spine."

"It was a story of my mother's."

Arthur turned to Lance. His whole focus settled upon him, unsettling as a hawk's. "You've never spoken to me about her."

"Nor to anyone."

"How did she know, do you think—about the dragon?"

"It was only a story. But her beliefs were old ones, Art. Every month when the moon was full, she and some of the other women of the village would go up to a cave in the cliffs, to meet and talk to something they called the dragon there."

"I want to ask you things. What your mother was like, what it was like to have one. But the time isn't right, is it?"

"No. Not yet."

The grey eyes remained, steady and kind, on his. "Do you follow in her ways, then? Or those of Father Tomas's new god?

Lance swallowed. "There was never any... punishment, in my mother's ways. She would leave that to our consciences, and help us out with the back of her hand if we did wrong."

Art sighed. "Blasphemous, our priest at home would say."

"And what do you say?"

"That to me, it makes perfect sense. This beautiful lough of yours—is it sacred, or can ordinary mortals wash away their visions and dark thoughts in it?"

"Both. At least... one thing doesn't mean that the other can't happen. My mother would say."

Art nodded. He threw Lance a scapegrace, understanding smile, then unfastened his jerkin and tugged his shirt over his head. "Let's go swimming, then."

All his life, Lance had come up here with his brothers and friends to bathe and splash about in the water. He'd never thought twice about watching one of them undress: they'd just been skinny moorland lads like himself, sinewy and pale with lack of sun. Art's bare back was the colour of sandstone on a summer afternoon. He was unfastening the crotch-lace of his deerskin trousers. For the first time in his life, Lance had to look away.

Swiftly he dealt with his own clothes. He knew from experience that, no matter how tempting at the surface, the lough retained a chill from the time of Elena's tales of ice and rain. He drew a warning breath, too late: Art had plunged through the reeds and dived.

He surfaced a heartbeat later. His voice rang out like music. "Holy Belenus! Sacred Dark Mother—Gog, Magog and Lleu Llaw Gyffes!"

Lance broke into laughter. He forgot his shyness and his sudden prickling awareness of his companion's body, and strode in to join him. "I told you it was cold."

"You did... not!" Art was treading water, his breath coming in painful gasps. "You said my flesh would encounter my spirit in here, or... something of that sort."

"And isn't it true?"

"Only in as much as I'm going to... die!"

Lance snorted. He put one hand on the tawny, wet head and pushed Art under: got time for half a yelp as Art's warm grip fastened round his waist and tugged him down too.

The water was full of shafts of light. Lance and the prince tumbled through them, rolling and scrapping like otter cubs. Lance's world went sun-over-soil with the force of his rolling dive. He evaded Art's pounce, stretched out his limbs in a pure ecstasy of flight.

A little further down, the light faded out to peaty bronze. Seizing Art's arm so that he wouldn't become lost or entangled in the reeds, Lance guided him to the place where the pale hand had risen from the water. They were back within their depth. He found a foothold on the bulrush-matted mud and broke surface for air. "It was here," he said when he could, still keeping his hold on Art. "This is where she gave me the sword. Who was she, Art? What did it mean?"

"I don't know. I wish you didn't have to be part of it."

"I am, though. You and Sir Ector knew the legend, but it happened to me. You don't have to be afraid, I'm certain. Viviana was strange, but she was kind to me. She saved my life."

"I'm not sure that she'd save mine."

"Did I do the wrong thing? Was the sword meant for you after all?"

"No." Art shook his head, sending water flying. He stared off over the water. "Look, Guy will come searching for us soon. Then I'll have to go back and help with preparations for our journey, and we'll have no more time. Come with me."

Lance followed him onto the shore. They were still hand in hand, and he wondered if Art had ceased to notice. His grasp was frank as a child's, but a bright new heat was coursing through Lance. They settled on the flat outcrop of rock which Elena said had been scoured smooth by the ice. Over untold thousands of years, he suddenly remembered, and tried to fit that with the life of the world as Father Tomas taught it: a mere *four* thousand, surely not long enough for dragons to sleep and make hills, and great majestic walls of ice to come and go.

The rock was sheltered by small, scrubby birch. When next the breeze blew—blessedly warm on goosepimpled skin—the shift of light and shade caught the bronze of the sun sign Art wore on his new chain. "*You* don't think the world is new," Lance said, reaching out with his free hand to catch and hold the heavy pendant. "You don't believe in this new god."

"I do as far as Ector and Guy are concerned. They were confirmed in the new faith before they took me in, and they've given me everything. But..."

A reed-music hush came over the lough. Gently Art drew his hand away. Lance didn't try to stop him, though letting go made him feel sick. "We should probably get dressed," he said. "But... what?"

"Do you have anyone, Lance? A woman, someone who's had your children, or... well, anybody?"

"Children?" Lance echoed in wonder. "Father Tomas still tries to whip me with a birch rod if I've done wrong. He's insistent that I'm still a child myself."

Art gave him a sidelong glance, so warm it made him glad that the rock beneath his backside was cold enough to prevent any of his body's recent awkward reactions to pleasure. "Not hardly."

"Well... all right." He chuckled. "My ma didn't think so either. She and Tomas used to go at it hammer and tongs, about children born out of what he calls wedlock. There were so few of us here even before the raid that she couldn't understand his objection to *any* healthy bairns coming along. But no, I don't have someone like that. There's time enough, isn't there?"

"Not for me."

"Oh." Rapidly Lance strung ideas together. Here was Arthur Pendragon, eldest son of Uther of Cerniw, already launched into a battle for his kingdom, a fight which could veer from diplomacy to deadly violence any day. Lance steadied his voice and tried to sound far more worldly than his years and experience of life allowed. "You... have to get yourself an heir?"

"Steady on. First I have to get myself a lawful Christian wife."

"Do you?"

"I know. It didn't bother Uther, did it? But times have changed since then, and Father Marcus says it must be so."

"Your village priest?"

Art grinned. "If only he'd confine himself to the village," he said. "He'd have travelled all the way up here with us if Ector had let him. He doesn't beat me with a birch rod, but he does tell me things. About what will happen to my immortal soul if I don't toe the line. So Ector made him stay at home, to give me a break." His smile faded. "Because if it were... only a case of getting a child, that's been seen to."

Lance felt an odd twitch of shock. He and Art had compared notes, and although neither knew his exact date of birth, had concluded that they must be more or less the same age. "A boy?" he asked tentatively, and waited until Art nodded. "Where is he?"

"In Ireland with his mother. I, er... I went to a Beltane fire."

"Oh!" Lance couldn't hide a grin. Children from the May Eve rites were a foregone conclusion. Father Tomas had made half-hearted efforts to repress them, but even up here on the moorlands, before the great winter had come, the early summer nights had been too sweet. "Was she nice? The girl, I mean?"

"Yes. Unfortunately she was also my half-sister, Modron." Art twisted round to face Lance, urgently, as if afraid of his judgement. "I didn't know her, I swear. She's Ygraine's first daughter, by Gwrlais. She was six when the Merlin took me away, and I'd never clapped eyes on her since."

Lance sat still and quiet. In some ways, as his mother's son, he was worldly enough. "Well, was the child… all right?" Art nodded again, his eyes still downcast, his handsome face strained in the dappled light. "You were lucky, then. Listen, Art, don't let the Christian priests tell you you did anything worse than take a risk. My people—my mother's, anyway—took consorts from amongst their brothers, time out of mind. The bloodlines are sometimes too close when the children come, that's all."

Arthur looked up. His brow had cleared a little. "Is that true? Father Marcus berated me so, I thought I'd be blown off to hell on the next high wind."

"I don't think so." Lance smiled. "Not for that, anyway. How old's the boy now?"

"Two this coming winter." He shuddered. "Priests aside, Lance, it doesn't feel right."

"Will you acknowledge him? When you become king?"

"I'm… under pressure to do so, yes. No-one can deny his blood is royal. His name is Medraut. I wish Modron would let me see him, but she's taken him off to Cell Dara—Kildare, I think they call it here. The sanctuary of Bride."

"Oh. Is she a priestess?"

"Yes, although nobody talks to Marcus about it."

"Then… did you ever consider that it might have been arranged?" Lance leaned forward, reaching for his discarded shirt, and gave Arthur a look of sympathy and mischief mixed. "After all, how dead-out-of-luck would you have to be—to pick the one girl in a Beltane crowd who turned out to be a relation?"

Arthur snorted with laughter. "If only there'd been any picking involved," he said. "They gave me a draught of poppy wine, and I woke up flat on my back in the greenwood, with Modron sitting over me, and..."

Lance blushed from the marrow of his bones, diving into his shirt to hide the reaction. "All right. I get the idea. But in that case, it *does* sound deliberate." He emerged, fringe in his eyes. "My mother said that a priestess can take whomever she chooses for her consort—her brother, and after that, if she so wishes, even the son of their union."

"She *told* you that?"

"No. It was one of the moon rites, and I was eavesdropping. But it sounds as though the women of your family might have their own ideas about who should be king after you."

"Wonderful. I haven't been king yet myself. You do know, I hope, that all of this depends on my getting horribly slain in battle, poisoned, struck down by disease or..." He paused, eyebrows rising. "Wait. What on earth have the women got to do with it?"

Lance was briefly too surprised to reply. Art had grown up among men, he supposed—Roman men and soldiers at that. "Well—nothing, maybe. Not if the priests of Christ have their way. You sneaked off to a Beltane, though, Art. You call on the old gods when you're upset, not Christ. And you wear..." He reached for the sun sign again. Picked out in silver on its reverse was a gleaming crescent moon. "You don't wear that for nothing. In my home, before the raid, my mother made decisions about everything."

"And your father allowed this?"

"Of course. They were comrades and friends."

He thought he had managed to swallow down the tremor in his throat. Lights of comprehension filled Art's eyes, however, and he put an arm around Lance's shoulders. "I can't imagine how that must have been," he said. "I'm fond enough of women, and you don't have to dose me with poppy to get me into bed with one. If I have a choice, though..."

His voice scraped to silence. Lance became aware, as if he'd climbed a steep hill and his ears had popped, of the breeze-washed stillness all around. *If I have a choice...* If Lance missed this, let these words with their load of longing and hope blow away on the wind, his loss would be greater than the northern earth's when the summer had failed to come.

He would miss out on the springtime of his own life. "If you have a choice," he whispered, sinking his fingers into the moss for purchase on one side, letting his weight ease against Art on the other. "What would you choose?"

For answer, Art put a hand beneath his chin and gently raised his face. Lance closed his eyes. A moment later, a warm mouth descended upon them: left, right, swiftest moth-wing touches. Then the prince of Cerniw was holding him most fiercely and tenderly still for a kiss.

Too much. Lance's world had been too narrow to hold the idea of such rushing joy. He knew about hunger, winters, ice, not young sun gods come to earth to plant honeyed fruit-flesh blessings on his lips. He jerked away, shuddering. "No."

"No?!"

Lance would have laughed if he hadn't wanted to weep. What a face! How many times had anyone been fool enough to turn him down? His astounded disappointment cut Lance to the quick. "How can I?" he asked roughly. "You've bedded Goddess knows how many girls—priestesses, at that. Boys, too, I should think."

"Of course. I'm not one of Father Marcus's slack-cocked saints. What difference does that make?"

"I haven't had anyone at all."

"Oh!" The red-gold eyebrows flew up. "How... How on earth have you managed that?"

"I just haven't wanted to. Nobody made me feel that way—like the bull covering the cows in May, like my brother with the dairy maid up in the hayloft, both of them yelling their heads off."

"Forgive me, dear Lance, but you're still only wearing your shirt. Is there any chance at all that you feel that way now?"

Helplessly Lance glanced down at himself. Oh, he'd been what his mother had smilingly described as a late-blooming sprig—but the time had come for him, this beautiful prince bringing it on like thunder in a summer storm. "Arthur," he choked out. "Yes. But I don't know what to do."

Chapter Twelve

"I would choose you." The words fell from Art like stones, a weight of truth he couldn't have known he was carrying inside him. He couldn't have known that this skinny boy, with his handful of acres and a kingdom's worth of pride, would bring down his walls. "I would choose you. Oh, Lance."

They lay together in the wind-shaken shadows of the birch. Lance, whose uncertainty had lasted only until they'd wrestled each other flat onto the rocks, pushed onto one elbow to look at him. "Arthur, my king. You look like a golden-eyed wildcat. Am I enough for you?"

"Enough for ten thousand wildcats. I'm not king yet, remember. I may never be."

"You'll always be so to me. What can I give you?"

Your allegiance. Your promise that, when I leave this place tomorrow, you'll be riding at my side. Art bit back the words. Lance had already said—indicated, anyway—that he'd consider it. Ector had warned him time and again not to push, to try and close his grasp on a privilege on its way to him anyway. "Give me your skin and bone," he said roughly, pulling Lance on top of him and clasping his chilly backside. "Give me your seed."

Lance drew a shuddering breath. He pressed his face to Art's shoulder, and Art felt the impassioned opening of his mouth, the graze of his teeth. The narrow hips bucked between his hands. Art, who had come erect from the first moment of subsiding with him onto the stone, cried out at the joy of it. He surrendered his grip and buried both hands in Lance's hair instead.

***

"I'd be a poorly-made knight, you know."

Art looked up and smiled. He'd just given Lance a leg-up onto Balana's broad back. "What makes you think that?"

"I can handle a weapon, as you're kind enough to say." Lance ran a hand over the pommel of the sword from the lake, making both of them grin at the hopeless suggestiveness of the caress. "But you'll need experienced soldiers, and much more than that—educated men, who can help you with strategy. You won't be the king of a hilltop, like my father was. You'll have a proper court."

"Much you know. Guy and Ector are going to help me take over a hillfort once held by the Durotriges, as soon as we return to the south. It's enormous, overlooking a big sweep of the River Cam."

"Defensible?"

"Oh, yes. Own spring-fed water source, ready-made embankments. I shan't be living like a tribal chieftain there—we'll build with stone, like the Romans—but without my ill-made knight, I'd still just be king of the hill."

"Come on, then. Gaius will be eating all our lunch."

Arthur gathered up Hengroen's reins and made ready to spring into the saddle. Then he went still, his attention once more captured by the waters of the lough. "Oh, no," he said faintly. "That's what I get for ignoring him."

"Ignoring who?"

"The vision. The old man."

Lance brought Balana round in a sweeping movement to shield him. "Never mind him. Just come with me. Come away."

"Avoiding him makes it worse."

"In that case..." Lance stilled the mare, who was capering and snorting as if she too would have preferred to run. "In that case, I think you should face it like a man, and tell me what you see."

Like a man?! Arthur wanted to turn on him in rage. *What would you know of it, farm boy? Prince of sheep?* But running through the matrix of his visions was always a sense of utter solitude, as if he had lost or driven from him everyone he cared for. Oh, if he couldn't avoid his fate, at least he need not hurry it on...

"All right," he rasped, taking a firmer grip of Hengroen, stepping a little way out of the shelter Lance had created for him, untaught and unprompted, a natural battlefield manoeuvre. "All right. I see the waters darken. I can smell blood, and I hear the cries of dying men. My flesh too is pierced, from my gut to my backbone. I am still young, and there's so much more I need to do. But my death has been decreed, so that my people can live. So that... So that I can return."

"What does it mean, Art?"

"I don't know. I've tried and tried to understand, but he—the Merlin—says it doesn't matter whether I understand or not. So long as I make the sacrifice."

Lance's hand fastened in his hair. He drew him back, close to Balana's warm flank, and Art, who had manfully faced as much for one day as he could, turned and rested his brow against Lance's thigh.

Still he saw the boat approaching. It didn't come naturally through the water, but formed itself out of black cloud and floated just over the surface. Art knew the shape of it. In Ector's Christian world, the dead were buried safely out of sight, but Art's Kernowek ancestors had given them back to the waves. He knew this, just as he knew so much more about Pendragon and the wild Cerniw shores than he'd ever been taught. He knew he was looking at a black-sailed funeral barge.

Cold terror seized him. The ship was no vessel of timbers and pitch, but a hole cut out of the universe. He would not die peacefully. He would disappear into that hole and be dissolved into its nothingness. On the prow, straight and still, a hooded figure stood, long robes unruffled by the gale. The old man, Arthur knew. The shadow that had dogged his life, come now in his last minutes to ensure that not even his spirit would escape the howling dark, come to bear him forever away from the sun. "No," he said wearily. "No."

Lance's grip tightened. "No," he agreed, drawing him closer. "This is some illness, surely. You've had too much weight laid upon you too soon."

"Do you think so?" Art raised his head. "Perhaps you're right. Why should it be this way?"

"Maybe it doesn't have to. Maybe it's only a warning, or... or a dream. I wish we could ask Viviana."

"Oh, damn Viviana!" Art yelled suddenly back, making Lance and the horses jump. "Damn her, and damn the Merlin. Father Ector and his prophecies, too." He seized Hengroen's reins and leapt effortlessly into the saddle. He grinned at Lance like a well-favoured demon. "Blast all whispering in corners, all flapping robes and Celtic mysteries. I'm a Roman and a Briton, and so are you. Neither of us believes in this nonsense. I can see Guy right up on the crest, beside the old Wall. Come on, Lance o'lough—I'll race you!"

For an instant, Lance wondered where they were going. As far away, he guessed, from the dark visions as Arthur could possibly get. Then he lost all thought in the excitement of the chase.

They tore along the shore of the lough in a rainbow of hoof-shattered spray, Art always a few yards ahead. Lance had never dared ride his borrowed mount hard, but now that caution was hurled to the winds, how sweetly she responded! When Hengroen got some distance on her, she snorted and lengthened her stride without urging, seeming to take joy in their bounding dash across the moor.

Lance laughed aloud between deep gasps for air. The turf and the heather were deadly, pitted all over with badger holes, scattered with grassed-over rocks, but he felt immortal. Arthur had loved him, had said *give me your skin and your bone, your seed*, and when Lance had given and done all that, had surged up on top of him and given him all those things too.

Far up ahead on the crag by the Wall he saw Guy gesturing frantically, his voice reaching them in tatters on the wind. *Probably wants us to slow down*, Lance thought distantly. *Poor fellow*. He felt sorry for everyone not privileged to be as he was now, for everyone earthbound, everyone not flying into the sun on the heels of the future king.

He saw their destination just as Art changed course and set a full-pelt dash towards it. The very crest of the dragon's spine. All his life, it had been Lance's landmark, that heartlifting shape on the sky. It had risen above the mists in the valley when he was making his way back from a day-long hunt, telling him that he was nearly home. It had haunted his sleep, a shape he had never recognised until Viviana had shown his dreaming mind the dragon. He had gone there often, to escape the scuffling chaos of his family, seeking refuge in its bareness, its bleak calm. It was like a mighty scale projecting from the earth, a ragged upthrust of rock where even the gorse struggled to find a niche for growth. The highest point for miles around. Lance smiled, wheeling the mare to follow in Art's wake. *Of course.*

The way to the crest from beneath the crags was up a steep and twisting path. Lance thought Art must have seen it, perhaps on their way down: it was invisible from here.

Then he realised that the prince had no intention of following any path at all. He had set his horse's head direct at the cliff face. At this point, before the walls of black rock leapt up sheer, the route was impossible.

"Art!" he yelled. "Not here!" But if Arthur heard him, he gave no sign. He set Hengroen's head at the last few yards of level ground, covered them at a flat-out dash.

Lance understood. Thoughts that should have unfolded slowly flashed at him in lightning blades. *You are outrunning your fate. Riding for your life, and you don't care how short that life might be, if only you can choose its ending yourself.*

Then, as certainly as he'd grasped that truth, he knew that his own fate was inextricably tangled with Art's. The distance between them increased, and he felt a physical tugging inside him. Where Art went, he had to follow. On the heels of his fright came a wild exultation. There were certainly worse ways to die. Throwing aside everything he'd ever learned about the care of himself and his horse, the brute common sense of survival, he turned the mare's head and rode her straight after Hengroen.

They made the climb somehow, in terrible wrenching leaps and bounds. If Lance slackened momentum for a second, the earth would pull him down. Under the thud of his heart, the percussive breathing of the horse, he could hear poor Gaius, shouting in what sounded like despair.

They broached the crest together, in a clatter of hooves on rock. Sparks flew as they reined in, both doing their best to pull up the snorting, wheeling horses before they shot off the crevasse on the far side. They came to a halt at the same instant, and faced one another, eyes wide with questions.

Lance got his breath back first. "What was that supposed to be?"

"What did it look like? A race!"

Lance hesitated. If he denied it—accused the prince of trying to destroy himself in a fit of half-insane terror—many things would be over. Was it his duty anyway? Surely Arthur needed friends who were too wise to accompany him into his madness… But, Lance knew, that was what he had just done. "A race," he repeated unsteadily. "Well, who won it?"

"We were equal," Art said, then added with absurd solemnity, "which means that I must fight you for it."

"I don't want to fight you."

"It's a challenge. You must. To show me your allegiance!"

"That makes no sense at all. Anyway, haven't I…" He paused, trying to make him smile. "Haven't I shown you more or less everything today already?"

A broad, loving grin rewarded him. But wild forces were whirling about the crag still, a storm with Art at its eye. "Nonetheless."

The wildness was catching. Lance didn't want to be Art's conscience, his counterpoise. He had Gaius and Ector for that. And if Art could only purge this strange mood through combat, better it be with a friend. "Very well, then. Foot or horse?"

"Horse, I think. They're all right. We just gave them a bit of a scare."

"Gave *them* a scare?" Lance said it for form's sake: at no point in the chase had he been afraid. There was no reason, he thought, unsheathing Excalibur. Harm couldn't reach him in Arthur's wake until Arthur's time had come. "Have at you, then, if you must. On your guard!"

Chapter Thirteen

They were too evenly matched. Such a fight could go on forever. At first Lance was afraid that Art was going easy on him, allowing for the difference between a boy raised as a warrior king and one who'd had to tend sheep between his father's infrequent lessons in swordsmanship.

But Art's eyes were too brightly intent for that, and anyway Lance didn't think it lay in his nature: he'd refuse to fight him at all rather than insult him by lowering his game. The horses circled like dancers on the rock. As if from a great distance, Lance heard Gaius clatter up onto the crest. Guy was shouting, but after a moment his voice faded out to the thump of blood in Lance's ears.

The sword sat so light in Lance's hand that he scarcely had to exert strength to wield it. It did his bidding with no gap between thought and act, worked almost ahead of thought, leaping to block Art's every move. Lance couldn't have held him off otherwise. The sword was the answer: with Excalibur, he was immortal, could join Arthur's forces and be worth something...

Just as this happy thought struck him, Balana—who was not immortal—slipped and went down like a rockslide.

Lance hit the ground first. A heartbeat later she fell on him, in a flail of legs and mane. The sword took flight. Pinned, winded, Lance watched it flash end over end and vanish off the edge of the crag.

He minded, but not half so much as he minded having hurt the horse. Her knees and flanks were bloodied: he saw it in dazed flickers as she scrambled to her feet. "Poor beast! Poor beast!" he gasped, pushing up onto his knees and holding out a shaking hand to catch her reins. She was battle-hardened, trained not to leave a fallen man, but plainly she'd been put past patience—stood staring and blowing at him with such an expression of disbelief that he almost laughed. Then pain caught up with him, and he dropped back onto the rock.

Art dismounted neatly. His weird fires were gone, quenched absolutely. Only the sweet-natured, sober lad remained. Quickly he caught Balana's rein and stilled her. "Poor beast?" he echoed. "Poor Lance, I think. What a fall! Are you still alive?"

Lance gave it thought. "Too stupid to die," he said, looking at the surface of the outcrop around them. "We shouldn't have fought here, Art. It's like glass. But never mind me. The horse…"

"The horse comes first," Art finished for him, grimly. Gaius had appeared beside Arthur, expression unreadable, and taken the reins from his hands. Only then did Art come and crouch beside Lance. "She's fine. They're scratches, that's all. You, however…" He ran both hands down Lance's shin, glancing at him in wry admiration when he didn't cry out. "If you were Balana, your outlook would be grim. That's broken. Guy and I will set it for you." He smiled pallidly. "At least, he will sit on you while I do it. Where's your sword?"

"Went over the crag. It doesn't matter." For the moment, it was true: Lance knew by now he'd gladly barter immortality for five minutes at the centre of Arthur's regard.

But Art's face shadowed. "I'll fetch it for you," he said, and before either Guy or Lance could respond, had leapt to his feet and was running for the edge of the rock. "Guy, look after him!"

Lance flipped over onto his stomach, oblivious to the sunburst of pain in his leg. He watched in horror as Art hesitated, assessing the drop, then slipped lithely over the precipice and vanished. "Gaius, stop him!" he gasped. "It really *doesn't* matter. Gods—not that much, anyway!"

"The sword from the lake?" Gaius roughly demanded. "It damn well should. As for stopping him…" He unfastened his cloak, took it off and dropped it on Lance without ceremony. "As for stopping him, you've surely seen by now how easy that is." He gave Lance a look that made his face burn with shame. "You've been a big help, by the way." Then he too was gone, leaving Lance almost too mortified to cover himself with the cloak.

***

Climbing rocks. It had been the one game Guy could win against Art. At first all their contests had been easy: Guy was older and bigger, and angry enough not to give Art an inch on either count, no matter how hard Ectorius scolded him. Then the prince, the Pendragon's son who could do no wrong, had fledged like an eagle, and overnight, it seemed to Guy, with a minimum of training, had become a natural expert in archery, swordfighting, horsemanship, all the arts of war in which Ector was having them trained. He hadn't forgotten being crushed by the bigger boy, either, and Guy had suffered accordingly.

For some reason, though, Guy remained better at scrambling up and down the cliffs that towered along Dumnonia's coast. Brute strength, probably, he bitterly reflected, beginning his descent. Big limbs, harder to break than his royal highness's: Art had grown into the length of his bones but would never be husky. Guy glanced down the crag and saw him making a decent job of negotiating the pitching, jagged slope, but as ever he was headstrong, not stopping to plan his route. Guy could see a better one. He steadied himself, undid his own sword belt lest the blade unbalance him, and sturdily began to scramble down.

The sword was lodged tightly in a deep cleft between two massive outcrops of the ridge. *Two scales of the dragon's spine*, Art thought, shuddering. It was cold down here, and damp, as if the sunlight had despaired of the place long ago. He wouldn't have seen the hilt if it didn't have a weird light of its own, if its spiral, didn't seem to dance in the corners of his vision, then go still when he looked at them direct. But for all its gleaming and dancing, Art couldn't reach it, not without a leap across four foot of empty space over a sickening drop.

The sword was all Lance had. It was his pledge, his promise, from the Lady of the Lake, and he'd lost it through Arthur's own fault. He had to try. Bracing himself to the rock, he glanced across the gap, swallowed hard and made ready to jump.

"Arthur Pendragon! Don't you bloody dare!"

Art froze where he was. Guy was growing into his father's voice, and that still had power to halt him in his tracks. He glanced up to the source of the roared-out command, and saw his foster brother making his way down toward him. The sight of him, the rugged solidity of his bearing, which for all his teasing Arthur secretly envied, made him feel like a child again, and he hated the tremor in his voice when he called out, "But the sword, Guy! We have to get it back for him!"

"I know. I don't think he'd want us to kill ourselves doing it, though. Stay where you are! There's an easy way over from here."

Art frowned up into the distant, blazing sky. Was there? Ah, yes—an obvious one, too, if he'd bothered to look. Ectorius accused him sometimes of making things hard for himself on purpose, and he'd always denied it, but perhaps it was so. Certainly life tasted best to him when he was riding full-pelt against it. No old men or visions assaulted him then. He watched Guy step over the gap where it was only a big stride across, and begin to scramble down to the sword.

He almost jumped anyway. His pride had been dented by Guy's common sense, and it would be a coup to spring over the abyss and get there before him.

Squinting, he looked up to see his brother's expression. There was no malice there, no trace of triumph. There hadn't been for years, he realised. Guy was just trying, as usual, to take care of him. He'd risked his neck in the process, too, and not for the first time—even the more sensible path he'd taken down the crag was fraught with danger. His homely face was concentrated with the effort of staying upright. Art felt a surge of affection for him, and began with care to make his way up to the safe path he'd been shown.

"Damn thing's stuck," Guy observed as Art slithered down the last few feet of the scree to where he was sitting. "Blade's gone clean down between these two rocks."

Arthur came to a halt and surveyed the scene. He rested one hand on his own sword hilt and ran the other through his hair, blowing out a puzzled breath. "How did he manage that?"

"I don't know, but I bet you he couldn't do it again."

They broke into brief laughter. "I'm sorry, Guy," Art said. "I picked the fight with Lance. He didn't want it at all. And I just got carried away."

"You two are meant to be friends. That's why I left you alone this afternoon—to use your diplomatic skills to persuade him to come with us tomorrow."

Their eyes met. Guy's were tranquil, but didn't hide a faint gleam. Arthur blushed like a rising sun. "We *are* friends. And, er... thanks."

"My pleasure. Come and help me try to shift this thing."

They both tried, Art clasping his hands round his brother's on the hilt and lifting, first of all directly upwards, then leaning against the wall of rock to get some angle and purchase. Gaius gestured Art aside and tried it again by himself, bracing his thighs and pitting all his considerable muscle against the blade's entrapment.

But the sword was balanced there as if in a perfect-made scabbard of stone, as if it had grown in place. "Sorry, Bear," Guy said, after another few efforts. "I think we might have to leave it."

Bear. Arthur smiled, eyes stinging. Guy hadn't called him that since their arrival at Vindolanda, as if aware of the changes the place had wrought in him, the sudden scramble to adulthood. Why did the old name touch him so deeply now? Art couldn't have said, except that some moments felt more than others like knife edges, like forks in the road when he knew that his path and Guy's would divide unimaginably far, and he had grown to love him dearly. "All right," he said roughly. "Thank you for trying. We'd better go and see to Lance."

He was turning away when the skies darkened. Guy was ahead of him: Art was tired, and only too willing now to follow his brother's better idea of how to get back to the top. "Wait," he said. "I have to try it again."

Guy shook his head. "I gave it all I had, and you're two thirds the man I am. Don't bother. It really is caught fast."

Had the light changed? Arthur shivered, and ran a hand over his eyes. No—the jagged patch of sky between the jaws of the rock above them was still diamond bright. The hairs on his nape prickled up. His eardrums popped as if he'd galloped too fast downhill. He'd scarcely known a day's illness in his life, and couldn't identify the horrible weakness undoing his joints, the cold sweat damping his spine and his palms, at the thought of leaving the weapon behind. Evading the hand Guy had put out to steady him, he went back.

He took hold of it lightly, just beneath the guard. He didn't brace to pull. There was no need. He simply stepped outside his flesh. He let all his bones turn to rock, breathed through lungs made out of the sweet north wind. He watched with the eyes of the sun, as the white-faced boy who was himself effortlessly pulled the sword from the stone.

Chapter Fourteen

"That's ridiculous," Guy said. "I must have slackened it. Put it back and let me try again."

Art stared at him, one disbelieving eyebrow on the rise. "You are kidding me, aren't you?"

"No, I really want to have another—"

A tremor shook the ridge. Guy flung out both hands to stay upright. A baker's dozen of ravens shot up from their nest-ledges into the blue. "Guy," Art whispered, when the cawing and the shudder of the ground had ceased. "Take the sword back to Lance."

"Take it yourself. What was that?"

"Can't you hear it?"

"Hear what?"

"The song of the dragon. Uther tried to seize it—that inheritance, that old magic—but he could only ever pass it on. The song of the sacred earth."

"For pity's sake." Guy strode to catch him before he could drop. "Sit down. Put your head between your knees. Give me that wretched sword."

"You have to take it back to Lance, Guy."

"All right, all right. In a minute. Are you going to faint?"

"Of course not."

"Then sit still while I look at the crack in the rock." Cradling the sword, Guy knelt to examine the place where the blade had been wedged—forever, he'd thought. "I don't understand," he said after a moment. "It's gone. The whole surface here is in one piece, as if it..."

"As if it healed itself?"

"Yes, but that has to be nonsense."

"It doesn't matter. Will you just take it up and give it back to him?"

"Arthur, it's yours," Guy said harshly. His father had always made him swear not to burden the lad with the prophecies, but Art had ever been too bright and inquisitive for secrets to stay covered long in Ector's small, ingenuous household. "You must know that."

Art turned on him. He was sweat-damped, shivering, and yet when his grey gaze met Guy's, there was command in it. "Didn't you hear me? I must rest here for a while. Take this sword and restore it to my friend."

Gaius climbed carefully, the sword tucked awkwardly through his belt. Occasionally he glanced down to see that Arthur was safe. After a while the boy began to follow, but slowly and at a distance, as if he didn't yet want to emerge into the light.

As he hauled himself over the edge, the beauty of this strange countryside seemed to strike Guy for the first time, with almost painful force. His focus had been on Arthur, on keeping him safe and returning him in one piece to Ectorius after each ride. The hills to the northeast caught his breath—endless, marked out in cloudshadows. Guy, not overly sensitive to landscape, was bemused by his sudden awakening now. The air smelled so sweet. It was as if the whole earth was silently laughing at him. He stood for a moment, distracted.

Then he turned, and his heart dropped into his boots. Lance was there on the outcrop where he'd left him. Standing over him, complete with horse, weaponry and three tall grooms, was Sir Ector.

***

"Inexcusable. Irresponsible, feckless, unjustifiable."

Lance tried to sit up. He'd been comfortably propped on the grooms' saddlebags, given water and wine by Sir Ector's own hands. He'd attempted several times to intervene, but to no avail so far. The old knight was punctuating each of his words with a poke at Guy's chest with one forefinger. "Sir Ector," Lance cried out in desperation. "It was my fault just as much as Art's, and Guy's fault not at all. I lost the sword, and Art knows what it means to me. He went to fetch it."

Ector spared him a glance. Then he swivelled back to face Guy. "Unforgivable!" Another poke, hard enough to rock sturdy Guy on his feet. "Hours past your time of return, and no sign of any of you. That sharp-eyed old priest it was who saw the flash of sword-blades up here, and raised the alarm. The Picts! A raid! The whole damn village up in arms, or hiding under their beds, according to their nature. I take to horse, and come up here like thunder with these good lads to rescue my sons and this prince from the jaws of the invader, and what do I find? Squabbling boys! My fine Balana with skinned knees, and..." He ran out of breath. After a moment he looked at Lance again. The life seemed to drain out of him. "The sword is lost?"

Lance made one last effort. "It was I who hurt Balana," he said. "Forgive me, Sir Ector—all this is down to me. As for the sword..."

"I have it!" Guy interposed, his voice cracked and raw. "I have the sword, Father. Here, Lance—take it."

Sir Ector's arm fell to his side. When he spoke again, he sounded like himself once more, but chastened and ashamed. "For God's sake, Gaius. That's good, but... where is my boy?"

"On his way up, Father. He isn't hurt."

Stiffly Lance took the blade from Guy. As soon as his fingers closed round the hilt, he felt the cold recede from his limbs, felt new life stir in him. He remembered the touch of a hand which had somehow come warm from the depths of the lough. "Thank you, Gaius. Had it fallen far?"

Guy glanced nervously at his father, who nodded curt permission to proceed. "The strangest thing happened. The sword fell into a crevasse. I... I pulled it free."

Lance was a rotten liar, but Gaius was worse. Lance wondered if he'd ever before in his life told a deliberate untruth. He was bullfinch-red from his brow to the neckline of his shirt.

Sir Ector, instead of exploding once more with rage, took him gently by the shoulders with both hands. "Is that what really happened, dear Guy?"

"Yes, sir. I..."

"Father Ector?"

The whole group turned, Lance twisting round as far as he could to see. Arthur struggled back onto the crest. He was dishevelled and grazed, and looked as if the climb had taken the last of his strength. Nevertheless he lifted a hand to wave at them all, and flashed Guy a rueful, self-mocking smile.

Guy closed his eyes in shame. "Father," he said. "I am a vain fool. The sword was caught between two rocks. I tried and tried, but could not pull it out. Then Arthur put one hand to it and lifted it free. The earth shook, and I heard a huge, strange voice singing, and now the sun shines more brightly than it did before. I don't understand these things," he finished humbly. "I told a lie. I wanted to be part of it all—this strangeness, this miracle—but I am not. Am I?"

At Ector's gesture, the grooms ran to help Art. Then the old man put his arms around his son. "Let me tell you what you are," he said roughly, as Guy hid his face on his shoulder. "You are my Gaius, my firstborn. My good, brave boy."

Art stumbled over. He looked at his father and Guy in dismay, then dropped to his knees beside Lance. "Are you all right?"

Before anyone could stop him, Lance pushed up: got onto one knee, using the sword as a dangerous prop. Once he was steady, he held it out to Art. "This is yours," he said. "Your brother knows it, and your father too. The very earth knows it, Arthur. Take your own."

He held on for long enough to see in Arthur's eyes the scared child, who'd fled his destiny at every turn and been run to ground at last on these northern moors, on the dragon's spine, bow his head and let the cloak of adulthood descend upon his shoulders. In unbreathing silence they shared the knowledge of how much that garment would weigh—how magnificent it was, how crushing, how impossible to remove. A shudder passed through Arthur, a last flash of grief and rebellion, and then he reached to take the sword.

It was done, and Lance, knowing his duty discharged, dropped back to the rock, the grey edge of a faint threatening his vision. The day became ordinary. Art, promptly practical, shoved the sacred blade into his old sword's scabbard. "Quick," he said, glancing up at his father and Guy. "Let's get that leg set while he's too weak to fight us off."

Chapter Fifteen

Earlier that day, Lance had instructed Edern and his family to prepare a fine dinner for the departing Roman guests. He didn't see why a broken leg should interfere with that, or any of his other duties, and so he fashioned himself a crutch from one of Elena's brooms, and as the sun was setting in red-gold splendour over the crags to the west, he set off on his usual inspection of the village boundaries.

For once—*on the subject of red-gold splendour*, he wryly recognised—the prince of Cerniw didn't appear from the shadows of an alley or the stables to accompany him. Lance was sorry. This would be their last time. Arthur had given him a ride home on Hengroen's majestic back, leading the stallion contritely by the rein. After doctoring Balana, the prince had brought Lance a draught of poppy mead and served it to him with his own hands. Although he'd been gone when Lance woke, through the poppy's kindly veils he'd been aware of his presence, silent and watchful by the bed.

They would have time, he and Art. Lance reached the eastern edge of the settlement, the bare stretch of land where Father

Tomas had built his church, and time seemed to spread out like a richly laid board before him, each shadowed valley a chalice brim-full of the joys and adventures he and his prince would share. *Much use I'd be to you like this*, he'd tried to protest on the way back down from the crags, but Sir Ector himself had leaned to pat his shoulder. *We're only going as far as Caer Lir, lad. You can rest and heal there before we head south.*

South, to the Forest Wild, where trees grew to five times the height of a man, and Art's great fortress of Cam would rise beside the river! Where golden sunlight flickered in silent glades, and there would be other lake shores, and the prince of Cerniw would once more say to him, *I would choose you. Give me your skin and bone, your seed.*

Lance shivered. He offered a silent prayer of apology to his lost older brothers, who'd pursued their dairy maids and strapping farm lads with a determination that had made him laugh. Oh, he'd been a child then, hadn't he, a caterpillar, deaf and blind, sound asleep in childhood's dream...

His leg was aching, so he made his way over to the steps of the church and sat down. He'd broken bones before, and was aware of how expertly his shin had been set. Sir Ector had said he'd be taught the arts of battlefield medicine, as well as many other skills and graces. He'd thought himself sophisticated to be able to speak Latin, but Arthur and Gaius could read it too, an accomplishment beyond his imagination. Sir Ector had a whole roomful of enormous leatherbound books, their parchment pages overflowing with tales of strange travels and encounters with mythical beasts beyond the seas.

Only a handful of books were left at Vindolanda, although Ban had used to tell stories of the praetor's house at the height of its glory. Only Father Tomas ever touched them, and kept them hidden in a chest beneath a slab in the chapel whenever they were out of his hands. Belatedly Lance noticed that the old priest was present and reading now, perched on a bench in the doorway of the church. With his bowed head and earth-brown robes, he almost disappeared against the candle-lit darkness within.

"Is it a good part, Father?" Lance asked. Elena had taught him to be polite about the teachings of the new god, even if he found them strange. "I like it when Joshua's army goes round Jericho blowing their trumpets, and all the walls fall down."

"You would, you wildcat's child," Tomas said absently. "Those are ancient tales, though the very word of God, and of course beyond dispute. I am reading now in the books authorised by the Council of Laodicea, confirmed by the Easter letter of Athanasius, bishop of Alexandria. The teachings of Christ. Ah, it's you, Lance, is it?"

Lance smiled. "Who else?"

"I don't know. Sometimes, at the end of these long days— perhaps because I am nearing the end of mine—I think I see your mother, striding about the fields. I think I hear the heathen babble of your brothers and sisters, and..."

Awkwardly Lance levered himself upright. Arthur had splinted his leg with sturdy cuts of wood, and he could bear a little weight on it already, or use it for balance, at any rate. He would take horse tomorrow with the best of them. He limped up the steps, and sat beside Tomas on the bench. "Don't be afraid to speak to me about Ban, Father."

Tomas snorted. "Afraid? Don't talk nonsense. What's that on your leg, you wretch?"

"A splint. I broke it."

"Broke it? While we have distinguished guests? Where are your manners, boy?"

"I was out riding with the prince. He was giving me a lesson in swordsmanship on horseback, and I had a fall. It was rude of

115

me, doubtless, but you wouldn't have had me refuse the instruction, would you?"

Tomas spared him a wintry smile. "Enjoy your joke, stripling. We down here in the vicus thought you'd been ambushed by Picts. That..." His smile faded, replaced by grey fear. "That we'd be next, if it were so. Everyone remembers how it was. Some of the farmers ran to fetch pitchforks. Your mother's women— savages, of course—were clamouring at doors of Ban's armoury, wanting his short-swords and spears. But today, most of them were simply afraid. They stood with empty hands in the doorways of their houses. They knew they wouldn't stand a chance. That they'd been once more abandoned."

Lance went cold. Tomas, naturally garrulous, had barely spoken about the night of the raid. Lance had taken his silence for shock. Now it struck him that the old man might have been showing a kindly and determined restraint. "Once more abandoned?" he echoed. "Tomas, do you know what my father did, that night when the raiders came?"

Tomas shifted uncomfortably. He folded down the cover of the vast leather book in his lap. "Why?" he demanded, almost harshly. "Do you?"

"Yes. I've been... I've been told. He ran off like a frightened deer into the smoke."

"Then I grieve, that you've lived with the shame of it. Your mother... My last sight of your mother, she had a Pict by his long barbarian plait and was smiting him with a frying pan."

"It was his shame, not mine!" Lance pushed the image of Elena out of his mind: already his voice was raw with the threat of tears. He paused, knowing the words building up on his tongue would change the whole world for him, shrink the joyous spread of the future to a few dozen acres of muddy moorland earth. It could make no difference. He got to his feet, the better to deliver his dreadful truth. "I thank you for your silence, for honouring his name, but the shame was his. I will never abandon you."

***

When Art met him in the courtyard of the praetor's house, he knew at once that something had changed. But Lance looked too lost and sick for interrogation. Instead, Art fell into step at his side. "That leg must be hurting."

It was an excuse, kindly offered. Lance nodded, his gratitude plain. "A little now, yes."

"You shouldn't be on your feet. I tell you what—I'll help you upstairs, and you can have a rest before supper."

First Lance had to manage the steps up to the main door. They were majestic in the Roman style, broad and shallow, their crumbling marble patched by moss. Deftly Art relieved him of his broomstick crutch. He ducked beneath his arm, got a grip around his waist. "There. That's better, isn't it?"

"Where have you been all this time?"

"With Sir Ector, getting hauled over the coals for conduct unbecoming to a soldier. Wasting resources, risking valuable lives, that kind of thing."

"I tried to tell him it wasn't your fault."

"I know, and thank you. I don't really mind it, though." Art tightened his grip and began to hoist Lance up the steps. The fire had been lit in the praetor's great hall, and dancing shades of crimson met the last of the sunset in the cooling air. "To tell you the truth, I'm more afraid of the day when he stops doing it. He'll feel he doesn't have the right anymore. And that means..."

"That means you'll be king."

Art came to a halt. They'd reached the footworn passage beneath the portico. "That's right." *Just for a while, I'd thought I wouldn't have to do it alone.* "More importantly, supper smells good. Who's coming?"

"Oh, who isn't? Everyone's still ravenous after the winter. If the word of free food goes out, we'll have everyone from shepherd boys to squires. The butcher, the baker, the candlestick maker—and their women and children. It'll be chaos."

"It sounds like you've done this before."

"Many times, in Ban's better days. He was generous, and would feed people when he could. He was a good master, a good father."

Nobody had denied these things. Arthur examined the pale, set profile studiously avoiding his gaze. "Of course," he said gently. In the kitchen beyond the hall, men and women were bustling about: Lance's housekeeper Edern and his family, who had continued their faithful service, it seemed, through famine and long winter. Arthur doubted that Lance could have afforded to keep paying them after the catastrophic raid. All kinds of things about this lonely, far-flung household were good. "In that case, you can help solve a domestic problem of Sir Ector's. A future one of mine, at that."

"I doubt it, but go on."

"Come indoors where it's warmer. All these squires, farmers, shopkeepers... I suppose they have their own ideas about their importance, just as the knights and landowners do who come to visit us in the Forest Wild?"

Lance smiled reluctantly. They'd entered the friendly dining hall with its long trestle table, where he, Tomas and the Roman visitors had taken their evening meals for the last fortnight. "You've no idea. The miller would come to blows with our blacksmith over whose wife had more of a right to sit nearest the head of the board."

"And whose wife does?"

"Neither of them, of course. We shan't be eating in here tonight—come with me." He detached himself from Arthur's grasp, took back his makeshift crutch and set off across the hall. He pushed open a door Art hadn't noticed before. "There," he said. "My mother solved the problem long ago."

Rushlight torches had been set in cressets all around the walls. Arthur stepped into the flame-lit space, and burst into laughter. Occupying the centre of the room, skilfully crafted from peg-tied sections of brightly polished oak, was a perfectly round table, nobly set out for dining. "Wonderful," he exclaimed. "I shall have one like this made for my fortress at Cam, only five times the size. If I have nothing else, I'll have this, even if they have to build the place around it."

"It does help. You do know they'll still squabble for the privilege of a place at your right hand?"

That place ought to have been filled. Arthur bit back the words fiercely. If he didn't push, he didn't have to know—not yet, not yet. "Perhaps I'll fashion mine with a hole at the centre," he said thoughtfully. "I'll put my throne there, with some kind of wheel and mechanism to turn it. Then I'll sit in splendour, command myself to be rotated, and shed my kingly beneficence upon each of them in turn."

Lance was laughing now too. "Please don't do that. You'll look like the sack of grain they put up on a pole at the fair, for the lads to shy down with stones and clods of mud."

"Thank you very much. Maybe not that, then. Your mother was a clever woman, though."

"She was. She died fighting, I'm told."

Art turned to him, suddenly as serious as he. "Oh, Lance. I'm sorry."

"Don't. It's better that way, isn't it—to go down with honour and pride?"

119

"Far better, I'm sure. But fearful too, and far from easy. I hope it won't ever be asked of me—or you either, my friend. How long do we have before these guests of yours arrive?"

"None at all. I can hear cart wheels on the cobbles right now."

"And here come Ector and Guy, all dressed for feasting." Art pressed a hand into Lance's back and began to steer him out of sight of the handsomely turned-out pair striding through the main hall. "They can take care of things for a while."

"Arthur, no. I have to do the honours of the house."

"Come and do them with me. My blood's warm, and so is yours. How can we get out of here without being seen?"

"We can't. But Edern's too busy to notice us, so... Quick, through the kitchens. There's a flight of wooden steps from the yard at the back to the bedchambers. It's more like a ladder, though—you'll have to help me up."

Art beamed. "If I have to carry you. Come on!"

***

Down amongst the deerhounds and the furs.

Lance lay crushed and unbreathing. He wanted to hold this instant forever: his heartbeat racking him, his friend's warm weight pressing him deep into the skins and hides where he'd huddled alone all winter. The dogs, sleepy and fat with kitchen scrounging, had barely moved aside for them. A haze like dawn on the lough covered his vision, and Arthur gave a shuddery laugh and sat up a little way. "Breathe."

"I don't want to. I want... so much, and I don't know how to begin to get it. If you were a girl—"

"Oh, if I were a girl!" Art cut him off with tender scorn, turning to kiss the palm caressing his cheek. "I'd have eaten you alive by now, my Lance, and sucked out your core and planted your pips to make more of you. I can't think what your village maidens have been playing at, leaving such sweet fruit as you on the tree all this time."

"Maybe I was... on a high branch. I wish I hadn't broken my leg coming down!"

"Girl or boy, broken or whole, there's ways of doing things." Quick as an otter, sure as a cat in the dark, Art dipped down to press warm lips to the side of Lance's neck. Each place he touched should glow, Lance thought, should leave a pattern like the dragon's molten footprints on his skin. Slowly, with a quivering strength too sweet to be borne, Art moved his hips, throwing Lance beyond speech. How could he ask about the ways, the magic by which a broken boy might find the end of desire?

No need. Art took his weight on his arms. Elena's embroidered coverlet stretched above them, the arcane signs she'd stitched into it gleaming like the signs the stars made on a clear summer night. Within this shelter, this upturned bowl of stars, Arthur put down a guiding hand.

Lance felt tightness—hot, clenched resistance—and tried to recoil. But Arthur gave a gasping moan and rocked forward. On joyous instinct, Lance let his spine arch, the burning cage of his hips push up. Pain from his broken leg met a bolt of pleasure so sharp that he lost himself, hanging on to Arthur's arms, crying out again and again until Art, laughing softly, put a hand across his mouth.

"Hush, now. Hush. You'll make the dogs howl."

"Oh, Art. Forgive me."

More laughter. "What on earth for?"

"I should have... held on, surely. Waited."

"I can, usually. Not with you, it seems. Pass me my linen."

Limbs heavy and passive, as if honey had got into his bones, Lance watched Art clean them up as best he could. "I didn't know there could be anything as good as that. Not in the whole world."

Arthur glanced up, a half-smile gleaming. "Oh, there's all kinds of good things in the world. I would love to be the one to show you."

"Art..."

"Hush," he said again, lithely scrambling away. "Stay where you are. I have to get something for you from our rooms."

Lance and Edern had given the visitors the best of the praetorium's sleeping quarters, on the leeward side of the building, looking out across the sweep of the valley to the east. He waited, counting his heartbeats, until they blended with the brisk sounds of Arthur's return. Then he sat up in the stormy wreckage of the bedding. "Oh, no," he said, when he saw the beautiful thing Art was carrying, held out towards him in both hands. "I can't take that."

"It was made for me by master-smiths in Cerniw. You haven't seen it before because I'm supposed to carry it on state occasions only, to impress and terrify the local chieftains. It's not ceremonial, though—it's a battle sword, through and through."

Unable to help himself, Lance lifted the weapon from his grasp. The hilt and blade had been forged from one beautiful length of bronze, burnished to a mossy sheen in the last of the sunset. Gold and silver chasings glimmered around the pommel and crossguard. He drew it a little way out of its leather sheath, and saw that the groove of the fuller was marked with interwoven dragon's heads. "This is your father's sign."

"Yes, the pen-dragon."

"What is this metal? The one that glows like gold, but looks like the sun at winter dawn?"

"Copper, they call it in Cerniw. They take it straight from the earth."

"What would Sir Ector say, if he knew you were trying to give me this?"

"He *told* me to give it to you, Lance. Considering what you've given us—given him—it's very little."

"You mean the sword from the lake? That's a fine weapon, but it's crude by comparison with this. Why does it mean so much to him?"

Arthur sighed. He leaned to help Lance lay the bright ceremonial blade aside, and climbed back into the bed with him. They subsided against Elena's fragrant, reed-stuffed pillows. "He wasn't just ripping strips off me earlier on tonight. He wanted to know, in exact detail, how I'd taken your sword from the rock in the crevasse. He thinks it answers part of the prophecy the Merlin gave him all those years ago."

"Did the Merlin describe such a sword?"

"Not exactly, and poor Ector was confused when we learned from you that you'd taken the sword from a lake. A *lough*," he amended, grinning, before Lance could correct him. "Here, rest your head on my shoulder—it's good to be like this after love."

"It's too good. I can't go to sleep here, Art."

"I know. I won't let you." Art brushed a kiss to his brow. "In Ector's words, I didn't just *take* the sword from the stone—I freed it. And if you avoid the obvious Latin words for stone like *petrus* and *saxum*, and use *calx* instead, like lime or chalk—which is a bit of a stretch, but are widespread rocks in the south..."

Lance yawned hugely, causing Art to chuckle and prod him. "Sorry. It's not that I'm not interested—"

"In my geology lesson? I should hope not. The point of all this is, though, that Ector says your sword was *ex calce liberatus*, freed from the stone. And the Merlin said the sword would be named Excalibur."

Another helpless yawn. "That's right."

"What? You know this already?"

Lance surfaced from the shallow, sunlit waters that fringed the edges of sleep. Excalibur... The word and its strange, blood-deep familiarity dropped away from him into dream's ocean as he opened his eyes. "Not... Not in any way I can explain. But that's right. The sword is called Excalibur."

"By all the gods! Don't tell Ector, or he'll have us both up all night with his myths and prophecies."

"It's still just a rusted old chieftain's sword that's lain in the mud for who knows how long. What you've given me is worth a king's ransom."

"All the more reason for you to keep it. You might have to ransom me one day. At any rate, you can use it down in Dumnonia, when Ector's sergeant-at-arms starts to give you proper lessons, and..."

Arthur faded out. Lance, sitting up, could only stare at him in fraught silence, and there was no hiding from the truth anymore. "Oh, Lance," Art said at last. "Oh, no."

Chapter Sixteen

The day was barely past dawn, but the party from the south were almost ready to ride. The grooms were loading up the horses, checking tack and buckles. Ectorius, Art and Guy were waiting out these final preparations in the chilly courtyard outside the praetorium. Ector, fully aware of his foster son's restless pain, had set him to sword drills, thinking he could do no better with the poor lad than distract him.

"No," he cried, as Art missed an easy thrust from his brother. "Guy would have had the guts out of you there. Lift your arm. Keep your weight on your back foot. Concentrate!"

"Perhaps if you let me use Excalibur—my destiny-appointed blade," Art returned breathlessly, "and not this blunt-edged toy..."

"You may bear Excalibur as you did your sword of ceremony, and not otherwise."

"Really?" Art squared up to his brother, who was edging round him, looking for his next avenue of attack. "On your guard, Gaius! May I not bear it in whichever battle it is where I'm supposed to spill out my lonely, stupid, useless little life in order to save my people, or whatever miserable fate it is the Merlin has spelled out for me?"

"Arthur Pendragon!"

The boy turned red with contrition. He put up his blade, and Guy mirrored the gesture, stepping back from him. Poor Guy's face was creased with a mixture of annoyance and sympathy. "Forgive me, Father," Art said. "I didn't mean to speak to you so."

"I know you didn't." Ector eased up stiffly from the mounting block where he'd been sitting. He went to the frowning lad, who was clearly fighting tears, and put a hand to his shoulder. "What are the qualities I have taught you to seek most earnestly in your companions?"

"A strong arm. Nerves of iron, ready for the fight. Lance has all that and more."

"*Arthur.*"

He sighed, slid his practice sword into its sheath. "Loyalty. Quickness of vision to see the needs of others, and to put them ahead of his own."

"So..."

"So the very traits I most need and admire are those which hold him here." He looked at the ground, scuffed one impatient foot over the hard-packed earth. "My lesson is humbly received, Father Ector."

Humbly, my rear end! Well, as long as it is received. "No-one said you had to like it. You will be a king soon. It becomes you to try hard to get what you want. However, when you fail, it also becomes you to act with grace towards those who've baulked you."

"I have, damn it." He met Ector's eyes, his own clouded with necessity and pain. "I will."

"Not just Lance, either." Ector looked across the yard at Father Tomas, hovering anxiously on the edge of the bustle of men and horses. "That old priest can't be left alone to guard this place against another Pictish attack."

"He wouldn't be!" Art burst out impatiently. "If that's what he's said to Lance, it isn't true. There's farmers here, blacksmiths, strong field-hands. With a little training at arms—"

"None of those blacksmiths and farmers are leaders of men," Ector interrupted him. "You of all people must understand the difference. And as for what old Tomas may or may not have said—you must also know that Lance will have made his own decision."

"Lance couldn't guard the place either, not now. He can hardly walk."

"That's why I'm leaving Marcus with him." Ector nodded to the burly, crop-headed groom holding Hengroen by the rein. "For a month at least, or until Lance is well enough to take his rightful place here again, as his father's son and a true prince. Put your chin up, Art. Here he comes."

Ruefully Ector surveyed Art's rumpled hair, the marks of sleeplessness and sorrow beneath his eyes. Lance, whatever effort it had cost him, was freshly turned out in a clean shirt, his spine as straight as his limping progress across the courtyard would allow. "You could take a lesson from this friend of yours, my Bear. Go to him now. Tell him he may keep Balana."

"For... For a month, like Marcus?"

"No. As his own horse." Art's jaw dropped, and Ector shook his head. "Yes, it will cost me dearly to leave her. But I have my reasons. Go on."

He watched while the boy obeyed him. He saw Lance turn white, then red, then look longingly at Balana. He gave Art a fleeting smile of such sweetness that the old man understood with new poignancy what was causing his ward to grieve on this day of departure, and briefly spoke to him. Then Art returned, his own spine very straight, his bearing as soldierly as Ector could wish. "Lance thanks you with all his heart, but says he cannot keep the horse."

"Is he worried about her upkeep? Because I can leave some gold with him too, if—"

"It isn't that. He's afraid there may be another famine."

"What does that have to do with anything?"

Art cleared his throat and looked at the ground. "It seems that he and the villagers had to eat his last horse."

"Oh." The two exchanged a glance, in startled acknowledgement of what this moorland prince had endured. Then Ector recovered his poise. "Listen, Art. Put your trust in time. I'm sorry you've grown up in such a blasted thorn-patch of myths and prophecies, but the good side is this—the Merlin said you have all kinds of wonders to achieve before you die."

"And so far I've done nothing."

"I wouldn't put it so harshly, but... well, I'm happy to think we aren't about to lose you just yet. And whatever unnatural winter has plagued this land, it's gone. They won't have another like it."

"How can you know such a thing?"

"Because of the blasted myths and prophecies. You have achieved one of your wonders. *The blighted land shall blossom in the wake of the future king.*" Art's face became such a picture that Ector began to laugh. "Don't look so thunderstruck, boy—it's just as your brother likes to tease you. The sun really does shine out of your royal behind."

***

"He's not taking no for an answer. You'll have to keep the damn horse. Just try not to eat her, that's all."

"I swear it."

Arthur had taken the reins from Marcus and put them into Lance's hand. The groom had gone to hold Sir Ector's horse by the mounting block, and Balana, as if kindly disposed to her new master, had swung her broad flank to shield him and Arthur from the rest of the yard.

Arthur took Lance's face between his hands. He kissed him: gently, thoroughly, full on the mouth, tasting of promises and salt. "I will write to you."

Lance stared at him. The salt had been from his own tears. Fiercely he scrubbed them away. "I can't bloody read."

"You have a priest, haven't you?" Art shot one savage glance in Tomas's direction. "What use are they, if not for teaching? Bloody well learn."

Chapter Seventeen

One day in autumn, just as the fields had been scythed of the last of their gold, a letter arrived in the village.

Like all such messages, this one had reached its destination by a mixture of goodwill and pure chance. The drover who'd brought it from Pons Aelius had never seen such a thing before: five thin squares of birch bark, neatly tied with leather, the knot encased in a crimson wax seal. He'd thrown it into his horse's pack, where over the next five days it had become buried beneath the farrier's tools, sheep cures and packages of herbs he'd purchased on his journey to sell, along with his flock, in the market at Caer Lir.

Lance stood thigh-deep in sheep. He was making rapid calculations. The summer had been long and dry, the barley crop good. The drover had two fine rams amongst his ewes. Allowing for the winter needs of the village, for bread and the seeds of next year's crop... "Give me one of those tups, Bryn, and by the time you get back from the west, I'll have six bags of grain for you."

The drover scratched his head. He'd known Lance for many years. He'd heard about the Pictish raid and was sorry for the lad, although at a glance, the vicus seemed tidier and better organised than ever it had been in Ban's time. Still, business was business. "What, one of my white-faced hornless, still as pure as the day they stepped off the Roman ships?"

"That's right. They breed well with our little brown soays, and the lambs give good wool and meat and are tough enough to survive up here. What do you say?"

"Ten bags."

"Seven."

"Lad, you'll have a beast in the flesh, while I have to hope that no raiders come to burn your barns, fine and..." The drover shielded his eyes to peer through the open door of the nearest building. "Fine and full as they are. Your soays look half-decent, too. How did you come by so many?"

The boy's face clouded. "They were a gift. From friends who saw that our fields were almost empty after the long winter." He pushed the shadows aside. "Come on, Bryn. You won't find better grain between here and the coast."

"Nine bags."

"Eight bags."

"Done. And because it's you, I'll throw in this cure for the bloat from the cunning woman down in Rivers Meet. Never been known to fail, the old girl says." He reached deep into his saddle pack. "Oh, and... this thing, too. One of the old boys still holding on at Pons Aelius fort said it should go to you, or someone at White Meadows, anyway."

Lance took the leatherbound package from Bryn's hand. He blew wisps of wool and grain-dust off it, turned it into the bright morning sun. "Tertius," he said, squinting at the scrawl of fading ink on the uppermost leaf. *"Tertius, filius Bani, rex Vindolandae."* He looked up in wonder. "Tertius, son of Ban, king of Vindolanda. That's me!"

Bryn looked him over doubtfully. He was dressed for a hard day in the fields, and one of the ewes was chewing contentedly at the hem of his tunic. "If you say so. What do you think it is, then?"

"Why, it's an *epistola*. A letter."

Bryn had travelled many times along the line of the old Wall, and felt he knew a thing or two. "Bless you, no. You get your epistolas on parchment, don't you? Or vellum, if it's definitely calfskin."

"There's too many uses for animal hides to leave much over for writing. The soldiers stationed here used strips of birch, my father said. Who did you say gave this to you?"

"One of the old Batavian lads. I know him well—soldiered here so long he couldn't be bothered to go home when the rest of them did. Besides, he has a wife and bairns, and he says the weather's not *that* much worse here than—"

"Yes, I see. But who gave it to him?"

"The skipper of a trading boat from Londinium, he said. And *he* had it from a tin merchant all the way from Cerniw, he claimed, although that must be a story."

"Why?"

Bryn shook his head pityingly. "Everyone knows the Cerniw tin comes from dragons. They lay it with their eggs, and burn up any man foolish enough to come near them with their fiery breath."

Lance seemed delighted by this information, or by something. He was ablaze with joy, and suddenly looked like the son of a king despite the mud in his hair. He thrust up a hand, took hold of Bryn's and shook it vigorously. "Thank you for this. Thank you!"

He turned away. Bryn frowned in confusion. "Here," he called after him. "Don't you want your tup?"

"What? Oh! Yes, of course." He beckoned to one of the workers in the nearest field, who climbed the wall and began to make his way through the bleating flock. Then he put his hand to his chest, and offered the drover a shy, formal bow. "You must stop for a while. Water your beasts, and if you go to the kitchen, my housekeeper Edern will give you a meal and some wine."

Bryn raised an eyebrow. The last time he'd passed through here, this boy had been a lanky-limbed pup, barely distinguishable from the rest of the litter. "Thank you, Your Majesty," he said, but if Lance heard, he gave no sign. He was walking away, absently pushing the sheep to one side, the birch-strip letter cradled reverently in his free hand.

***

"Father Tomas! I need your help."

"You do indeed, child, or the kingdom of heaven is closed to you. Have you come to me to shrive your heathen soul?"

"Er... no. Not exactly." A pile of Roman epistolary birch-strips landed on the page Tomas was reading, obscuring the text. "I need you to read these."

Tomas sat up. His back was aching, his eyes sore. He'd been oblivious to these bodily discomforts all the time he'd been left undisturbed with the satisfying story of God's vengeance at Gomorrah. "Why must you pester me? Don't you have work about the farm?"

"I do, but I've had..." Lance tailed off to catch his breath. "I've had a letter, and I can't read it. Please."

"Can't read it? Have I not, by your own most unexpected request, spent hours every night instructing you?"

"Yes, you have. But he... Arthur doesn't write like the scribes who made your books."

"This letter is from the prince?"

"It is. It's from the prince, to me. Please, Father."

"The prince was very kind during his visit. His foster father Ectorius paid me particular kindly attention. I shall always remember it."

The bible was laid out on Tomas's little lectern, in the draught-free corner of the chapel where he liked to retreat at sunny noontides. A shameful indulgence, he supposed, but the chapel's one window was filled with blue-green Roman glass, and the warmth and the underwater shimmer of the light was soothing to the flesh and the mind. Tomas gave a croak of dismay as bible, birch and lectern disappeared, to be replaced a moment later by Lance himself, passionately kneeling at his feet.

The croak became a dried-up laugh. "Miracles in our days! That's the first time your stubborn knees have bent in this place."

"I know. I don't understand the things you preach, Father, and I don't think I ever will. Don't make me say I'll come here and kneel and pretend, because I will, if that's what I have to do."

"Of course not. Of what value would that be to me?" Tomas examined the first of the birch strips. "The prince writes in a courtly hand."

"Oh, no. Can't you read it either?"

"Insolent! You think I've had no dealings with courtly men? I was at the shrine of Brocolitia, you know, after—"

"After the Emperor Theodosius ordered the temple of Mithras there destroyed. Yes, I know. Is this how they wrote, then—the learned men you knew there?"

"Hmm. A little." Tomas turned the strip sideways, then upside down. "This is what I would call a *very* free hand, but it's befitting to someone of the prince's station. *Carissime Tertie*, he begins. That's you, Lance, and he properly refers to you by your formal name. *Tertie* is the vocative singular of Tertius, although *carissime*—most dear—is very informal indeed. Hmm."

"Really? *Most* dear?"

"And he goes on, *quamquam semper Lance meum*..."

"He says I'll always be Lance to him?"

"*My* Lance, to be accurate. My Lance, who became *plus quam frater*..." Tomas looked up, storm clouds beginning to gather on his brow. "Who became my more-than-brother on the shore of the lake?!"

Lance smiled helplessly. "Well, you know Art. He's very affectionate."

"And again, upon that... *lectum*... Well-remembered bed?!" Tomas sprang to his feet. With the energy of a much younger man, he strode to the corner where he kept his rod of punishment. He hadn't dared lift it to Elena's one surviving child, not after the prince of Cerniw had come and gone and left the boy cloaked in his new adulthood, but enough was enough. "Heinous brat!" he rasped. "Spawn of corruption! There's better use for birch than the scrawling of such monstrous tales. Thou shalt not lie with man as with woman! Thou shalt not..."

Lance jumped out of his reach. He grabbed the birch strip Tomas had dropped, gathered up the others and clutched them to his wicked heart. Unpredictably, he was laughing, not with mockery but a kind of pure joy. He leapt beyond the sweep of Tomas's rod and bolted for the chapel door.

Tomas gave chase. It was beneath his dignity, but this was a special occasion. *More than brother*, on the lake shores and in the bed! He didn't much care if he saved the wretched boy's sacred soul or whaled it out of him. Corruption! The lusts of the flesh, shamelessly written in ink for all eyes to see! Lance, whose leg had healed nicely, was running at full pelt across the stable yard, causing Balana to stretch her head out of her stall and whinny a greeting. He seized a low-hanging gutter, made an improbable leap and vaulted up onto the terracotta tiles of the roof.

He was laughing still. "Father, forgive me," he managed, as Tomas approached. He was just out of reach of the long, whipping rod. "If I'd known, I wouldn't have asked you to read it. I swear."

"What difference does..." Tomas leapt as high in the air as he could, cassock flapping wildly. His swipe with the rod brushed Lance's knees. "What difference does *knowing* it make?"

"I just didn't know he'd write something like that down. I wasn't even sure he'd remember. He's had lots of lovers, you see."

Another impotent swipe. "Close your wicked mouth!"

"He has to. He's going to be king, and he might not live long, so he has to get heirs."

"He won't get them with you!"

Lance slid down to the edge of the roof. He caught the end of the whip and held it fast. He'd stopped laughing, and his face was oddly gentle. "There's more to love than that."

"That's just where you're wrong," Tomas gasped, trying to twitch the rod away. "Procreation is the sole reason for the lusts of the body. All else is wickedness."

"How strange it is. I struggle with Arthur's writing, but I have read most of your holy book by now. I've never found such a thing written there."

"Nevertheless, it's... it's what I was taught."

"Who would teach you such a thing?"

"My preceptors from Rome. Holy men!"

"They must have faced a quandary, I suppose."

"What on earth do you mean?"

Lance tugged the rod out of Tomas's hand. He put it across his knee, and without any sign of effort or anger, snapped it in two. Then he jumped down off the roof. He was taller than

Tomas by now, beginning at last to fill out into the length of his bones. He turned to face him, and any authority the old man had held over him vanished at that moment, like dew on the sunlit gorse. "If all joys of the flesh are wicked as you say, where are the children to come from who will carry on your church? I suppose that was the compromise. I even understand it in a way. But already you make no distinction between the words in your book and lessons taught you by men, with no better idea of what's right and wrong than you have yourself. And that makes me afraid."

"How dare you?" Tomas rasped. But the time for remonstrance was past and gone for him. The wicked child—a fine young man now, straight as a reed, a far-seeing clarity in his brown eyes—was gently and kindly dusting him down. "Terrible things come out of your mouth," Tomas said wearily at last. "But your actions contradict them. Why did you stay with us, when your prince has offered you so much?"

"You read past his sinful words of love, then? You didn't go blind?"

"They're all words of love, it seems to me. The court is established in the south, in a place he calls Cam. He says he's keeping a place at his side for you, a seat at his right hand. You'll leave us now, won't you? You'll go."

Lance looked away. He reached for the strips of birch that had slithered into the dry stable gutter, carefully piled them up and bound them once more in their leather ribbon. He fastened the hoop of the ribbon around his wrist. "No," he said hollowly. "I will not."

"Why not? The teachings of my book mean nothing to you— not even the words of my new and gentle god."

"Did my mother need a book to take you in and shelter you, and not... feed you to her dragons, as must have been a sore temptation? Even my father, whose life should be judged for what it was, not just its miserable ending—he built you your church and fed you at his table. It seems to me that men shouldn't need a book or a god to make them good."

He opened the stable door, and Balana came nickering out to him, snorting and lowering her impeccably trained Roman head for her bridle. Lance unhooked it from the back of the door and put it on her. Ector had left him the beautiful horned saddle too, but that was locked up in the armoury. Balana widened her eyes at his unaided leap onto her back, but stood foursquare and still for him, just as she would have done with battlefield spears raining down around her.

"Don't misunderstand me, Tomas," he said. "I know what I've given up. I don't mean the honours and the place at his side in Cam. I'd just give my immortal, wicked soul to be with him once again by the lough." He touched the mare's sides with his heels. "See to it that Bryn the drover's fed, and have the farmhands settle the new tup. I'll be back by sundown."

Chapter Eighteen

Dearest Tertius, who will always be my Lance to me, who became my more-than-brother on the shore of the lake, and again in that well-remembered bed, with the deerhounds looking on! I hope you have learned to read Latin for yourself, or I will by now have scandalised your priest.

The court is settled in Cam. I am holding a place for you at my right hand. I commanded my round table to be built as I told you I would. I joked with my sawyers and masons that the hall would need to be built around it. Alas, they have not your sense of the ridiculous. Upon my return from Cerniw two moons later, the job was done. My latest recruits—four brothers from an island so far north of Scotia that the sun never sets during summer, nor rises in the winter, Bors, a lord of Gaul, whose land has been seized by the Saxons, causing him to throw in his lot with mine, and Drustan, an old friend from Cornwall—look like lost children around its vast edge. But it does solve quarrels over precedence, and because I believe the brothers from the Out Isles to have been driven slightly mad by their long, unnatural days and nights, it has spared much bloodshed. I have caused your mother's name to be graven in gold at the rim.

The battle for Cam was a sharp one. Warlike descendants of the Durotriges had settled there. We were outnumbered, but Excalibur was like fire in my hand. The fort is desirable, the water supply from a spring so deep it cannot be tainted or stopped from outside. In these autumn dawns, badgers shuffle about in the woodlands all around. In spring, I am told, these same woods are the haunt of cuckoos. Deer and boar are plentiful.

Dear Lance, I would not often wish to experience such pain as I knew at our parting. Having learned to read Latin, you must learn to write it! Send via my tin merchant Landry, who trades in Londinium at the full of every moon. Aldegund, the Batavian commander in Pons Aelius who sent this on to you, knows him well. Place a direction on the outside, as I have done on yours. Artorius, filius Pendraconis *will find me. We call this place Cam, for the river, but it must have been an island in it once, or an islet. You'd better use the old name, which is Camelet.*

Discharge your duties, my dark-eyed moorland prince, and come to me.

Lance sat up. His eyes were burning, the back of his neck stiff. There was no chance of reaching Aldegund and Landry in time for the next full moon, because—apart from his utter, miserable, thrice-damned inability to write a word of Latin—it had taken him the best part of a fortnight to decipher his letter from Art. He had done it, Tomas remaining wrapped in highest dudgeon, by borrowing one of the old man's Latin texts, copied by some long-lost scribe whose hand resembled Art's. Lance knew the story from Tomas's many wistful fireside readings of the tale, wherein a prophet named Esdras went forth from his house and offered his soul to God for punishment rather than let the divine wrath fall upon his sinful neighbours.

Poor Tomas, surrounded by men and women who barely knew they were sinning, let alone in need of a priestly lightning rod! Lance had almost felt guilty, coming up here to the lough every day when his farm work was done, picking out the Latin words he knew, connecting them one to the other through the fibres of the tale, matching the shapes on the parchment to those on the pieces of birch.

But he'd have raided Tomas's library a hundred times over, pillaged his texts without mercy, to find the key that would unlock Arthur's words. Breathing a prayer of thanks to the long-lost scribe, he leaned back against a rock. Balana, who'd been peacefully cropping the turf, came and nudged his shoulder, as if aware that he'd finished his task. "I should have asked *you* to read it," he told her, rubbing her velvety lip. "You'd have managed it faster. And now—look at this!—he says I have to learn to write to him, too."

If wishes were learning, the work would be already done. He stared into the sunlight, Art's lettering and the scribe's entwining and dancing in the bright air, creating new shapes that would be his own. *My most dear Artorius—carissime Artorie*, he would write, correctly using the vocative singular. *Art, to me, from the hour when we laid down our arms and rode together into Vindolanda...*

"Oh, and the sun fades to nothing in the beauty of his smile, and he walks on water, and brings back the spring to the earth, I suppose."

Lance leapt to his feet. He whipped round, trying to locate the source of the reed-thin, crackling voice. Only a moorland hare was poised on a rock a couple of yards away.

Out in broad daylight and asking for trouble. Blindly Lance drew his spear from its loops on Balana's saddle. Pictish raider seeking to distract and ambush him, the breeze playing tricks, drawing words from the water and the rustling birch, or nothing more than a good hare stew on the table tonight—he was ready for anything, if only he could get his heart out of his mouth and the tremor of fright out of his arm...

"Cures piles and warts, no doubt. Frightens the ticks off sheep."

Lance wheeled again. "Where are you?"

"Why, here, boy. Just as I always have been."

He rubbed his eyes. The hare was gone. In its place was an old woman, wrapped in a ragged black robe. Lance dropped his spear with a clatter onto the rocks. "Viviana!"

"Well, what of it? Why were you poking that twig at me? Where's the sword from the lake?"

"I... I thought I'd never see you again."

"Nor did I think you'd hand over your destiny to Uther Pendragon's stealth-begotten son, young man!"

Dry-mouthed, unaccountably filled with joy, Lance made a cautious approach. He bowed to her shyly. "Will you come to the vicus with me, my lady? I'd be glad to offer you shelter and food."

She looked him over, eyes bright. "Shelter and food, eh? This isn't the starving brat I met up here half a year ago."

"No, ma'am. I have changed greatly since then."

"Two inches taller, chest and shoulders broader. Handsome, too—the very spit of his mother. Not a virgin anymore. Has a fine Roman horse. Still bearing Ban's old sword, which is strange, for a boy who was entrusted with Excalibur."

Blood ran hot and cold beneath the surface of Lance's skin. He didn't know where to begin to reply. On balance, the sword seemed the easiest place to start. "Arthur drew it out from a rock. That was *his* destiny—*ex calce liberatus*."

"Oh, I see." She flickered him a mocking smile. "I suppose he wrenched it from your hands."

"No, by no means. I gave it to him, with my..." His voice scraped, and he waited until he was sure it would be firm again. "With my whole heart."

"Poor Lance. He did land on you like a cartload of rocks, didn't he?"

"If I had the time I again I'd do the same, my lady, but... was it wrong?"

She got up and stretched. She was just as withered and ancient as Lance remembered, but there was a vigour to her movements, a deep-rooted, earthy power. "I'd have said so, once upon a time."

"And now? He *did* bring the spring to the earth."

"Ah, well. He's his mother's son, as you are yours. So much depends upon him, and what he understands—about the dragon and her ways. What he doesn't, you'll have to teach him."

"What? I don't know anything."

"You'd be surprised. The Merlin says the new world's coming to destroy the old, but he's a curmudgeon. What if your future king could be the best of both?"

Lance forgot himself. He seized her shoulders, distantly relieved when she didn't seem to mind, gazing up at him fearlessly. "You know the Merlin?"

"Of course. Pendragon's son will rise in England's darkest hour, the Merlin says, and maybe he's right."

"England?" Lance tried the strange word carefully. His head was still full of Latin, of the strange, compulsive business of learning to read. "Where's that?"

"*Here*, ignorant boy. Or it will be, once these tribes of Angles settling up and down the country name the place after themselves."

"Nonsense. They'll never get that far. Not the Saxons, either—Arthur will raise an army from Cerniw and the old lands to the west, Caer Lir and Rheged and..."

"Ah. Outraged, are you—about these damned invading foreigners?"

"Of course. The land is ours."

"Did you ever stop to think about what the Picts think of you?"

"The Picts?" Bewildered, Lance let the old woman go. "What have they got to do with anything?"

"Little more than animals, aren't they? Blue-painted savages who sweep down out of the dark to pillage and burn. And you, orphaned lad, have better reason than most to believe it so."

"How could anyone deny it? Father Tomas told me the whole story of the night of the raid. One of the savages slew my mother from behind."

A look of pain crossed the old woman's face. It was ordinary, human: surprising and piercing to Lance, who had grown used to her eldritch smile. "Ah, my poor Elena," she said. "I shouldn't think she took that in good part."

"No. But you told me truly about her, all those months ago when we first met. She was holding another of them by the hair and smashing his skull with a pan. Did you know her too, my lady?"

"Never mind that. Look at this toy, which I picked up on my travels."

Lance was getting lots of practice in dealing with his elders. Tomas, relieved of the prospect of looking after the vicus alone, was becoming more eccentric every day. Patiently he took the little stone she'd handed to him from some pouch within her robes. It was flat, no bigger than the palm of his hand. On it was carved, with a jeweller's mastery, a kind of crescent moon, pierced through its horns with a V-shaped staff. Beneath it was a sign like a lightning flash, and two circles connected by a narrow, elegant neck. The whole was bordered by a pattern he recognised, a kind of knotwork Elena, when intolerably bored by winter confinement, would irritably embroider onto bed coverings.

"Beautiful," he said, following the hypnotic shape of the circles with one fingertip. "What does it mean?"

"Ah, who knows? Not even they know, not anymore. Maybe once, before you Celts arrived, seized their lands and scattered their culture to the winds."

"Are you saying this is Pictish work?"

"It is. You should see the full-size stones. Bigger than you are, and covered with serpents, boars, horses with beaks, fish-tailed dragons... Of course they learned the knotwork from you."

"I'm not a Celt. I'm a—"

"Oh, a Briton! That's right, I forgot. *Brittuncuh*, the Roman lads on the Wall—right here, as it happens—used to call you lot. Dirty little Britons! That was before they started recruiting you, getting men like your father to farm their land for them, marrying your women and putting their fine long legs and noble faces into the stream of life for princely souls like you to inherit." She caught hold of the front of his shirt, her fist the size of a sparrow but strong. "Listen to me, Lance. I'm not telling you this to shame you or to pull you down. He came to you, didn't he—this future king, with his smile and his sunlight, and his gift for making men want to follow him to the gates of death, and after?"

"Yes," Lance said. His throat was sore and tight. "But he had to go, and I... I had to stay."

"Nothing's forever, boy. Remember these words, if you find yourself at his side again. His people will call him Arthur of the Britons. He'll come to think of himself that way, and so will generation after cascading generation of fools—some romantic, some vicious beyond understanding—who believe that there's one purebred race in this land, or ever could or ever will be."

"He doesn't think that. He's travelled too much, seen too much."

"Oh, I grant you he's bright. And he's more the politician than I thought any lad of sixteen summers could be—old Ector did well with him. But you're the clever one, Lance. Tell him that the Celts took this land from the men who lived here in shadowy time out of mind, and the Romans took it from the Celts. The Angles and Saxons will take it from you, and there'll be pain and bloodshed, loss and gain, and eventually, in a time even I am not permitted to see, one people standing in the sun—cross-fertilised over and over again, vigorous, all their arts and learning shared."

"My lady, I don't understand."

"It doesn't matter. Tell him, if you love him, that this sacred island of his lies on a natural westbound invasion route, and his life doesn't have to be the price of pretending that's not true. Don't let the Merlin sell him that miserable dream."

Lance stumbled back from her. "I can't tell him anything," he said hoarsely. "I'd give my soul to send him one line in reply to the words he's given me, but I'm too ignorant even for that. Probably I'll never see him again."

"Put your trust in time, as old Ector would say. And get your priest—as *he* says, in that lovely epistola you carry with you everywhere, and sleep with under your pillow—to teach you how to write."

"How do you *know* all this? About Ector, and Art, and me, and—"

"And your mother, too."

"What?"

"You'd better turn away, boy. It's rude to watch an old woman while she's changing."

Sharply he obeyed. All around him the air was thickening, pressing on his skin and the depths of his ears like the shift before a storm. "Please, Viviana. My mother?"

When her voice resumed, it was wild, weirdly low to the ground, words from a throat not designed for them. "Don't fear death, Lance. Dying can be bad, but death... We come from the earth on the spine of the dragon, and she takes us home again, that's all. Tell this to the king. Let him not sunder the contract, the ancient, loving kinship between men and the land. It's not too late. That's what your mother says. Oh, and the usual—what a fine boy you are, and how proud of you she is, and all the rest of it. Yes, yes, my dear priestess. We know all that. He knows."

Lance knew, but still he wanted to beg the old woman to go on. He was breathing a scent he'd thought had passed forever from the world: warm fur and meadowsweet, the fragrance of Elena's winter cloak. Still there was something he wanted more. "I will learn to write," he said, his throat hot and painful with yearning. "But it's weeks since Art sent me my letter, and will be many more before he'll receive my reply. Is he... Can you..."

"Oh, you think I can just lift the roof off his Great Hall at Camelet and peer inside, to see him feasting with all his hard-won allies at his round table—trying to stop the brothers from the Out Isles from killing one another to gain that empty place at his right hand?"

Lance shivered in pleasure. Now he could smell crushed moss on the lough-side rocks, and taste, as if Art's mouth was pressed to his once more, the promises and salt of his farewell. "Yes," he said to Viviana, or the creature she'd become. "I think you can."

"Looks that way, doesn't it? There he is. He's well, never fear, only tired of carousing in the name of diplomacy, and wishing more than anything else under heaven that..." She paused, then gave a sudden shout of laughter. "Ah, the poor bearcub! A girl in each arm, the world at his feet—and nothing in his head but thoughts of you."

Book II

The Dragon's Tale

Harper Fox

Chapter One

My dearest Lance, now that we are settled at Cam, I can write to you on this fine parchment instead of birch. Everything here is abundant. I lack for nothing except my moorland prince.

I am glad that the eggs we gave you are healthy, and breeding well with the rest of your flock. Is it not an inconvenience, however, when they roll down the hills?

Dear friend, forgive me. Ova *and* ovis *are so similar, anyone could mix them up. The rest of your* epistola *was perfect. How did you get your priest to teach you so many words of love? On still, starry nights, I go onto the earthwork fortifications of Camelet and look north to find the Bear and Arcturus, which are my stars, and then I find the lights of the great Shepherd, which are yours. I sense that you are watching over me—and your eggs, of course. A bear should not need such comfort, and nor should a future king. Nevertheless, I seek you out.*

Saxon incursions continue from the east. I am recruiting, but the sons of the chieftains here are bred to a life of ease and plenty. I must strike north again soon, to remind the kings of Rheged and Gododdin of my existence and our shared interests, and seek men of true heart, with fire and ice in their veins. I am fortunate in that I have found one already, so at least I know what to look for.

I don't know where your next letter will find me, but write it anyway. Better still, come to me. Can it be a year since we rode together on the wild heights, and since I knew the joy of your touch?

Two years. The drover who brought news, sheep-cures and messages from the east coast had handed Lance a parchment that looked as though it had come to him through water, mud and hellfire. Arthur's tin merchant had been set upon by pirates during his voyage north, the drover said, his vessel run aground and its salvaged contents left to make their way overland as best they could.

Two years! Lance paced the floor of his study, the fragile parchment in his hands. A miracle that he'd received it at all, but he could gladly have balled it up and tossed it into the fire in sheer frustration. Anything could have happened to Arthur in that time. His own missives to Cam could have ended up anywhere. He came to a halt by the window of the bright upper-storey room he'd taken over for his books, writing implements and the peace in which to learn how to use them. Instead of ripping the letter up, he raised it to his lips and kissed the wild, freeform scrawl of the signature. Then he sat down at his desk.

He wrote his reply in less time than it took for the early summer shadows to mark out the flight of an hour. He was full of thoughts, brimming over with words of love. All was not abundant at Vindolanda, so he worked through strip after strip of the birch bark he'd cut and prepared for the purpose. His gull-feather quills scratched and caught on the wood, but his hand remained lucid and clear. When he was uncertain of a spelling or a form, he picked up one of the volumes for which he'd vigorously traded in the markets at Rivers Meet and Corstopitum. He knew each of these from worn leather cover to cover, and exactly where to find the example he required. He could have kicked himself for mixing up sheep and eggs, but he'd been barely literate then. Reading a letter from Art had taken him a fortnight: writing one in return the task of a whole month.

Thoughts, words of love. Two years since he'd parted from his future king, two years and five days—he was counting—since he'd known the astounding, transformative joy of being touched, from head to foot and skin to soul, by Arthur Pendragon. No doubt Art had had dozens of girls and boys since then: it was his nature, and he'd never said he wouldn't. It wasn't his fault that for Lance, there was only one source and focus of desire.

Even if Bryn the drover made it back from Caer Lir this month and took Lance's letter in safety to Pons Aelius, the tin-trader's vessel was gone, that line of communication snapped. Even if he found another way, what direction would he mark upon the outside of his hopeless little heap of birch? Art could be anywhere between the Forest Wild and the Old North.

He laid down his quill. When he put his hands to his face, he thought for an instant that he could detect a trace of the scent that had lulled him to rest on the sun-heated rocks by Broomlee Lough. Warm skin, crushed moss, promises and salt... "Oh, Art," he said softly to the empty room. "I miss you."

The day was still young. Lance had given orders that, when his morning tasks around the farmsteads were done, he was to be left in peace until noon. These were his hours for study. He now possessed a wide, unfiltered knowledge of a world stranger than he could possibly have imagined, rising into his startled mind's eye from the pages of his books. He knew that there were sea-creatures so vast they pretended to be islands, and when unwary sailors landed and made fires upon their skin, would suddenly dive, taking men and vessels with them. He knew that giants walked the earth. From underneath a stall at Rivers Meet, a trader had handed him a thing called a *necronomicon*, and he knew, in theory at least, how to summon a voluptuous female demon to satisfy his every need.

Perhaps one day he'd learn a spell to summon Arthur. He rested his chin on his hand. A sweet May-time breeze blew shimmery essences of gorse and sunlight into the room. How would he be, when so conjured? As Lance had first seen him, in his handsome but well-worn travelling clothes? Or would he come fresh from the lough, wearing nothing but his sun disc on a leather strip around his neck?

Lance stood up. Shivers were tugging at him, heat like summer lightning flashing across his skin. All he'd managed to conjure was his own hopeless yearning. There was a bench against the far wall, left over from the time when the room had been used for storage. If he could stretch out there, allow his memories to inhabit and direct his whole body, so that his hands and touch became Arthur's own...

"Lance? Lance? *Lance!*"

So much for peace. As for his orders, they were met with nods and smiles, and then cheerfully ignored. Wearily, dreams and visions blowing away like thistledown, he went to the window. "Yes, Dana? What's wrong?"

"The pig has got into the midden-pit, Lance. She's up to her snout in muck."

"Can't Farmer Alun get her out?"

"He tried, but now he's fallen in there too. It's been raining, Lance. The mud's hip deep, and everything really stinks."

Lance examined the girl. She was staring up at him, face solemn as an owl's. She ought to have been a priestess by now, but times had passed and changed. Her mother was only the baker's wife, and she herself a skinny farm girl, frail and at a loss.

Once upon an enchanted moor, Lance had no doubt, Elena and her women would have gathered round the midden pit and sung the damn pig out, and Farmer Alun too. "Oh, good," he said. "I'm so glad you came to get me. Have Edern and Bryn fetch ropes and planks, and I'll meet you there."

He ran down the outside steps into the yard. It was like swimming through a tide of memories. Here Arthur had half-carried him, broken leg and all, away from the clatter of incoming guests and up to the firelit bedchamber. By the bed, Art had hoisted him up into his arms with a grunting effort: stood laughing at his outrage, and then laid him tenderly down.

He set out for the midden pit. One day these flashes of perfect, vivid recall would cease to plague him. On his way across the courtyard, he paused once, as he always did, by Father Tomas's grave. The old man had taken a fever in the depths of winter and died. Lance had caused his resting place by the chapel to be marked with as fine a stone cross as his village mason could carve. For himself, Lance had never seen the light of the new god, but it wasn't what he thought that mattered. Tomas had never forgiven him after Art's first letter, or consented to teach him another word of Latin, but after his fashion, the old man had tried to help hold the fort, and by then Lance had learned enough to teach himself. Now—more keenly and crucially than ever—he was alone.

***

My dearest Lance, we are at Din Guardi. Do you remember the story you told me, the tale of the dragon who came from the stars and lay down to sleep in the earth? You showed me the scales of her great spine, on the moors above Vindolanda. That spine stretches right across the country, and ends here on the east coast in a splendid outcrop. The name of the place means the hill of the fortress, *but the people call it Dragon's Head. So you and I are connected. The countryside is dangerous, filled with strange tales of monsters, but that would not deter my bold Lance.*

Is it not strange that Arthur Pendragon should come to Dragon's Head? The fortress is not mine, however—not yet. I have come in peace, as an ally to one of the kings of the Old North. He is besieged by Anglian invaders. The times and the affairs of men are exciting. Three years have passed now, and I'm sure your mother taught you the magical power of threes. You have a place here. I say this in every message I send you, and I always will: come to me.

***

To the son of King Ban of Vindolanda—

Lance, I pray this missive finds you. My brother has sustained a wound in battle and lies desperately ill. The journey is a week's ride. The horseman who brought you this will return with you. I beg you to come.

Gaius, son of Ector, Din Guardi.

Chapter Two

A year to the day since Tomas had died. Nights growing longer, the longest of all on its way. Slaughtered beasts salted away, precious grain stored in the barns. Vindolanda like a beacon fire, calling out to raiders all around: *here am I, full of wealth, defended only by my prince and the handful of farmers he's trained to lift swords as well as ploughshares. Here am I, such rich pickings, women and children and beasts, protected by such a frail shield. You took me before: here am I.*

No man could leave such a place. Lance had grown up with these people, known them and loved them for as long as he'd understood what love was. To leave would be to throw them to the wolves. The thing was impossible: could not be done.

And yet here is Lance in Balana's lamplit stable, settling her saddle blanket with tender care. You lift it onto the withers first, then draw it back towards the tail, so that the hairs don't get rubbed the wrong way and irritate her hide. Then you place your prized Roman saddle, supple from years of polishing, on her strong spine. You fasten the girth, wait until she's tried her trick of bloating herself out—lazy old girl, unwilling to leave her quarters on such a night!—and deflated again, and then you tighten the strap. You check her bridle and her bit.

Lance laid his brow to her neck. Dana was sobbing in the corner. She was the only one who'd dared come in. The open half door of the stable was filled with pale faces, watching in silence. One of them belonged to Guy's messenger, who'd clearly been coached to treat Lance with respect. "Forgive me, sire. The night is deep, the road dangerous. Don't you think we should wait until—"

Lance jerked his head up, making Balana snort and sidle. "If I delay by so much as an hour," he said roughly, "and by such delay cause Arthur an hour's needless loneliness or pain, may my soul be forfeit." He fixed a scorching look on the messenger. "Yours, too. Edern! Where is Edern?"

The old housekeeper fought his way to the front of the crowd at the door. "I'm here, Lance."

"Fetch my father's old sword and spear from the armoury. When I am gone, you are to take the sword Arthur gave me and sell it at Rivers Meet. The melt value alone will be considerable. Use the money to buy more winter grain if we need it, and to hire men to help with the planting in spring."

"I will, Lance. But... you'll be back by then, won't you?"

Lance couldn't answer. He led Balana out of the stables and leapt into the saddle like a drowning man finding a rock. If Arthur lived, the threads that bound their destinies together would tighten, would begin once again their intricate weave. And if Arthur died... "Sell the sword. If there's money left, get some of the lads from the militia at Corstopitum to come up and see you through raiding season. May all the gods bless you, old friend. Goodbye."

Lance and the messenger clattered out of the courtyard together. Lance didn't allow himself to glance down at any of the faces, any of the reaching hands. There was just enough moon to travel by, a chilly first quarter hanging high above Hadrian's old Wall. He turned Balana's head eastward, touched his heels to her side, and he rode.

***

"That horse of yours—she used to belong to Sir Ector, didn't she?"

Lance returned with an effort to his skin. He'd been sitting by Art's bedside in a chamber in Din Guardi, and Art had just opened his eyes. This beat all hell out of the other fantasy, the one in which a white-faced, weeping Gaius showed him into a crypt. "She did," he said tersely. "Although what business that is of yours, I can't imagine."

"You should be kinder to such a noble beast."

Startled, Lance turned to look at the messenger. The man's eyes were fixed on him fearlessly. The countryside had changed beyond recognition. The hills had smoothed out to broad flatlands, the turf and gorse of the moors replaced by mile after mile of featureless mile of salt-grass. The eastern sky was pink as wild strawberries. "Where are we?"

"Still on the road the Romans made. It stretches from Pons Aelius to the river the Scots call Uisge Thuaigh, fifty miles north of here. If you gallop for a few more days and nights, you can ride your horse right into the water."

"Is that the dawn?"

"Yes, sire."

Lance reined Balana in. She dropped to a trot, then a stumbling walk, then came to a halt and stood wearily, head down. "Heaven forgive me. I *should* be kinder—not just to her, but to you. What is your name?"

"Drusus, sire."

"Pardon my discourtesy, Drusus."

"You'd better pardon mine, or Gaius will have me publicly flogged."

Lance smiled despite himself, despite the sick yearning he felt to be moving onwards, closing the gap between himself and Din Guardi at any cost. "Is there a place nearby where we can rest the horses?"

"And ourselves, sire, or we'll be useless to the very men we so wish to aid. There's a settlement a little way west of here—Anglian, but they're not hostile. All manner of traders and travellers pass through here."

Stiffly Lance dismounted. Only when he was on the ground did he realise his own exhaustion. The horse pushed at him with her nose, a gesture of forgiveness he didn't deserve. "Go ahead. Not too fast, though—I'm going to lead Balana on the rein."

Lance had never seen anywhere like the settlement before. In many ways it was primitive, a couple of dozen timber huts roofed in thatch, none of Vindolanda's crumbling Roman grandeur. The track running through it was made of hardpacked earth, ringing beneath the horses' hooves after a frosty night. In wet weather it would turn into a swamp. And yet there was a bustle and brightness in the air, even at this early hour. The forge was open for business, the baker shovelling fresh loaves out of an open-air oven. The two streets, marked at their junction by a fine round-headed cross, were already busy with men and women, some dark like himself, others strikingly fair. Most wore wooden pattens and thick tunics against the cold. It was hard to tell who was a villager, who was just passing through. Hard to tell where anyone came from at all.

There wasn't time to wonder. Lance had taken the messenger's point, but he didn't think he could linger here. Drusus and the horses needed rest. For himself, he'd hire a fresh mount and ride on, if he could find anything bigger than a market-cart pony to carry him. He'd barely taken enough gold with him to cover his journey, but surely someone here could help. He drew a breath to ask.

"Here, sire. It's not much, but at least it's shelter."

One of the huts, larger than the rest, had been fitted up as a kind of hostelry. A brazier burned in the middle of the floor, smoke curling upwards through a hole in the roof. A sturdy, yellow-haired boy appeared at Lance's elbow and took Balana's reins from him: dazedly he allowed this, then followed Drusus into the warmth.

Broad wooden benches surrounded the fire. They were covered in sheepskins that looked as though they'd been there since the hut was built, but were no less comfortable for that when Lance sat down. He hadn't even meant to do that much: stiffened immediately and tried to get back up, but Drusus placed a large hand on his shoulder. "Rest," he ordered. "Gaius would be angry to know you were driving yourself and the animals so hard. And he's a general now, so you have to mind what he says."

"A general?" Lance echoed in amusement. He sank his fingers into the sheepskin to keep a grip on reality, but all that served to do was plunge him back into memories of the firelit bedchamber at Vindolanda. "He'll be a good one, I'm sure. What about Ector?"

"You have to sleep. Close your eyes, at any rate, while I fetch food."

"All right. But then I have to move on."

"Very well, very well."

"What happened to him, Drusus?"

"To... To Ector?"

"No. To Arthur. Was his wound very bad?"

"No worse than he's had before, but he took an infection after it. Still, you know how strong he is."

"I should have been there with him. I should have gone the first damn time he asked."

"You'll be there soon enough." Drusus gave him a shove, and Lance, who for all he burned and longed to be on horseback and flying north once more was still a lad of nineteen summers, at the mercy of his body's demands, rolled down onto the bench, asleep before his head touched the sheepskin.

He had a strange dream. In it, he was the dragon who had come from the stars to rest in the moorland earth. He coiled his tail around Caer Lir in the west, and he laid his great head on the sands at Din Guardi.

No rest for him here, though. The people at his centre were hungry, the men and women of Vindolanda. He tried to curl himself protectively around them, but he was stretched too thin. He lost the sense of himself as male, slipped into a dark, blood-hot knowledge of his mother, of Viviana, the very land itself and the dragon-force within it. The dragon waited. She could feed everyone if she herself was fed, if the ancient contract of friendship and trust was fulfilled. If the women came to the cave...

But the women were gone. Starving, the dragon tried anyway. She rubbed her great snout around the fort at Din Guardi, causing panic and earth tremors there. She pressed one vast eye to the chamber where the future king lay dying, the magical weave of his ongoing life snapping thread by thread, falling into disarray. She'd have wept over him, and her tears would have washed away his fever and pain like the dust from a long weary day, but he was sealed away from her. She cried out his name, and the soldiers herded the women and children inside, barred the gates and dropped a portcullis of iron, a terrible new barricade through which she could not pass.

Fading and sick, the dragon retreated. She shrank as she coiled herself back into the earth. She became as an adder, then a tiny grass snake, and then she was nothing but a worm, her powers reduced to the small mindless ever-task of eating and turning the soil. When the hare appeared, the creature seemed vast, blocking out the sun. "Ah," said the hare. "Which miracle do you need, child—the small one to stop you breaking your poor coils in two between your past and your future, or the great one concerning the sword from the stone?"

"Both. I need both, Viviana."

A distant chuckle, the feel of a gnarled old hand on his hair. "Greedy boy! Well, well. We'll see what we can do."

Lance jolted awake. He couldn't have slept long: there was a bowl of broth on the ground by the bench, still steaming. Half a loaf of bread, too, warm to his touch when he reached for it. Drusus, seated on the bench next to his, was tearing hungrily into the other half. He grunted as Lance sat up, silently gestured to him that he should eat.

He picked up the bowl. He was ravenous, dreams scattering to windblown rags. He dipped a wooden spoon into the bowl, and finally noticed the figure on the other side of the fire.

Just another traveller, resting from the road. He was hunched over his broth, and he too had stopped, spoon in hand, to stare at Lance. He was gaunt, long-limbed. Once he must have been handsome. His cloak was ordinary, but beneath it he wore the shabby remains of a Roman army uniform. He put back his hood, and Lance found himself staring into the face of his father.

Chapter Three

"Much I gained by running away from you. The emperor Constantinus was recruiting. I met one of his generals in the east, and he hired me, along with a shipload of other poor fools who could lift a sword and had reason to leave these shores. This island's finished, as far as Rome is concerned."

Ban still had a fine head of fair hair. The longer Lance stared at him, the more the years dropped away, and the more he struggled to fit the familiar face to the dead-leaf words falling from its mouth. "I didn't even know there'd *been* an emperor Constantinus," Lance said, and wondered at his own stupidity. His first words to his father in four years, and he sounded like a dolt.

Ban gave him a tiny smile, as if he'd read the thought. "You wouldn't have. He was gone before news could have reached you here—the usurper usurped, by a puppet of the Vandals called Jovinus. You won't have heard of him either."

"No, I haven't. What did you do?"

"I was on the Rhine when Jovinus made his move. Jovinus looked good for a while, so I deserted, along with a lot of the other troops."

Noble King Ban, who would once have recoiled at the thought of such treachery! He wasn't even seeking to defend himself. Lance, who was growing up in fits and starts, leaned his elbows on his knees and suddenly found he could lift away his memories of his father from the man sitting opposite him now. Ban had been noble because Lance, as a boy, had yearned for nobility, and had thrown that longing upon him. Believed all his stories, gazed in admiration at his army cloak and sword. He'd been a kindly, easygoing father, more concerned with hunting and carousing with his friends than heroic displays of courage. None had been demanded of him, until the night of the raid. "I take it," Lance said flatly, "that Jovinus was defeated, too."

"By the Visigoths. They put his head on a spike outside Ravenna. The Western Empire is crumbling, Lance. That's why Rome's jettisoned Britannia. They're trying to protect their heartland, but I don't think even that can last for long."

"Why are you telling me this?"

"Because here you are, with a squire and two good horses, if the beasts I saw in the stables are yours. If you mean to try your fortune in the service of Rome, I caution you against it." In the silence that followed, Ban examined his son's face. He gave a dry chuckle. "You never could keep your heart out of your eyes, boy. Look at you, wondering what right I have to caution or command you, and too polite to open your mouth."

"I am not too polite. You're a stranger to me, and there's no point, that's all."

Ban didn't try to hide a flinch. "I wonder, would it help you to know how I paid for my sins? I spent three years fighting my way home across the Rhineland and Gaul. I was a soldier for hire to whichever tribe of Vandals, Franks or Visigoths would pay my wage. I laid my head in marshland villages infested with cholera, and at the end of it all I barely had the price of my food and the boat when I got back to Gaul's northern shore."

"And now what?"

"Now, after my travels, I hope to go home."

"Home's a heap of ash on the moors, for all you know."

"No. Not for all I know. News of the rise and fall of emperors might not have reached you here, but I met a soldier in the marshes who'd travelled from Caer Lir. From him I learned that Vindolanda was still standing, thanks to a fine son of mine." Ban held out a placating hand. "I don't think to flatter my way to forgiveness, boy. I'm only curious. You stood by the place for all this time. Why are you leaving now?"

"To join Arthur Pendragon at Din Guardi fort."

Ban's eyebrows flew up. "Artorius?"

"You've heard of him?"

"Everyone's heard of him by now. Old Uther's dead. Artorius seized the crown from his claimant half-brothers last year and made a great march north, drumming up troops for his campaign against the Saxons. He's to be married, too, I hear, so there's great doings in hand. You're a grand boy, Lance, a hundred times the man I'll ever be—but what would the king want with you?"

Lance put his bowl down so Ban wouldn't see the tremor in his hands. His last letter from Art—the worn, much-folded parchment folded in his jerkin's inner pocket, as close to his heart as he could carry it—was more than a year old. He glanced up at Drusus, but the messenger's face was impassive. With swift, subtle instinct, Lance understood that he mustn't spread word of Art's illness, that such news would reach his enemies like the scent of blood. "I'm not sure," he said—and it was suddenly, painfully true. "Possibly he'll want nothing. But I owe him my allegiance, and I'm going to him." He turned to Drusus again. "Now."

Ban held out a hand. "A moment, son."

"I owe you no moments."

"Agreed. It's I who owe you. I have my cloak, and the shirt on my back, and you wouldn't want either. But I was a soldier once, and I do have something to give you. You'll need it, if you're off to fight the Saxons for the king." A smile lit Ban's face, erasing decades. "I recall you trying it on when you were five years old, and falling down the stairs under the weight. I thought your mother was going to kill me."

Lance sat stiffly while Ban unfastened the pack at his side. Metal jingled, and Ban took out a chainmail shirt. *Lorica squamata*, the soldiers called it—tiny plates of bronze sewn onto a linen backing, in a Celtic design grown old before its adoption by the Romans. "I had a newer one," Ban continued, shaking out the shirt so that its disks glimmered dully in the firelight, "but I traded it for food on the way home. You might've seen 'em. Bands of metal that go all the way around you, the *lorica laminata*. I'm not sure they do much better in a pinch than this old thing. Stopped a few spear-tips for me, anyway."

He held out the garment. After a pause, Lance took it. "Won't you need it," he asked, his voice unsteady, "if you're travelling west? The hills are still full of Picts."

"Nothing ever changes, eh? No, I'll be all right. And you can go to your king with an undivided heart, because I know you'll have torn it in two to get this far."

"*How* do you know?" Lance demanded fiercely. "I don't understand. How did you come to be in this place of all others, at this very time?"

"It's not so strange, is it? This is the only place to rest between the coast and Pons Aelius." Ban tipped his bowl to his mouth to drain the rest of his broth. Then he sighed, and looked properly at his son. "I will tell you the truth. Your mother always said you were one of the dragon's brood, even more than your sisters, and perhaps you won't think I'm off my head. I had a dream in the early hours of this morning, when I was sleeping by a campfire three miles south of here. And in this dream an old woman spoke to me, and then…"

"Then she turned into a hare."

"That's right. May the gods of the Romans and the dragon's cave forgive me for what I did at Vindolanda, Lance. I don't know if they ever will. But I'm going back there now, to care for the place as best I can."

Lance rubbed his eyes. What did Ban have left? Ten or twenty good years, he supposed. For all his trials, he was barely forty summers old. He was thin and wiry, much of his strength undiminished. Even stripped of his heart, he would make a good village chieftain, by rote and by habit… Yes, it would do. Lance could reconcile it to his conscience. His own heart leapt and started to race. Old angers and fears fell away. "I'm glad we met," he said truthfully. "Can I help your journey onwards? I can pay for your horse's feed and keep here."

Ban pulled a rueful face. "And grateful she'd have been for that, if I hadn't had to sell her, too."

"Oh." Lance pulled open the pouch at his belt. He took out the coins he'd have used to hire a mount for himself and ride on. "Take this, Father. A king shouldn't have to return to his people on foot."

Chapter Four

Lance would never forget his first sight of Din Guardi fort. In all the years that followed, rich with joy, blood and sorrow as they were, his memory never lost that shape on the horizon, the proud crest rising from the wild coastal flatlands, as he and Drusus left the Roman road and began their approach through the maze of Celtic lanes, lined with tangles of frosted hawthorn at this time of year. Hawthorn trackways, and then vast sweeps of heath, scattered with gorse thickets, a few dried-out blossoms holding on still. A confusing country, lonelier even than the Vindolanda moors, home only to the clean sea winds.

His instinct was to point Balana at the great rock in the distance and set her to a gallop. Drusus laid a restraining hand to his rein. "Wait a moment, sire."

They had halted on a crest of high ground, where Din Guardi dominated the whole seaward horizon. The shape of it resonated deep inside Lance's mind. He was looking at the dragon's furthest stretch, her vast sleeping head, lapped by white sands and the cold north sea. "How far away are we, Drusus?"

"No more than ten miles. But this is the most dangerous stretch—we have to take care. The land's half overrun with Anglian settlers and pirates, and... Well, you'll see for yourself. We'll approach through the villages where we have friends. Follow me."

Lance started to obey, then drew Balana to a halt again. The question he hadn't meant to ask was in his mouth before he could prevent it. "Is it true that Arthur's to be married?"

Drusus frowned. He gave Lance a curious look, not unsympathetic. "Once more, it's a thing that you'll have to see for yourself. But, yes, his marriage is planned. If he lives."

The last words blew away unworthy thoughts—disbelief, a first ache of jealousy—like sand from wind-scoured stone. Art could marry a hundred times, if only he would rise from his sickbed whole. It was his duty as king. Who knew what political alliances he would seal by taking a bride from among the tribes of the Old North?

Or perhaps he'd just fallen in love. A shiver ran through Lance, and he settled his cloak around him before following Drusus downhill and back onto the track. After all, what had Lance been to him? A day and a night, Art's hands on him so tender and skilled that his experience, all the lovers he'd taken before, had shone out of him like sacred light. He'd never said otherwise. He'd told Lance the truth of it easily, with all the sweet pride of his nature. Except for the Beltane with his half-sister Modron, he was untouched by priestly fears or restrictions. It was better so.

When he and Drusus broached a seven-mile radius of the castle, he began to notice strange changes. The flatlands were sparsely dotted with small farms and hamlets. In these, the travellers were given a cautious welcome. Until the coming of the Romans, this land had been Votadini territory, and, just as at

170

Vindolanda, these fierce Celts had absorbed their conquerors. They worked the sandy soils for a living, called themselves Britons just as Lance did. They had recognised Lance and Drusus as their own, Roman credentials displayed in their dark hair and the fine horses they rode. The women brought them bread and wine, eager to tell them how some of their own sons had gone to try their fortunes in the army of King Artorius.

This close to Din Guardi, though, many of the farms were deserted. Lance saw no smoke rising from their chimney holes, and no dogs came running to bark around his horse. The silences near the dwelling places were strange. Lance, the cautious hunter, eased ahead of Drusus and began to lead them down tracks with better cover, avoiding the open heath. If Drusus was amused by this takeover bid from the newcomer, he gave no sign.

The empty fields and houses didn't look like the work of invaders. The buildings were mostly untouched. The damage seemed confined to the fields. There were odd barren places in the stubble, broad streaks where the earth was exposed. These marks gave Lance a weird pang of fear at his heart, stalwart traveller as he was, and the horses snorted and boggled at them too, and carried their riders past at a gallop.

Simpler on the face of it were the bodies of dead cattle they encountered from time to time. Cattle raids had been a fact of Lance's life since boyhood. If the thieves were too few in number to herd the beasts away, they would catch one and kill it on the spot, butcher from it as much as they could carry, and disappear, leaving such sorry remains as the ones he and Drusus were seeing now, half-decayed and tainting the breeze with the stench of decomposition. But when he looked more closely—pushing Balana's flanks with his heels, because she didn't like these corpses any more than she had the poisoned fields—he didn't recognise the wounds on them.

Surely Anglian raiders would be no less skilled than Pictish ones at stripping down a cow. They wouldn't randomly rip and tear. One of the beasts had been cleaved clean in two, only the hindquarters left behind, the rest nowhere to be seen.

If this was the work of pirates, they were savage ones. Lance, on full alert now, began to make his way with more caution still, gesturing to Drusus to keep behind him. He hadn't come this far to be ambushed in the shadow of Din Guardi itself. And yet, as they approached the dune meadows that rolled and gleamed to the south, he forgot his bewilderment and unease. There it was. The fort on the rock.

From this distance, it was hard to see that there was a fort there at all. The kings of the Old North had no desire to blazon out their strongholds. They hadn't won; they didn't own Britannia. They were under siege. The castle was only a group of single-storey halls, enclosed behind a wooden palisade. A couple of the buildings had a second floor, and the tower a precarious third, but that was all.

Lance loved it. He couldn't define the sense of welcome that shone out from it. Arthur was there. A joyful conviction took hold of him: Art must still be alive. Once more he conquered his impulse to break cover and gallop on. He and Drusus had no guarantee that the stronghold remained in allied hands. In the time it had taken the messenger to reach him and return, Anglian raiders could have seized the place, and he knew the kind of welcome he could expect from them.

He trotted Balana into the lee of one of the dunes, gestured to Drusus to stay where he was, then dismounted and scrambled up onto a crest to take a better look. Stretching out in the prickly marram, he smiled. There were so many harebells you could almost hear them ringing in the wind. And all he could think about, looking at Din Guardi rock, was that he had come home.

No, not bells. The percussion of galloping hooves on wet sand. Two horsemen emerged from the dunes in the distance. They weren't trying for concealment—to attract his attention, rather. Lance shifted to get a clear view. Then one of the men rode right out onto the beach, and hoisted a white flag adorned with a proud red dragon. He was waving it excitedly from side to side. Lance broke cover, Drusus following at a more sedate pace behind him.

Once the horses were within yards of one another he reined in hard, scattering sand. It was Gaius, all right—older and heavier, his homely visage not improved by a new scar that gaped down one cheek, but his old friend from Vindolanda still. "Guy!"

Gaius passed the Pendragon flag to his companion and heartily caught Lance's outstretched hand. "Lance! I knew it was you. No-one else crosses open ground like a weasel chasing a snake. I laid a bet with that fool Garbonian that it was. And I'm short on cash. I staked my horse on you."

"In that case, I'm doubly glad to be here. And... I can tell from your face that I needn't have galloped quite so hard. Please tell me I'm right."

"When my brother heard you'd been sent for, he got out of bed, told everyone he was fine and went back to work, knocking the warlords' heads together in the debating hall."

Lance lifted his face to the frail winter sun. Its light seemed to fill him. The fear that had driven him relentlessly across moor and dune fell away. "Thank God."

"Yes. We had a sharp time with him, though. Forgive me for taking you away from your people."

"You didn't. At least—that problem's been solved for me. I'll tell you about it later."

"You can stay?"

"For as long as I'm needed."

Gaius nodded. He was smiling, but his eyes were shadowed. "That's good. Drusus, ride on. You did well to bring our Lance home in one piece. I'll see him the rest of the way."

He waited until the messenger had set off down the beach. His own man fell back to a discreet distance, and he and Lance turned their horses' heads toward the castle. "I have to tell you something," he began, his voice unsteady for the first time since Lance had known him. "We lost Ector."

Lance went cold with shock. He hadn't known the old man for long, but he'd seemed as permanent as rocks and earth. "I grieve with you," he said awkwardly. "What happened to him?"

"He was killed in a raid on our camp further south. It wasn't the ending he'd have chosen for himself—they slew him in his sleep, his sword undrawn." Guy negotiated the crest of a dune, and shot Lance a tired, anxious look. "I mourn for him, but my brother took it worse. I don't know if he blames himself or the Saxons more."

"Poor Ector."

"I used to think sometimes that Art fought for the fun of it, or the principle—Britons versus Saxons, all that. Well, there's blood on it now for him. He misses the old man, but he won't talk about it, and other matters trouble him too..." He shook his head. "Never mind. Come along, and let's get out of this cold."

Lance rode on at his side, up through the last of the dunes and onto the meadows at the foot of Din Guardi rock. Now that he needn't draw every breath in fear for Art's life, he had to learn the story of his friend's presence here, so that he could find his place and begin to make himself useful. "I'll help in any way I can. How long have you been here?"

"Almost three months now. We came at the request of Coel the Elder—Coel Hen, in the old tongue. He used to rule over this whole land of Bryneich, from Din Guardi to the river Thuaigh in the north. The Romans even made him *Dux Britanniarum*, he was so useful to them."

Lance knew about the coveted *duces* posts. Once the Romans could no longer spare their own men to hold them, they had begun to offer them as a reward to whichever of the brawling British kings would best support them, and Ban had held out hopes. "That's a fine thing, isn't it?"

"Certainly used to be. Coel's losing his grip on his dukedom, though. He's got Pictish raiders in the north, tribes pouring in from Hibernia in the west, and Anglian pirates washing up from the east every day. He's got so many troubles, and his face is so long, that some of my lads made up a song about him. *Old King Coel*, they call it."

Lance grinned. "I think I heard the children singing that in one of the villages we passed."

"Well, he's not a merry old soul, and he's liable to prove it with an axe. When he heard that Arthur was travelling north with an army, he offered us shelter at Din Guardi and treated for talks with him. The trouble was, Coel thought Art was a potential recruit for *his* war, not vice versa."

"Oh. What did Arthur do?"

"He summoned the lords of Ebrauc to the south— Eboracum, the Romans called it—and of Rheged, from the mountains and lakes in the west, to take part in the debate. Mor and Ceneu, their names are, and poor old Coel lies awake at night grinding his teeth at the thought of sharing his castle with them both. They've all been enemies since birth."

"But Coel needs Arthur, so..."

"That's right. Art's no more than an upstart, as far as these old codgers are concerned, but men listen to him. There's the very faint chance of an alliance."

And that would change everything. Lance and Gaius exchanged a glance of understanding. If the kings of the Old North could set aside their differences, the realm of Britannia might step out of the shadows of a mythic past and become a reality. *A dream kingdom only*, Viviana breathed in Lance's memory, but he pushed her cautionary words aside. He was here now. His goals were Arthur's.

By this time they had reached the outskirts of the Pendragon army's camp, and Lance looked about him alertly. This would be his home, his life, if he could be useful and earn his place. God knew it looked ordinary enough—rough tents made of sewn leather, mutton being roasted by the cooks over a massive open-air fire, a hubbub of men and horses and servitors from the castle bustling back and forth with messages and pots and pans. But it was huge. Lance put away certain hopes, desires and assumptions, as firmly as he'd hushed Viviana's voice in his head. He might never see his king, except at a distance or on the battlefield. But a time might come when he could serve him, and that moment, when it came—even if it were only the heartbeat flash of stopping a sword for him—would mean more to Lance than a lifetime as prince of Vindolanda. "Where's your recruitment tent?" he asked Gaius, looking around. "I'll go and present myself."

"What?"

"Your sergeant-at-arms and your quartermaster. I have to go and—"

"Oh, for heaven's sake. Art would skin me alive. He expects you in the stronghold—your own chambers and everything. Come inside."

Here at its south end, the great rock crouched down low, like an obedient horse trained for a child to mount. A ditch and earthwork followed its curve, crossed by a narrow, defensible timber bridge. Gaius bellowed to the gatekeepers, who began the laborious task of hauling up a vast portcullis to admit them. "Sorry," he said to Lance. "We're having to keep it closed. Do you see those clusters of huts and tents to the west?"

Lance shielded his eyes against the last of the midwinter sun. His heart was beating low and fast with joy, warm blood driving the chill from his fingers. "Aren't they ours?"

"You'd think so, as close to the castle as that. They're Anglian. They're getting bolder every day, and unlike us, if they get cut down, there's thousands more to sail in and replace them."

That must be the cause of the dead fields and farmhouses, Lance thought. The gate was up now, Gaius gesturing him through with a smile. "Good heavens," Guy said suddenly, focussing on his horse. "Is that old Balana?"

"Well, I found myself short of fine Roman warhorses this year, so... yes, it is."

"She doesn't look a day older. You've cared for her well." Guy shook his head. "I remember how blisteringly jealous I used to be when Ector gave away anything I thought should one day be mine—especially to poor Art. I envy him nothing now. I only wish the old man was here so I could tell him so." With an effort he threw the shadows off. "Never mind. We'll give our horses to the grooms and get some breakfast, and then you should come to the debating hall. It's the best way to see what we're up against here, and he'll expect you to learn. I'm glad you're come, Lance. He's bored me blue with the sound of your name for the past three years."

Chapter Five

For all that, when Gaius ushered him into the great hall, Lance doubted Art would even notice him. He could see nothing but the burly shoulders of warlords and their bodyguards, forming a wall in front of him. Guy tapped his arm, and pointed to a flight of wooden steps to the right of the door. "Up there," he whispered. "There'll be room in the gallery, or if not I'll throw someone out."

Hesitantly Lance scrambled up. There was just space for two on the end of the first long bench. He sat down quietly, Guy thudding into place beside him a moment later. Then, when he was settled, he dared to raise his eyes.

The hall was no more than a great bare space, but was perched high on the Din Guardi rock, and the sun flooding into it was beautiful. Dozens of small windows pierced its upper courses, just beneath its timber-thatch roof, and through each of these a pale winter radiance was pouring. In the centre, in a pool of dust-moted light, Arthur was addressing the chiefs.

Lance barely recognised him. He was plainly but richly turned out in the full panoply of a Romano-Celtic statesman who might get called onto the battlefield at any minute, and there was no

178

mistaking him for anything other than a king. The boy Lance had known was gone. He had gained about a foot in height and broadened into it: his shoulders were wide beneath his gold-threaded tawny cloak, his stance solid and poised. At his side, in a beautifully worked sword belt and scabbard, Excalibur hung, and did not look decorative.

His hair was long, and a more pronounced shade of red-gold than Lance remembered. He bore no signs of his recent brush with death. Lance, disoriented by travel, wondered if his terrified moorland gallop to get here had been a wild dream. Would he wake up in his makeshift reading room at Vindolanda, ink-stains on his cheek, nothing more to care about than sheep and the pigs in the midden?

He forced himself to concentrate. He and Guy had arrived in the middle of an intense debate. To Art's left and right, in stiff wooden thrones, sat the kings of Yr Hen Ogledd, the Old North. Lance recognised the tartans of Rheged, of Ebrauc and Srath Chluaidh brightly patterning their britches and cloaks. The eldest of them was speaking now, a rugged old Celt of such grim countenance that Lance knew him at once, and struggled not to laugh. He shot a sidelong glance at Guy, who was grinning broadly and nodding: yes, that was Coel.

"And the little rat beside him is his eldest, Prince Garbonian, who now owes me a horse, thanks to you, dear Lance."

Guy had made no effort to keep his voice down. Just for a moment, Arthur glanced up from his pose of polite attention to the old man's speech. Lance read the message of pained amusement, of reproach—and then Art's focus widened. He jerked up his head. A vast smile cracked his solemn mask.

Coel tailed off into silence. Then he shifted on his throne, banged his staff and growled, "If I am boring you, sire, please do feel free to let me know."

Arthur turned back to him instantly. "Forgive me, Your Majesty." His smile was fading, but it remained in his voice as he added, loud enough for Guy to hear, "I did ask my guards to keep out the louts and layabouts. Will you please go on?"

"Very well. As I was saying… I must deal with my kingdom's troubles in the north and west before I can think of joining your campaign against the Saxons, lad, noble though it is. I had hoped that you'd divert some of your forces to assist *me*."

Arthur nodded. Lance, up in the galleried distance, noticed even from there how he did not immediately respond, how he took the words and thought about them, unashamed to be seen to be taking his time. "I understand," he said. "It may be that we have to fight our separate wars, Coel Hen, for the time at least. I would help you gladly if my numbers were greater."

"Did I ask you to spare me a whole army, boy?" Coel got stiffly to his feet and leaned on his staff. He looked as if lightning was ready to strike from under his grizzled brows. "A few raiding parties, that's all, some good actors who'll go up there in the guise of Picts or these damned Scots, stir up trouble and create divisions between them. That's my only hope of keeping my borders secure in the north."

"With respect, sire, that won't work. I've seen them. They'll squabble amongst themselves day and night—until an outsider provokes them, and then they'll drop every blood feud and cattle war they have, and come together like brothers to fight a common enemy."

"Me, you mean."

"Yes, sire."

Coel's reputation had reached Lance, even in the wilds of Vindolanda. He was a stern, stubborn old warrior, and all his life he had upheld Roman interests against the incursions of the native tribes. It would be his instinct to bring them down by any means at his command. But he was an able administrator, too, a statesman and legislator, and whether or not he liked it, plainly he could hear the sense in the young king's words. "Very well," he growled. "What is your suggestion, then, Artorius?"

Before Art could reply, the occupant of the throne next to Coel's rose smoothly to his feet. This was Garbonian, the king's eldest son. Watching, Lance wondered at his own instant surge of dislike, then saw it reflected in Arthur's expression, and wondered still more. The prince of Din Guardi was as fine and mannered as his father was rough. When he laid a hand to old Coel's shoulder as if to restrain him, Coel snarled like a bear and shook him off. Garbonian retreated, palms raised wryly, eliciting a small wave of laughter among the men opposite. Art, who had certain ideas about filial duty, frowned at him. "You should not raise mirth against your father, prince," he warned.

Garbonian shrugged. "It wasn't intended," he said easily. "The fact is that I agree with you, Artorius. We shouldn't engage the Picts and Hibernians at all in their own territory. That war is lost." Coel glared at him, but Garbonian turned away and addressed the whole room, spreading his pale, well-manicured hands as if to invite support. "We Britons can only defend our own heartlands, now that the Romans have abandoned us. And the means to do so lies within our grasp."

Coel reddened. "Damnation, Garb! Did I not forbid you to spew out your treachery inside this hall? Bad enough I have to hear you over dinner. I won't have Artorius think the House of Coel supports this nonsense."

"Sire," Arthur interjected gently, when the old man paused to draw breath. "I would never assume the prince's views are yours. But we agreed—did we not?—that all men should be heard."

"Hah," Coel grunted. "You *demanded* that, then wouldn't take no for an answer, as I recall." But he subsided wearily onto his throne. "Speak, then, Garbonian."

The prince gave a small, sarcastic bow of thanks. "I'm much obliged to you, Father, and to His Majesty of Cerniw. The truth is, gentlemen, that we cannot control the ancient tribes. Nor can we stem the tide of invaders from over the sea." He waited until the outraged mutters of dissent had subsided. "That's the truth of the matter. I don't like it any more than you do, but my answer is simple. Let us set our enemies one against the other. These Anglian settlers may be unpolished, but they're fine soldiers. And they love the sight of gold. I propose that we treat with them— use them, employ them to protect us, and repay them in coin and in settlement rights."

Instantly the hall was full of murmuring voices. Lance felt a change in the air like the coming of a storm: his nape and his skin prickled. Out of the dangerous rumble, Coel's great voice boiled up, deep and harsh. "You're a fool, my son. And your proposal will cut all our throats for us. However…" He paused, shaking his head. "I might even have considered it, if I believed for a moment that you'd thought it up yourself."

The rumble became a roar. Laughter was woven through it: Garbonian's milky skin had mottled puce with embarrassment. Arthur gestured the crowd to silence, but his eyes were cold. To Lance, that made him look like a stranger, and he wondered if it was Ector's death that had driven such iron into his soul. "Your father is right," he said to Garbonian. "I *have* insisted that everyone be heard, even when that goes against my own inclination. Continue."

"Very well," said the prince. "I'm not ashamed that I use the words of men wiser than myself. You must all know that this is the policy of King Vortigern of Elmet in the south. You, father, with your nostalgic dreams of Roman rule, should not oppose it. It is simply a *foederatus*, such as the Roman administrators on the island made for centuries with the tribes. And it has worked well. He has used the Saxons not only against the raiders in the west but against their own kind, arriving by sea! They are savage fighters, cowed by nothing."

Lance looked quickly at the men around him. They were all dressed as Art was, in the rich, muted colours of the Cerniw court. They must have marched north with him, fought with him in heaven only knew how many battles. They hadn't liked Garbonian's final words one bit, and were issuing an array of snorts and other derisive noises. Guy, with greater rights to express himself, clapped his hands to his knees and let go a wild, hooting laugh.

Arthur stood quietly, arms folded over his chest, letting the reaction run its course. Then he raised his head, and his men— Guy, too—knew him well enough to fall silent without being told. "You're partly correct, Garbonian," he said. "But your news is old. I gained mine two moons ago, when my army engaged these very same Saxons, who broke treaty with Vortigern when he could no longer pay their raging demands for gold and land. I tell you with shame that we were defeated, driven back by their greater numbers. You are quite right—they will turn on their own kind. Their hearts are as empty as their pockets are full. I have heard you, but I do not advise you to speak kindly of Saxons—or of Vortigern—in front of my men."

Lance expected Garbonian to sit back down. If Art had turned so icy a gaze upon him, he wouldn't have known how to bear it. But Garbonian seemed unruffled. He took a moment or two, as if readjusting his ideas. Then he looked up at Arthur without fear. "Will you permit me to say, Your Majesty, that your views on these newcomers have been coloured by the death of your good stepfather, whose fate I learned with the greatest sadness?"

A faint gasp went through the crowd. Guy's hand flew to the hilt of his sword. Old Coel surged to his feet and actually caught his son a clip across the shoulder with his staff. "Garb!" he thundered. "You wretched, unfeeling boy."

Then he turned to Arthur, and stiffly dropped down on one knee before him. "Artorius," he growled. "Forgive this insult to your grief. Forgive my child. I was much away on campaign during his youth, and left his upbringing to fools and women."

Art leaned down to him. Something in the movement caused him to pale more deeply than Garbonian's words had done, but still he hoisted the old man back to his feet. "It's forgiven," he said, loudly enough for everyone assembled to hear. Then he turned to Garbonian with a calm, pleasant smile. "It's forgiven. But if your tongue ever forms my father's name again, sir, I'll cut it from your head. Finish what you have to say, and be quick about it."

Garbonian looked less startled by the threat than by the chance to carry on. Lance could read him easily: felt, despite his instinctive loathing, a kind of kinship. Lance too had been raised amongst hotheaded tribal aristocrats for whom everything was personal. He had never before seen a leader who refused to let his own feelings sway an argument. Garbonian, Lance, Guy, the gathered soldiers—everyone here was witnessing, would be forced to acknowledge, a new kind of kingship.

But Garbonian had learned something else too. Lance could see it in the very blandness of his expression. He was stowing away the discovery that Arthur could be hurt. Quickly he resumed the floor. "Yes, Your Majesty. The shame is mine, that I didn't know of the Elmet uprising. But things are different with us here in the north. For one, there aren't so many incomers, and never will be.

Further, apart from a handful of pirates, they are most of them settlers anyway. We couldn't stop it when they arrived, and now they have lands of their own to take care of. We should use that to our advantage."

"So you... seek an alliance?"

"I don't know if I'd dignify it with that word. They're not our equals. But a treaty, an arrangement..."

For the first time, Arthur looked uncertain. He shot a searching glance into a patch of shadows behind the row of thrones. "Excuse me," he said. "I must consult with my Merlin."

Lance wasn't sure if he'd heard him aright. Then the shadows stirred, and a kind of human scarecrow emerged into the light, which was just beginning to redden as the short winter day drew on. The frail, bowed figure was nothing but bones draped in a cobweb of cloak and robes, face invisible behind a cloud-grey hood.

It was Viviana, surely! Lance lurched halfway to his feet before Guy grabbed his elbow and pulled him back down. Lance turned to him, joy and hope boiling up fiercely. If anyone could counsel the king, guide him wisely in the paths of treaties, arrangements, alliances... After all, hadn't she told Lance that the blending of the streams was inevitable, as natural in the long term as the confluence of waters at River's Meet? "Guy," he whispered. "It's the old woman I told you about, the one who looked after me and showed me the sword from the lake. Viviana!"

Chapter Six

Guy made frantic gestures of hushing. "What are you talking about?" he whispered, staring down the haughty knight in the row in front who'd twisted round to frown at them. "That's our Merlin."

"Your *Merlin*? I thought he was a legend, something out of Arthur's visions."

"Well, sometimes he is. He's real at the moment, though, and we're very fortunate to have him."

"I don't understand. This is the old man who brought Art to live with you? How can he still be alive?"

"They're said to be immortal."

"They? There's more than one?"

"So legend says. There must be, or how could they appear as they do, in a man's youth and again in his old age, always the same?"

The haughty knight turned again. This time Lance raised a reproving eyebrow at him, and he blinked and looked away. "How can you be certain, then, that this one is real? Arthur's Merlin?"

Guy's expression became grim. "He is. He came to us during our useless battle for Vortigern's land, just after my father was wounded. Ector recognised him, or… Well, he was dying. But he said he was one and the same. And everybody listens when he speaks, so for heaven's sake shut up."

Lance obeyed, bewildered. He'd have bet his own horse that Viviana's gaunt face lay beneath the folds of the hood, but now the thin figure was straightening up, pushing the ragged fabric back. A harsh profile appeared, thrusting up towards Arthur's like a hungry bird of prey. His words were for Art only, even though a pindrop silence had fallen throughout the hall. Taut sibilants only reached Lance across the space between them, which suddenly seemed vast, a desert he could never cross. Then, abruptly as the old man had started, he was done, drawing his hood back into place. His retreat into the shadows was so subtle and quick that Lance rubbed his eyes, suddenly uncertain that he'd been there at all.

Arthur swayed. Lance had half forgotten that he'd hauled himself off what should have been his deathbed to come to the debating hall today. Now, suddenly, it was all too apparent. Old Coel, who'd never resumed his seat after rising to deal with Garbonian, took gentle hold of his elbow and held out a hand to his vacant throne. After a moment's resistance, Arthur gratefully sat down. "Thank you," he said, and looked around him as if unsure of where he was. Then he collected himself, using one elbow to push himself up straight. "Garbonian says the invaders aren't our equals. I don't know the rights and wrongs of that, but… Coel, why not seek alliance with men you *do* know are worthy to stand with you in defence of your realm?" He held out a hand toward Mor of Ebrauc, Ceneu of Rheged, Srath Chluaidh, Coel himself. "Right here in this hall with you are sovereign lords whose kingdoms, once united, could form a wall against any invasion."

Coel sighed. He seemed to have forgotten about any sovereignty of Arthur's: was patting his shoulder as if Art had been a tired, injured son of his own, and a much nicer one than Garbonian. "Yes, once united," he said wryly. "But you'd have better luck making three tom cats see one another's point of view. You're a southerner, Artorius. You don't understand how we've all fought each other, or for how long. They'd rather slit each other's throats than cooperate."

Art turned to look at them. "Is this so?" he asked, wonderingly. "Can it be that you'd all rather lose your whole world than learn how to govern it together?"

Mor, Srath Chluaidh and Ceneu carefully avoided his eyes. Lance watched, waiting for an answer, aware that everyone on the benches around him was waiting tensely too. Lance had been astonished to learn that the Hen Ogledd kings had come willingly to Din Guardi. Had Arthur been naïve? It seemed all too likely that each of the old men glowering at him from their thrones had simply come here determined to get Art's famous army behind their own separate wars. Perhaps that was the only reason why Coel had opened up Din Guardi to him in the first place.

But, oddly, it was Coel who spoke at last. "It has been so, Artorius," he said reluctantly. "Yes, it has been so. However, I for one am ready to talk."

A moment of possibilities. Arthur's cool grey gaze kindled, became almost boyish again with hope. Coel's own household and retinue looked as astonished as the rival kings. Out of all of them, Coel had been the most bloodymindedly determined to hold his realm without help from his neighbours. If he, of all men, would stand down...

But Garbonian laughed out loud. "If the day ever comes, father, I'll embroider the flag of the united kingdom with my own hands! Listen to me, King Artorius. What use is one old man who might just be willing to negotiate, if he doesn't change his mind next morning, when his gout bothers him, or Mor or Ceneu looks at him sideways? Outside in the settlements west of here, I have ten Anglian princes and nobles ready to come and make treaty with you tomorrow, for the joint defence of this land!"

The silence that fell was electric. It was also short-lived. Lance saw Art look round the hall, judging the mood of his men in one comprehensive glance. He would have picked out the best of them, the chiefs and commanders, to attend with him here, but they weren't without their boiling point. As for Coel, he was upright again, face livid, and Lance noted with alarm that he'd unshipped his battleaxe from his belt, to God knew what murderous end. "Is that where you spent your morning, you puppy?" the old man roared. "Grovelling and plotting with your pirate friends?"

"Enough, Coel," Art warned him. Then he repeated it, loudly, against the rising tide of jeers from the crowd. "Enough! Enough for today." This time they didn't attend him. His palm sought the hilt of Excalibur, and his voice rang out. "I said it's *enough!*"

Doves flew in the old hall's rafters. Lance barely noticed their sunlit flight, the absolute hush that fell down like loosened feathers from their wings. He could hear nothing but his own raggedly thumping heart. Then Arthur spoke once more, quiet and ordinary. "It's enough. Hot tempers offer bad counsel. I will speak privately with Garbonian. Tomorrow we convene again."

***

189

The crush around the doors was considerable. Garbonian, quite aware of the effect he'd produced, was amongst the first to shove his way out. Gaius pointed to him, ploughing a track past the gallery. "There he is, the weasel," he said, slapping Lance on the knee. "I'm going after him—I want to settle our bet before somebody kills him. You stay here and catch up with Art. See you later."

He vaulted the rail and was gone. Lance remained seated, waiting for the crowd to thin. It was good of Guy to make him so welcome. When he closed his eyes, he could see once again the sweep of Viviana's moorland on the day when he'd first taken Art there, to the untamed heights where he'd encountered his life's first mysteries. At the time, he'd barely noticed how Guy had sent them off together, wordlessly creating a safe hour for them—the sweetest of Lance's life—and setting himself to guard it from a discreet distance. Guy had been on his side, on *their* side, and as the lonely months afterward had unfolded, Lance had blessed him for it again and again.

But perhaps Guy had created such hours for his brother many times. Perhaps his duty of guardianship had included them, ensuring that the future king could roll around in safety with a boy or a girl of his choice. Lance's mother would have found nothing strange in that. By such encounters, a man increased his potency and skills, making himself fit for the honours his queen would one day bestow upon him.

Father Tomas, Lance's village priest, would have said his soul was hellbound. Lance smiled. If he had half the chance, he'd have joined Art in hell anytime. Art was still there among the thrones, listening patiently to Coel, who appeared to be tearing his hair out. Certainly he wasn't looking around for old friends. Guy had surely exaggerated the importance of Lance's arrival.

Lance didn't mind. *Of course I don't bloody mind*, he told himself sternly. He had come here as a soldier. Easing off the bench, he dropped down the gallery steps into the groups of chattering, quarrelling stragglers, and was borne with them out into the sun.

Outside, the day was ending in shafts of brilliant light. Lance had never travelled as far east as this coast, and although sometimes when the wind was right, faint tangs of brine had blown over the hills of White Meadows, he had never smelt the salt of the North Sea.

He followed the scent, shading his eyes from the sun. Blood and metal, he thought, trying to define its richness. Kelp, and the air before a storm. A big gale was galloping in off the water. He hardly had to breathe for the air to find its way to the depths of his lungs. It was stingingly fresh. He fought the impression that it was greeting him, buffeting him with its wings in boisterous welcome. He threaded his way towards its source, through the maze of small buildings that made up the fort, and soon emerged onto the cliff.

A low parapet wall bounded the seaward side. There wasn't much need for more here, Lance reflected, taking in the beautiful defensibility of it. You could almost see clear to Juteland, so clear and bright did the setting sun lie on the water. The invaders troubling Bryneich now must have found their way ashore elsewhere: no-one could ever surprise Din Guardi. From the seaward base of the wall, the cliff plunged a sheer hundred feet to the dunes. Lance leaned out to see the high-water mark. A fine chain of seaweed and shells traced the white sand about two thirds of the way up the beach from the water, but he wondered if, on stormy nights, the east wind ever heaped up the waves so high that they dashed themselves on the very roots of Din Guardi…

"Lance!"

He whipped round. He hadn't noticed the doorway behind him, or the rising ripple of voices and laughter coming closer. Coel's fort was a honeycomb, halls and chambers linked by unexpected corridors. Halfway down the curving stone stairway that led from the floor above to the door onto the parapet, Arthur was standing. He was holding fast to the banister with one hand. His other arm was around the waist of one of the handsomest women Lance had ever seen. Her face was kind, her bearing noble.

Art was to be married. That was good and right, and in the nature of things. A woman like this would be a companion to him too, if the keen intelligence in her eyes was anything to judge by. The shape of her brow reminded Lance of Coel's, and she was perhaps a daughter of the house. She was a dozen years older than Art, but that mattered little: an alliance was an alliance.

A huge pang of grief seized Lance. He told himself there was relief in it. He and Arthur had their separate paths—could live without each other, as they'd lived for the last three years. All was for the best. What would he have done, if Art had let go of the woman at his side and taken a step towards him, saying his name as he had by the moorland lake, in front of the courtiers and maids gathered round him?

Art let her go. He could barely walk without her support, but he clutched the stone rail with both hands and took one step down. "Lance," he said hoarsely, eyes clouding with tears. "Lance!"

Chapter Seven

He dismissed the crowd with a look. Even the queenly lady at his side whisked herself away in a sweep of scarlet cloak, casting only one concerned glance over her shoulder as she vanished up the stairs. The others scattered like leaves on the wind, and then he was alone.

Why couldn't Lance run to him? He'd ridden halfway across the country to get here, almost broken the heart out of a good horse. Why couldn't he climb a flight of stairs?

Arthur saved him the trouble. He half-stumbled, half-fell down them, and limped across the patch of windswept turf. The sun had gone down and the sudden night was cold. Uncertain lamplight painted the parapet wall. "For God's sake be careful," he said. "I lost two off there last week in a drunken scrap."

At last Lance could move. He strode forward, holding out his arms. Arthur walked into them, and their bodies met hard, a subdued thump of ribcage, flesh and bone. Art was shivering. "Lance," he whispered. "You came."

***

Three stars were rising over the North Sea. The stone archway framed them, making a new constellation. The *Trinity of Joy*, Lance would have called it, or *Journey's End*. He knew it was only the tail end of the Plough, beginning her nightly sweep up and away to the zenith, but he would take what he could get. The Plough was also called the Bear, and soon Arcturus would rise too—Arthur's star, the sign he'd watched for on clear nights over the moors. Red-gold, like the head resting now against his shoulder. The stone archway could be his own arm, a shielding curve. "We'd better go in," he said softly. "It's getting cold."

"I can endure it if you can."

"Yes." *Fire, ice, the mud of battle, whatever you need me to bear.* "Not very kingly, though, is it? To be sitting here on the back stairs?"

"No-one dares question me. And when I tell them to go, they stay gone."

More sorrow in that than pride. "Even the lady in the red cloak?" Lance asked tentatively. "She didn't seem to want to leave your side."

"Yes, even she, though she has more right to disobey me than any of the others."

"Because… Is she your chosen bride?"

Arthur sat up. He looked at Lance in undisguised amazement. A smile dawned on his face, pale echo of the blazing grin that had lit up Lance's summer three years before, putting the sun to shame. "My what?"

"Well, Drusus said—I hope it wasn't a royal secret—that you're about to be married. I wondered if that was the lady concerned."

"Lance, for God's sake. She's seen thirty winters if she's seen one, and she's a bony old girl into the bargain."

Was she? Lance had only seen strength in the woman's tall frame. He'd clearly put his foot in it, though, and was glad the shadows would hide his blush. "I'm sorry. I thought her handsome. Anyway, if she'd been your choice—"

"But she isn't. Good grief. She's my sister-in-law."

"Your... Oh! Guy?"

"That's right. Within two weeks of clapping eyes upon her. She's Coel's eldest daughter, the Lady Ardana."

Lance tried to sound worldly. "Was it... political?"

"Hardly. She decided she wanted him, and he returned the favour, so they marched straight off to the Din Guardi priest and tied their knot. I didn't mean to call her names. She's strong as an oak, and she goes about with me whenever she can to save me appearing with a crutch."

"That's good of her. Yes, I... I heard you'd been hurt."

Art shook his head. "You don't have to play things down. They thought I was dying, and I cried your name so often in my fevers that they sent Drusus to fetch you. I do *know*. And over the moors and dunes you came at the gallop, expecting no doubt to find me with one foot at least through death's door."

Lance couldn't deny a word of this. "I'm just glad to find you still on this side. All of you."

Art shifted on the cold stone step and winced. "It very nearly *wasn't* all. The reason for the mystery surrounding my injury— apart from the fact that I'm meant to be immortal—is that I took a knife blade through the top of my thigh and into what Gaius likes to call the family jewels."

"Oh, my God." Now it was Lance's turn to wince, in pure sympathy. "Ouch."

"You're not kidding."

"How did that happen?"

"I slew the Saxon who'd killed Ector. I thought I had, anyway. I was… distracted, though, and the bastard knifed me with his last breath as I was stepping over what should have been his corpse." Art laid a hand to Lance's mouth. His fingers were chilly and smelled of witch-hazel salve. "It's in your good and noble heart to tell me how sorry you are about my father, how you grieve with me. I take it as said, dear friend. I can't bear to speak of him, though. I can't."

Was it wrong for Lance to kiss the fingers pressed against his lips? Right or wrong, it was done before he could stop himself, and Arthur's gaze widened unfathomably. He caressed Lance's cheek before lowering his hand. "I won't breathe his name," Lance said. "Not until you do, I swear. This wound of yours—it has healed?"

"My physicians are sworn under oath to say it has. A king must be potent as well as immortal."

"And the truth of the matter?"

"I've been too sick to test the equipment. Too scared."

"Oh, Art."

"I'll be fine, I'm certain." He made an effort to brighten, painful for Lance to watch. "I'd better, hadn't I? For the sake of my future bride."

"There is such a creature, then?"

"The Merlin says so. He's prophesied her arrival soon."

Lance took this in, wide-eyed. "So… she isn't real?"

"Until the battle of Elmet, I thought *he* wasn't. But he showed up large as life, exactly as I'd seen him in my vision. And everything else he's foretold has come to pass, so…"

"Look, Art," Lance said uneasily, reading the lines of illness and strain in his friend's face. "I've no doubt he's a prophet. But one very old man with a long white beard can look a lot like another, and… my mother used to say that these hermit-magicians, for all their gifts, are caught between the old world and the new. That they don't really understand either, and would do anything to pull things back to a kind of dream of the way the kingdom used to be, or should have been, and maybe never was."

Art reached up to grasp the rail. Before Lance could stop him, he'd pulled himself to his feet. "You don't understand. He's the Merlin, the very one who brought me from the forest. I need him, especially—especially now that Ector's gone."

I won't breathe his name until you do. Lance hadn't had to wait for long. Art had been close to a decision in the debating hall today, and the old man had deflected him. "Ector loved the bones of you," he said firmly, getting up and taking Art by the shoulders. "He'd want you to heed any wisdom your Merlin has to give, but not to fear him. And he'd definitely not want you standing about on freezing staircases until your family jewels drop off anyway. Come inside."

"All right. Let's stay out of the corridors, though, then there's less chance of old King Coel collaring me."

"Does he do that a lot?"

"Every chance he gets. A merry old soul, my arse! Like it's my fault his son's a collaborator."

"And is he?"

Lance put out an arm. It was no less than the Lady Ardana would have done, and Art took the offered support with as much grace as he could muster. "Garb? Just an idiot, I believe. Thinks he can succeed where Vortigern failed."

"Can he?"

Night had fallen on Din Guardi, a wolf with icy breath. Slowly they made their way back down the track and past the wooden palisade that marked the castle's inner ward. Even this pace was making Arthur limp and bite back sounds of pain, so Lance stopped with him under the archway to a squat tower, ignoring the edge of his temper. "Is that the keep?"

"Yes. Sight lines clear to Alauna. Has its own well, too. I could hold the north from here, if the Hen Ogledd kings would stop bickering and join me." He released a long breath, and turned to meet Lance's amused glance. "Thank God you're here. My enemies won't say yes to me, and my so-called friends won't say no. You must be tired, though, after your journey. Come and I'll show you your quarters."

***

Lance, who had been ready to billet down among the soldiers, looked with pleasure around his bright-lit chamber. Coel had given Arthur's retinue lodging in the keep, the only structure in the fortress with a stone-built upper floor. It was the best and least draughty of all the buildings, with cloudy blue Roman glass in its narrow windows: whatever his motives in asking Art here, the old king had certainly meant to do him honour. The rooms in the upper floor were not large, but they had plain, comfortable wooden-frame beds and even their own rough corner fireplaces. A good blaze had been roaring in this one when Arthur had left him, and it was crackling still, sending ruby and orange flickers to blend with the world's-edge darkness beyond the glass.

Driftwood and sea coal, Art had said. A salty incense filled the little space. Unpacking his few possessions from a saddlebag, Lance knew he would never forget it—that fragrance, and the unseen, softly roaring sea-night. *I put you on the seaward side,* Art had said to him. *It's colder, but I thought you'd like it better. I have to speak to Garbonian now, curse him. See you at dinner.*

Lance went to the window. A single pane, it swung outward from its latch, letting in a wild rush of air. Art was right—it was freezing in this depth of December, and he doubted it was ever truly warm on this far-flung seagull's perch. But he did like it better. *I love it*, he realised, wonderingly.

The draught was making the fire smoke. Reluctantly Lance closed the window. He wasn't tired, he thought, not really. He could have gone with Art, or at least done something useful with his evening, to begin to pay for his welcome. Well, he'd seen archery targets in a hall on his way up here, even a big, torchlit yard where men were doing their best to knock one another off horses with swords. He could go and practise drill. From the look of things, he could even use what Ban had taught him from his Roman army days to make a few improvements…

He turned back into the room and looked at the neatly made-up bed. A huge yawn shook him. It hadn't mattered to him at the time, but now he came to think of it, he had hardly rested for days. He'd been like a loosed arrow himself, flying straight for Din Guardi, as soon as he'd known he was free.

The rough blanket smelled clean from its outside drying. Stretching out on his stomach, Lance tried to stay awake, long enough at least to feel guilty about falling asleep in his boots, barely an hour after the midwinter sun had gone down.

Chapter Eight

He slept on until late evening, only jolting awake at the sound of shouts and laughter down in the hall of the keep. A clench in his belly, and savoury scents in the air, reminded him that he hadn't eaten since his snatched meal with Guy before the debate. He scrambled up, washed as best he could in the bronze bowl of water by the fire, and changed into his one clean shirt.

At the foot of the twisting spiral staircase he met Guy and Ardana, involved in a scuffle that was making them laugh like children. Ardana looked up blushing when she noticed him, and Guy let her go, still beaming. "Ah, Lance! Have you met my wife?"

"Not formally, no."

"My Lady Ardana, I present to you Lance o'the Lough, king of the White Meadows and Vindolanda."

Lance bowed. Ardana, who looked as if she'd have liked to bow back, dropped an awkward curtsey instead. "We've heard a lot about you," she said, then caught Guy's eye and smiled. "An awful lot."

"I'm sorry about that. And I'm only the prince, I'm afraid. My father came back."

Guy's eyes widened. "He never did!"

"I'll tell you all about it, but not now. It looks as though we're going in to dinner."

"Aye, and you don't want to miss that. It's a grand affair."

"Every night?"

"Now Art's up and about again, yes. He thinks he'll make all these grumpy old men learn to get on, if he sits them down together every day and feeds them. Of course old Coel couldn't afford it, and we don't believe in billeting troops on unsuspecting landowners like that anyway, so we're footing the bill."

"Just as you did at Vindolanda."

Memories chased across Guy's homely face. "It was one of Ector's first rules, and Art obeys it faithfully. I know you have doubts about our Merlin, Lance, but he came at the right time." Before Lance could reply, he forged on, making an expansive gesture towards the dining hall. "Come, then! Your place awaits you. The king discourages talk of politics at the table, but all other subjects are safe. And he knows Coel is fond of music, so we'll have fine melodies to accompany our meal."

"Very well. I'm happy for you both, by the way."

"You'll never be as happy as I am," Guy said gallantly, holding out an arm to Ardana, "for there aren't two such women in the world." He set off. To Lance's amusement, Ardana held out her free hand towards him, and so they entered the torchlit space three abreast.

Looking around, Lance wondered if he was still asleep and dreaming. Coel's court musicians were working away in one corner, coaxing wild old music from their instruments—one of them a bone flute-pipe attached to a pig's bladder, three wooden resonating chambers strung with sheepgut—while a long-haired, blue-tattooed drummer, naked from the waist up, kept time.

There was a space at Arthur's right hand. As soon as he caught sight of Lance, he brightened, and no sight could have been more splendid than the young king in his gold-embroidered robe, effortlessly holding court amongst his nobles. He looked every inch the warrior still, his swordbelt still strapped round his waist, Excalibur's hilt gleaming. His hair had been twisted into a thick braid, and a richly jewelled torc lay at the base of his throat. Lance threw Guy an alarmed look. "Does he mean me to sit there?"

"Of course. No-one will think it strange—they've all been prepared for your coming. Anyway, see how Coel is seated at his left? That's the true place of honour, according to Bryneich tradition, being nearest to the royal heart. Coel's sons are lined up in order of importance after that, and the mob from Camelet are filling up the rest of the places any old how. They're used to a round table, thanks to you."

"Doesn't the Merlin eat with you?"

"It's a matter of conjecture whether he eats at all. No-one's ever seen him. He feasts on air and starlight, they say."

"I'm guessing your women don't, though. Where are they?"

Guy laughed. "Off in their quarters, where they belong! Even my Ardana has only accompanied us this far out of courtesy to you. Farewell for now, my beauty, and I'll see you later."

She left without a murmur. Lance had no time for astonishment. Arthur was gesturing to the empty seat beside him. Guy gave him a poke in the ribs. "He's waiting for you. Go on!"

Guy was right. The only man who looked up when Lance took his place was Arthur himself. "Here you are," Art said, a touch too heartily, and Lance saw that the brightness of his gaze had less to do with torchlight than fever. "Thank God. A civilised face amongst all these squabbling heathens."

Lance thought Art had the table under fair control, given the combative nature of the guests. The only jostling for position seemed to be taking place among Art's own men, the chieftains of the various tribes who had joined him on campaign. He noticed the direction of Lance's gaze and sighed. "Those are the brothers from the Out Isles—Gareth, Gaheris and Gawaine."

"You wrote to me about them. You said the endless nights of their northern winters had driven them mad."

"I can't believe you got those letters. I sent them off like doves across a wilderness. I can't believe you somehow managed to reply."

"Mixing my eggs up with my sheep."

"I don't believe you'd make that mistake now, my Lance. You have the air of a learned man."

"Well, I had little to do with my own long winter nights than to teach myself. And I had the best of reasons."

Once more Art's face altered, as it had on the stairs when Lance had boldly kissed the fingers pressed to his mouth. "I'd best tell you who the others are," he said, a little unsteadily. "On the other side of the table, looking properly appalled by the Out Isles brood, we have Bors of Gaul, who lost his land to the Saxons and came to help me defend what's left of ours here. Beside him, Drustan. He too is from Cerniw, though he's much better bred than I am, and rightly thinks he's too good for this mob. Gareth, for heaven's sake!"

One of the Out Isles brothers had actually succeeded in nudging his neighbour off the end of the long bench where they sat. Art gave the table an admonitory tap, and smiled as they all lapsed to shamefaced silence. "This is Lance, son of King Ban of Vindolanda," he said. "I've told you about him. He gave me

Excalibur. Please treat him as your brother—or better, if you could, Gareth of the Isles." A ripple of laughter went round the table, in which the squabbling princes had the grace to join. Lance stood to acknowledge the introduction, then was glad to subside back into the rising tide of music, chatter and argument.

"I'd like to think they're anxious to be close to me," Art said wryly, filling Lance's cup from a magnificent bronze mead jug, "but the fights are all over rank and precedence. Who should sit higher—the hereditary prince of a tiny rock off the coast of Cerniw, or a Roman client king who until five years ago was ruling half Gaul? I need another of Elena's round tables here, and in all my strongholds."

"They do solve many problems." He looked at Art slyly over the top of his cup. "Of course they mean nobody gets to be king."

"Have you been sent to cut me down to size, Lance?" Art enquired politely. "Did word reach you in White Meadows of my arrogance?"

"Surprisingly, no. Only of your success, like a riptide sweeping up from the south. How have you done it?"

"Oh, I've sold my soul a dozen times over. If only these damn kings weren't Christians—if only I wasn't—I could have married all their daughters, to seal up our deals. As it is, I've poured out more gold and oratory…" He paused, eyes kindling. "It's been such a three years, Lance! You wouldn't believe it. I've got a hundred stories."

He fell silent. Lance would have listened to every one of the hundred stories and more. But Arthur's attention had come to rest, with all its old unsettling thoroughness, upon him. "And I might just tell you a few," he went on eventually, "once I've heard yours. Mind you don't leave anything out."

Lance found it surprisingly hard. Unused to finding words for his own situations—for such a long time, he'd had no-one to talk to but children and sheep—he began to stumble through the tale of his own past three years, his journey here, his encounter with Ban in the wilderness outpost on his way. The telling of it all was hampered further by Art's expectation that he eat as well as talk: a whole pig was roasting on a spit over the fire, and generous portions of this, as well as other delicacies—rich, dark rye bread, slices of black pudding—kept making their way to his wooden trencher.

It was Lance who noticed that their neighbours at the table were growing restless. Art had already waved aside as many interruptions as he diplomatically could. Quickly Lance brought his observations about the strange, burned fields around Din Guardi to a close. "Now talk to Coel and Mor," he added quietly, "before you undo all your good work in the debates this afternoon."

"Nonsense, Lance. I'll talk to whomever I…"

Lance gave him a gentle kick to the ankle. Art's eyebrows went up, but he glanced around with a rueful half-smile of surrender, then turned to Coel. "Your musicians are in good form tonight, Your Majesty."

"Ah, yes. A pipe, a drum and three on the strings—there's nothing to beat it. I call for them whenever I feel melancholy. Now, did I ever tell you about the time when I travelled as far as Caer Lir on the western coast, just to hear a man play a thing called a rebec? Now, a rebec differs from the old *lira da braccio*, in that the number of strings can vary from one to five, and the tuning should be done in fifths, not…"

***

It was late by the time the meal was over. Even when the kitchen servants began to clear away the last remains, the warlords lingered, reluctant to leave the company and the warmth of the fire. Coel's long disquisition on instruments and tones had given Lance leisure to look properly at Arthur, and when the old man at last got up to order hot wine to the table, he reached out and touched Art's wrist. "Is this your first meal down here since you were injured?"

"I was propped on my pillows eating gruel at this time last night. See what a tonic you are?"

"I can't work miracles, though. You ought to be in bed."

Art pulled a face. "I can't, not until this lot clears off. A true king can down his tankard of hippocras *and* sit up carousing till dawn. I have to try and repair my reputation." He lowered his voice, brow creasing. "I tell you what, though—there's a prize for the knight who can make me forget I got pretty much speared through the bollock a fortnight ago."

Lance considered. There were all kinds of distractions he could offer—questions of military strategy, logistics, the sheer graft of keeping a standing army in hostile terrain. He rested one elbow on the table, laid his chin on his fist. "This duck walks into a tavern."

Arthur blinked. "A duck?"

"That's right. And he goes up to the keeper and orders himself a pint of ale. The keeper's astonished, but he serves him his drink, and the duck goes off into a corner, sits down and settles to read the bill of fare."

"This is ridiculous, Lance."

"Next day, the same thing happens. Duck comes in, orders a drink, sits down to read. So the keeper decides to talk to him, find out something about him. And the duck says he's only in town for a while. There's a building site over the road, and he's doing some plastering work over there."

"For God's sake…"

"Don't you want to know how all this turns out?"

"No, I... All right, yes. Go on."

"The next day, the circus comes to town. Not gladiators and horse-racing—clowns and performing animals, that kind of entertainment. And it occurs to the tavern keeper that they might be interested in this marvellous duck. So when one of the animal tamers comes into the tavern, he tells the man all about him—how the duck can speak, read, drink a pint. The animal tamer thinks this would make a great act. He tells the tavern keeper to get the duck to call in and see him."

Art shook his head. "I'll never get it back, will I—the time I've spent listening to this?"

"You won't regret it, I promise. Next time the duck comes into the tavern, the keeper tells him he might have the chance of a job with the circus. The duck says, 'The circus? You mean the place with the great big cloth tent that they take down every time they move on?' The tavern keeper says that *is* the place he means, yes. And the duck looks at him and says, 'What the hell would they want with a plasterer?'"

Art stared at him in silence for a long moment. Then he got stiffly to his feet and tapped his tankard off the table. His voice was steady enough: perhaps only Lance and Guy could have detected the tremor in it. "Will you excuse us, Your Majesties? My honourable lords and nobles? This day has been a long one, and I must retire."

He took Lance by the elbow. Lance scrambled off his bench with as much grace as he could manage and followed him through a narrow doorway at the far end of the hall. Silently Art limped ahead of him to a room little bigger than a cell, with the remains of a fire glowing in the corner. A guard's chamber, Lance guessed. There were no chairs, but like good soldiers they made do with the wooden stools on either side of the fire. Arthur was wiping his eyes on the sleeve of his robe. After quite some time—during which Lance watched him with the greatest satisfaction—he was able to speak. "Well," he said raggedly. "You succeeded. You did make me forget. What do you want for your prize?"

Desires and hungers ran through Lance's blood, glittering, fuelled by hot wine. Carefully he said, "I'll tell you at some other time. Come on, Art—you've heard every word of my tale, and the tale of the duck. How fares the legendary Arthur of the Britons?"

"I thought I wanted to tell you all about my triumphs and campaigns. Now I'm alone with you..." He folded his arms, shifted uncomfortably on the stool. "Now I'm alone with you, all I can think of are the times when I'd have given my soul for you to be there with me. I killed both my half-brothers in battle last year, the legitimate sons of Pendragon—contenders for the throne. In fact the first time I met one of them was when I split his head in two with an axe. Not very fraternal, was it?"

"No," Lance agreed softly. It was hard for him to remember that the boy he had met three years ago had been engaged since then in almost constant warfare. How many lives had he taken? Lance was not sentimental; had stabbed a sheep-raider to death and snapped his comrade's neck for him barely a month before, when a bunch of them had ambushed him on his way back from the moors. But Art had been a warrior. "You had your reasons."

"I had Ector's. He told me it was necessary, that I'd saved the kingdom. The Merlin had prophesied I'd kill them, he said." Art shuddered. Then he pushed to his feet and paced a few strides toward the narrow, barred window, where the night pressed in blackly from outside. "God, Lance!" he suddenly cried, turning by the wall like a caged wolf. "I wish I'd been Ector's son in very truth. I'd have flown his pennant a thousand times more gladly than Uther's bloody red dragon. I didn't even realise until he was dead."

"He was trying to guide you by what he thought was right. It cost him dearly."

"It's made me want to exterminate every Saxon and Angle in the land, pirate or settler. And that's wrong, isn't it?"

Not a question Lance was meant to answer. Arthur was looking into the silences inside, where he had to make his own decisions. "Bless you, Lance," he said fervently. "You won't ever tell me what I want to hear, will you?"

"Not unless I think it's right."

"Or advise me, unless…"

"Unless you ask for it." A double meaning there: he let Art know, with a lift of one eyebrow, that it was intended.

And after a thoughtful few seconds, Art threw off the shadows that had clustered around him. The effort was too harsh, and Lance could see that he was exhausted. "Well," he said. "Sufficient to the day, for these grave topics. What do you think of Din Guardi, Lance? It's beautiful, isn't it. But why?'

Because somehow life runs into it from the heart of the world, Lance thought. *The dragon of the ridge lives here, just as she does in my land.* But all Arthur needed right now were his thoughts on the military advantages of the fort, and he sat back, tilted his head and looked around. "It's beautiful because… it has a well, straight down and into the bedrock. Pure water, unfailing supply—you'd have to dig through solid rock for weeks to poison it or cut it off." He leaned forward a little, tracing with his finger the line of the walls beyond the guard's chamber, the height of the roof. "Also because… just there, you could run a dividing wall through and make the place independently defensible from north and south. I'd triple the width of the walls—about nine foot should do—and, nice as they are, I'd lose all the windows."

Arthur laughed. "I knew it would be so. You're a strategist, my friend, and you'll see what's to be done on the battlefield just as clearly as you have in here. Thank you for coming, for giving up your father's kingdom. You won't regret it. I'll make you a general, like Guy. You'll be my second-in-command."

Lance listened in dismay. "What—because I know how to quarter off a building?"

"You'd be astounded how many don't. Listen, Lance—"

"No, Your Majesty. You listen. If you put me at the head of your army like a bladder on a stick, the men won't respect me. They don't know me from King Coel's wolfhound. Thank you for giving me my own chambers, for welcoming me as a friend, not a recruit. But tomorrow, while you're in discussion with the kings, let me go and drill among your soldiers. Let me work with them, fight with them, and if I do well, promote me as you wish. Not until then."

"But I want you at my side."

"Yes, as your friend, as I am now. On the battlefield and in the conference chambers, too, once I've earned my place there. Don't make me into something I'm not in the meantime. That's all I ask."

Arthur turned pale. Had Lance overestimated his capacity to bear contradiction? He was much more imperious in manner than Lance remembered from their weeks at Vindolanda, the boyish airs he'd assumed to make Ector laugh replaced with the real thing. It suited him, God knew, like his new height, like the quiet royal splendour of his clothes. But Lance, a future king himself, and proud as death even if he'd been a swineherd, could not jump through hoops for him, not at any cost...

"Damn," Art said faintly. "I thought these visions had stopped."

Lance listened. It felt strange, exerting his senses to pick up the trace of another man's hallucination. But he'd almost managed it, back on the moors by the lough three years before: for an instant he had almost seen Art's spectral tormentor...

Ah, was it working now, too? A deep, low vibration began to make his eardrums flutter, as if a sound-below-sound was reverberating through the hall. A moan, from a throat unimaginably vast and terrible...

The wine cup he'd been drinking from rattled on the bench, tipped up and clattered to the floor. "Not a vision," he said, getting up and taking Art by the shoulders. "Not unless I and your nightwatchmen share it." Arthur's lost gaze focussed, and Lance indicated the soldiers, glancing at one another in confusion and running for the stairs. "It's something outside. Come on!"

Chapter Nine

The turf outside the keep was shaking underfoot. Stumbling out into the night, Lance first noticed that the stars were gone, that the night had clouded to absolute black. There was no moon, and the torches in the cressets in the archway to the keep trembled and threw harsh shapes of orange and shadow up the ancient walls. Dust was falling from their mortar.

He should have been afraid. A wild exhilaration had seized him, though, and swinging round to find Art, he saw the strange joy reflected in his face. "What is it?" he demanded. "It feels as though the earth is dancing!"

"Well, I don't think it's Saxons," Art replied, grinning, his hand nonetheless on the hilt of Excalibur. "What do you think? Is old Din Guardi about to come down around our ears?"

"Ah, would that it might!"

The great sorrowful voice cut across the grinding in the castle's foundations, the cries and chatter of the soldiery assembling before the keep. Lance and Arthur spun around to see a tall, gaunt figure, clad in a voluminous nightgown, lurching across the courtyard toward them. His hands were upraised, and the gown's fabric, none too clean, flapped round him in the wind. "Would that it might fall, and be done!"

"My God, it's Coel," Art said. Lance stared in disbelief. Yes, the dishevelled, wild-haired apparition was Arthur's dignified fellow diplomat of that afternoon.

Coel came to a frozen halt a few yards away. "The worm!" he cried. The rumbling and shaking increased, as if on cue, and Lance shifted uneasily at the strange oppression in the air, like storm pressure unable to find a release. "The worm! The worm returns after her routing, to burrow and nest in the bowels of my accursed home!"

He sounded distraught, barely sane. Lance, dismayed to see him like this, took a few cautious steps toward him, but he shrank away. A block or two detached itself from the keep's upper battlement, narrowly missing them both.

An elderly woman, also in her night clothes, ran out barefoot onto the turf. She hitched up her long skirts and dashed to Coel's side. The roar and the vibration were beginning to abate. "No, no, love," she cried, taking hold of his elbow. Turning to Arthur: "Forgive him, Your Majesty. He sleepwalks. These strange nights disturb him. Come, my lord. It's cold. Come back inside."

But Coel stood rigid. He looked at Arthur, then, not seeming to find what he wanted there, fixed a wild gaze on Lance. "The worm," he repeated. "She feasts, and kills, and nests in my castle." His face assumed an expression so utterly woebegone that Lance, to his horror, felt laughter strike sparks in his lungs. From the corner of his eye, he saw Art look away, as if similarly affected. "We are cursed," Coel finished. "I shall call this place the Gard Dolorous, my castle of sorrows."

His wife led him off, talking to him soothingly. Overhead, the clouds parted, and bright stars blazed out over the sea. Air moved sweetly over the turf, rich with seaweed and salt. Pressing both hands to his mouth, Lance turned to see the king of the Britons huddled against the wall, for the second time that night weeping with silent laughter.

***

Lance helped him back up the stairs. He was still wiping his eyes. "I'm sorry," he said, when Lance, who had recovered more quickly, chided him. "He was just such a sight. That song the men sing about him popped into my head, and… Oh, dear. *This is my Gard Dolorous.*" He shook with fresh laughter. "And what does he mean, he's cursed by a worm?"

Lance half-lifted him up the last few steps. He could manage fairly well on the flat, but neither let go. They made their way along the stone-flagged corridor and stopped outside the door to Lance's room. It was cold now, the night deepening, and Lance pulled his cloak tightly around both of them, frowning in thought. Arthur, like Coel, had used the Latin word *vermis*, and it resonated oddly in his mind. "My mother's people had a word not unlike that," he said, "but it meant something bigger. Is there one in Kernowek?"

Art considered. "I'm not sure. But I had a Breton nurse. The way she spoke—it was a tongue for fireside tales, for twilight, ancient things that could twist and turn out of their own darkness. *Ver*, she used to say. That's a little like *vermis*, but it didn't mean a worm." He stood thoughtfully, arm still warm around Lance's shoulders. Then he burst out laughing again. "A *dragon*, Lance?"

"Does it sound more deranged than a murderous worm?"

"I don't know. My whole life seems deranged to me in one way or another. The last thing that made sense was… riding with you and Guy, up in the hills at Vindolanda." He paused, and they both listened to the tramp of the guard changing watch down below in the keep. Carefully, deliberately, he let Lance go and stepped back. "It's very late. I must let you rest. Do you need anything else?"

"No. My chamber is very fine. You know I should be sleeping with the rest of the men, in a tent on the dunes."

"It's a cold night. You'll just have to cope. Do you have enough blankets?" He considered, then brightened. "Oh, would you like a girl? Coel has some very pretty maids and kitchen wenches. They're already gossiping about my handsome friend—you won't be refused."

Lance recoiled. The movement was small but impossible to repress. "What?"

Art's gaze faltered. "Or a boy? I remember you told me, back at Vindolanda—"

"Arthur!"

He hadn't meant it to come out as a shout. Never before had Art tried to avoid his eyes, but he was doing so now, trying to hide behind the long, thick fall of his hair. "For God's sake," he said awkwardly. "Don't wake the place up. What's wrong?"

It took Lance a moment to find words. "I'm trying to imagine," he began, "what my mother would have done to me, had I offered a guest a girl from her household as a... as a *toy* for the night." The girl concerned would have been, more likely than not, a priestess, accompanying her mistress to the ceremonies Elena took care to hide from the priest, at full moons and turns of the year. "I've hardly even seen a woman here, except scuttling about from one domestic task to another, or flirting with the soldiers at the gates. What's happened?"

"I don't understand."

"Art, you must." And yet Lance himself couldn't get any further with putting into words his deep, formless unease. Dragons, worms, a castle under curse. The sword that Art called

Excalibur, flashing end over end and disappearing over a cliff. Some power once strong in the land, now crippled and raging, a river thrust out of its course… "Something's changing, and it's not good. If we treat women this way…"

"Didn't you hear me?" Art interrupted him passionately. He pushed his hair back, lifted his chin and stared at Lance with all his old unbridled honesty and fire. "I damned well offered you a boy as well!"

"You are absolutely missing my point." If Lance let a ripple of laughter into his voice, he was lost. Nothing about this was funny, except Art's clumsy, generous, utterly misdirected efforts to share the resources at his disposal. "I don't want a girl—or a boy, for that matter."

"What *do* you want, then?"

Lance released a long breath. *Oh, let this long night play out however it must*, he swore inwardly. Let all dice be rolled, all chances seized like wild horses and ridden on till dawn. He leaned his back against the wall, folded his arms. "I think," he said, voice dropping to a soft growl, "I want my prize."

***

"Give me that, before you put paid to your other bollock."

"I can't. My hands have gone numb."

"Are you cold?"

"No, it's just that… all the blood in me seems to be heading elsewhere. Thank God. I wasn't sure I'd still be able."

Lance sat up on the narrow bed. There was barely room for two, and Excalibur and its gem-encrusted scabbard had already dealt them a few bruises. Deftly he undid the strap and buckles holding Art's swordbelt in place. "Lift up your hips for me."

Art groaned. "I can't. Everything hurts so damn much."

Lance eased a hand under him and tugged the belt free. He grabbed the hilt of the sword before it could clatter on the stone flags. Although the door to his chambers was thick, it had no lock. "Let me see."

"What?"

"Your injury."

"No, Lance. It shames me."

"It's a battle scar. Why should you be ashamed?"

"I don't know, but I am. And I'm sorry I angered you about the women. If it makes any difference, they're Coel's household customs, not mine."

"Are things so very different at Cam?"

"A little. Ardana's a widow. At my court, she'd be let ride out with Guy, to local skirmishes at least, just as she did with her first two husbands here. Instead she has to sit in the solar with the other wives and work tapestries."

"Come here. Let me help you sit up."

"Why?"

"What do you think happened—in the time between Ardana's first two husbands and Guy, I mean? Why can't she ride out with him?"

"Oh, God knows. The priests, I think. Not the old boys from Ireland and Cerniw—the ones they sent from Rome, or trained up at Canterbury and places like that. Lance, you think you're very cunning, but I am aware that you're undressing me."

"Is that something you'd rather I didn't do?"

Art shivered. "I've thought or dreamed about you doing something of the kind every night since I left you."

"I, too. Does this have any kind of fastening?"

"No, it comes off over my head."

"Put your arms up, then." Lifting the robe away was the work of a moment. For all its fine embroidery, the fabric was supple and light. "How beautiful this is," Lance observed, thoughtfully, almost as if to himself. "How beautiful *you* are."

"I'm not certain. Perhaps when you first saw me this way… But I'm scarred now. Skinny, too. This is the first place we've had enough to eat since we left Cam."

Lance kissed the colour he'd called into the pale face, just under the cheekbones, and then—more daring than he'd been before—lifted Art's chin and brushed his lips across his warm, half-open mouth. "Yes, you're thin. But your muscles have come up like corded ropes, and I can see the perfect shape of you underneath. And here are your bandages. Is it safe for me to move these?"

"Yes, I'm almost healed. But…"

"Hush." It wasn't a time for fear, although a horror he couldn't define—much more than the shrinking of the flesh a man might feel on sight of such injury to another—was trying to enter his soul. A song welled up from his earliest childhood. *The king is wounded in the thigh—so falls the kingdom, and the land must die…* Where had he heard it? The words were nonsense, he told himself fiercely, unfastening the linen strips that held the dressing in place. Art was trying to catch his wrist and stop him, but he had to see. "Oh, I remember."

"Remember what?"

"A rhyme came into my head, about a king with a wounded thigh. Some travelling players came to White Meadows, years and years ago, when I was just a boy."

"Oh?" Art enquired, propping himself up a little on the pillow. "And did they hire the duck?"

Lance snorted. "Be quiet, stupid. This is important. Father Tomas tried to send them away, but my mother insisted we give them hospitality and listen to their stories and songs, because old truths get caught up in such music like flies in amber."

"What was the song?"

"It doesn't matter. They didn't really mean *thigh*, though—it was just a polite word for…"

"Cock."

"Ah, you're so regal." At last Lance got the bandages untied. He grabbed Art's knee to hold him still, then pushed it back towards his chest, turning him a little so the flickering light from the lantern would shine on the damage.

A faint choking sound escaped him. The Saxon's knife had gouged a long trench out of the flesh and muscle of Art's inner leg. The blade tip had nearly castrated him in very truth: one testicle had almost been ripped from its moorings. Scar tissue was forming, and whoever had treated him had done it well, but still it was hard to see for dried blood. The force of the thrust had carried on upwards. He was lucky not to have been disembowelled. "This must have hurt you so much."

"I couldn't stop myself from crying out. I nearly got Guy killed, too—he had to stuff a rag into my mouth, or they'd have come back and finished us both off. I was so ashamed."

You were crying for your father, not this wound, dreadful though it is. Lance held him still. There was no hope that such a king could ever ride into battle again. Whatever excitement or blood-flow he'd been feeling was a dream: his cock was lying limp against his belly. Such a king could never bring a child to the world, or restore life to the land.

"Arthur. I want you to understand something."

"Let me go. I can't bear for you to look at me this way."

"In a moment. Are you listening?"

A flame-rustle silence filled the room. After a moment Arthur nodded. "Yes."

"You're perfection to me, just as you are. If I had my way, I'd carry you off with me back to White Meadows, and we could spend our days herding sheep, and swimming in the lough, and our nights in each other's arms."

"Oh, my Lance."

"But that's not your destiny. Pass me the sword."

"What?"

"Just do it."

Blindly, his gaze never leaving Lance's face, Arthur reached down to the side of the bed. He took hold of Excalibur by the scabbard and obediently passed it up to Lance. "Are you sure?" he whispered. "About my destiny, I mean? Because the sheep and the lough and the nights… they sounded good."

"You're sick and weak now. When you're strong again, that world would feel too small. Like the little glass globes the Romans make for their children, with models of tiny people and castles inside." Lance sat back on his heels. He was kneeling between Art's thighs. He was still fully dressed—their immediate, tussling engagement as soon as he'd managed to kick the door shut behind them had allowed for nothing else, although he'd wrestled Art off for long enough to get out of his boots. Made him take his own off, too, out of respect for Coel's bedlinen, or the queen's. How strange that he didn't know her name or her proper title, that he hadn't been presented to her first! Even if her life was confined to the castle, she ought to be the presiding spirit there, as Elena had ruled White Meadows. He shouldn't have encountered her for the first time as a defenceless old woman in a nightgown, pursuing her poor mad king.

These thoughts allowed his mind to drift away. He balanced Excalibur on the flat of his palms, then suddenly, with an impatient gesture, tugged the blade free and tossed the ridiculous scabbard aside. "She belongs in soft leather," he said. "The well-worn scabbard of a soldier, rich with oil and blood."

"That's how she goes into battle with me. That great gaudy codpiece is just to scare the warlords in places like these." Art swallowed hard. "What are you going to do?"

"I could never understand that the goddess of healing and of warriors was one and the same."

"The goddess Bride?" He said it in the old way, the rough growl of the R and the long *E—Breed*—sending a thrill down Lance's spine. His hair had come out of its braid and was coiling over his shoulders like copper snakes. The lantern light had turned the grey of his eyes to amber. He said, barely audible, "Do you understand now?"

I thought the power was in the sword. And she does bring it, but after that... after that it's down to me. Lance kept silent on the thought. He stretched over Art and reverently laid the weapon down on the floor by the bed. Heat was coursing through him, pulsing up his spine like the rise of sap in springtime. At the level of his heart it broke in two, a river dividing, blazed down his arms and into the palms of his hands. Art shuddered and cried out as Lance reached beneath him: closed a warm grip around his balls, then flexed down smiling and took his cock into his mouth.

Chapter Ten

Urgent shouting woke him just after dawn. He sat up, blanket in a tangle around him. He'd slept deeply: bright winter sunlight was painting his room's western wall, and he was alone. He got up and opened the window. Down in the courtyard below him, a group of villagers was clustering as close to King Coel as his burly guardsmen would allow. Art was there, too, hands on his hips while he listened, formidable despite his untucked shirt and sleep-tangled hair. The old king was fully dressed and businesslike once more, although whatever the crowd was telling him hadn't served to make his expression any less grim. The men looked like farmers: when Lance shaded his eyes from the sun, he saw that a few were brandishing pitchforks and scythes.

There was colour in Art's face. His spine was straight, and shadows of pain had vanished from his brow. Smiling, Lance went to pull on his britches, shirt and boots. Then he ran for the door.

He met Art stalking back through the gateway of the keep. Coel was behind him, almost running to keep up. Of the two of them, Lance thought Arthur's gaze was more bleak. He answered it in silence when it sought his, falling into step at his side. "I want them, Lance," Arthur said flatly. "I want them now."

"Saxons? Anglians?"

"Both. Either. What's the difference? I'm weary to death of diplomacy, of cold campaigning. I'm taking a party out now."

"Was there a raid?"

"Half a dozen. Those farmers lost cattle, sheep—even a couple of children. Their whole livelihood. The grooms are readying our horses. Go fetch your weapons and meet me outside." He paused, and Lance, who hadn't even thought of arguing, started back as he jerked to a halt and fiercely rounded on him. "Unless you want to go and drill with my bloody soldiers?!"

Lance folded his arms and looked at him calmly. It only took a few seconds. The night they'd spent reasserted itself, and a flush stole over Art's haughty cheekbones. "Sorry," he said. "God, sorry, Lance. How is it that I'm able to run around this morning without pain? That was your doing, wasn't it?"

"Your flesh was ready to heal, that's all."

"Nonsense. I'll have the truth out of you when we're alone. And now you think me a bloodthirsty savage."

"No. And if you are... I don't have any better ideas, not today. You're hardly going to *talk* these raiders into submission."

Art nodded gratefully. Lance was halfway up the stairs when he called him back. "Wait. Do you have armour?"

"I have Ban's chainmail shirt."

"That must have seen some action. Well, it'll have to do for now—the armoury can kit you up when we get home. Coel!" he barked, making the old man jump. "Choose your best men. I'll take them with me. And, you, boy, hanging about over there..." A stable lad, leaning idly on the wall nearby, scrambled to attention. "Send to the kitchens for bread and cheese, enough for twenty saddlebags. Now!" The master of the castle and its lowliest servant having run off in opposite directions at his bidding, Arthur flashed Lance a great smile. "Well, no reason we should miss breakfast, is there? Be ready to ride in ten minutes."

***

They pounded out into the bright morning, their horses' hooves ringing like bells on the earth. Lance let go his unease, lifted his face to the wind and enjoyed it. Bors, Guy and Drustan rode with them, as well as fourteen of King Coel's men, and, to Lance's surprise, Garbonian, too, looking every inch the soldier. All of them had stared in wonder as Art, who yesterday had barely been able to walk, had leapt unaided into the saddle and led them off at a gallop from the fort.

It was just as Lance had imagined, sitting alone and bored in the house at Vindolanda, or listening to Tomas's increasingly senile drone in church, a practice he'd faithfully followed right to the old man's very last sermon. That sad old duty was fulfilled. Now he was riding out at the side of his king, in the cause of justice and retribution. In search of a fight, he wryly admitted, confessing too, in the blood-beating silence of his mind, that he would enjoy it if they found one. He had been calm and good for far too long.

Art, flying along as fast as his fine Hispanic-bred stallion would carry him, shot him a sidelong glance as if sharing the thought, and smiled broadly. Then he looked again, and said, "Lance, is that still old Balana?"

"Of course. Going strong." Lance had made a vow to him, and so bit back Ector's name. *I never did thank him properly for leaving her. I know she was his favourite mount for ten years before you set out on your first journey north.* He saw the memories rushing like storm clouds over Art anyway, and put out a hand to give his wrist a swift squeeze. "I couldn't have had a finer horse. What happened to Hengroen?"

"Cut out from under me in Vortigern's accursed fight."

"Poor beast! I'm sorry, Art."

"I have my pick of horses now. There's no point in looking back."

"What's this one called?"

"Nothing. It's easier that way." Art rode on, concentrating rather fiercely on the dunes ahead. "Balana's a beauty, all right, but we'll have to get you better mounted. See my cavalry commander, after…"

"After I've seen your armourer, yes," Lance finished, grinning. Art didn't seem to have noticed that, other than a horseblanket and sheepskin, he rode bareback, preferring the deep-seated comfort of that to Ector's four-horned saddle for a ride like this. He didn't want to be told to see Arthur's saddler after his chief of horse and the armourer.

The morning was his. No matter what the future held, he'd spent the night in the arms of his king. He urged Balana to a flat-out gallop that soon began to challenge Art's stallion to keep up.

***

The flats to the south of Din Guardi were a grand place for mindless exercise. For a while the whole troop rode in contented silence. While talks were in progress, both Arthur and Coel had forbidden any private sorties amongst the Anglian populations, and Coel's men had been just as cooped up in the fortress as the kings in their debating hall.

Sun struck off the sea, flashing between dunes to their left, blue and bronze lights turned blood-red through Lance's eyelids as he tried to squint against it. Apart from Balana, the horses had been standing overfed in their stables for days. Soon they got into the swing of a good long pull, and scarcely needed urging. The air was rich with salt and gorse. Lance, whose world had contracted to the sweetness of pure action, to the satisfaction of flying wing to wing with Art, was sorry when the sight of a village in the distance ahead recalled him to his sense of purpose, the work they'd come out here to do.

Art had remembered it too. "Garbonian!" he yelled above the pounding of hooves. "Is that Spindlestone?"

The prince drew alongside. "Yes. The heughs, anyway. Hamlet's a mile or so south."

"Britons? Friendly?"

"Last time I looked, Your Majesty. Nothing but a mill, some crags—they call them heughs—and a few stone huts, though."

"I don't care how small it is, sir," Art said sharply. "Didn't one of the farmers who came to the fort this morning say he was from there?"

"I think so."

"That's where we start our search for these godless raiders, then." He signalled to the knights and troops, and Lance watched them fall into a rough defence formation around him. None of them seemed keen to take the rear, and after a moment, when Art's attention was fixed on the track ahead, he slowed Balana up to cover the gap.

The open turf became fields, divided by the lie of the land more than any force of ownership. The earth was good enough, but full of sand, and Lance read in the bare winter soil the signs of a struggle for subsistence.

He couldn't understand the Anglians' habit of raiding here. Yes, there was the odd stronghold like Coel's, tribal kings whom the Romans had left rich, but they were desperately thinly scattered. The spoils from the hamlets, the farms, must be scarcely worth the wear to their horses' hooves. They had a history of conquest, he supposed, a warrior's inheritance that drove them on.

And yet here too the damage did not look like the work of men. Lance saw a burned-out trail ripped through a wheatfield, just as he had on his way to Din Guardi the day before. Long, thin, twisting, leaving the soil bare, the stubble blackened. In the corner of a paddock, five sheep were down, raw chunks torn from them. How was it that Art wasn't seeing it?

None of the others were, either. They were riding like good Roman *equites*, eyes fixed and forward, now that the gallop had become a patrol. Lance thought about overtaking to point out to Art or Guy the strange destruction, but now they were being funnelled out of the fields and onto the track to the village, and their rear was vulnerable. He settled Balana down to a stolid canter, kept her on the middle stripe of grass that bisected the track, muffling the thud of her hooves so he could listen, and he kept the watch.

***

Three farmers, the miller and his brothers. A blacksmith who doubled up as a baker, and the wives and children belonging to these men. That was the population of Spindlestone Heughs. Prior to last night's raid it had been twice that—or three times or ten; it was almost impossible to tell. The survivors were in utter disarray.

Lance, arriving half a minute after the others, had thought the destruction complete. Doors gaped open, and the fire lay in ashes beneath the cold forge. A few skinny mongrel dogs ran out to snarl at the horses, but these were the only signs of life. Drawing Balana to a standstill in the little square around which the few houses were clustered, he was in time to see Arthur lower his head and clench his hands on the reins in a spasm of rage.

Then, one by one, the little crowd had emerged, from haylofts, ditches, the shadows of the wood that topped the crags, all the places they must have sought refuge the night before. Arthur dismounted, and the men and women clustered around him, telling him five different stories at once. Art looked round. "Lance!" he demanded. "Where have you been? None of these people speak Latin, and they don't understand me. What are they saying?"

Lance swung down from Balana and listened. He got a little further than the southern king, but the villagers' dialect was so obscure, their accent so rich, that he too was only picking out one word in ten. Coel's soldiers, some of them local, gathered round and tried to help, which somehow worsened matters, until Arthur made an angry gesture of cut-off. "All right!" he said. "It doesn't matter. I'll find the bastards who did this, I swear. If they've taken your children, I'll bring them back. I'll find them."

Chapter Eleven

He ordered two of Coel's men to stay behind and help restore order, and gave the eldest miller a pouch of coins, indicating to him with signs that he should distribute them. Then he sprang back into the saddle and rode off, Lance and the others in tow, leaving the villagers to stare after them, a small, bewildered huddle.

Lance let him be for a while. His profile was coldly set, hard to read. The lane that led from the village was even narrower than the one they'd followed into it, and seeing that Guy had taken up the rear, Lance let Balana draw abreast and canter alongside. He said, gently, "Arthur."

He came back from a great distance. To Lance's surprise, he found a smile. "Yes, Lance?"

"I didn't understand much of what they were saying. But…"

"But you did get some of it, and you've been waiting in the hope that at some point my face might start looking less like a boar's arse."

"Something like that," Lance admitted. "It didn't sound to me as if they were complaining about raiders. They said… They kept saying that the *worm* had come." Art turned on him an expression of blank incredulity, but he braced up and continued, "Also that… all their cows had been milked dry in the night."

The words hung strangely in the chilly air, like the reverberation of a bell. Arthur rode on in silence a few paces. "Are you saying to me you believe that these poor people are under siege by some… unnatural beast? Some dragon or giant bloody worm?"

Lance hadn't decided. He'd only been reporting what he knew. But hearing Art put it like that made him shake himself. What *did* he believe? In Anglian raiders, obviously. Anything else was absurd. "No," he said. "No, of course not. It was just strange."

"I know. But they were in shock, Lance. Half of what they had was destroyed last night. A kind of madness comes on ordinary men after that kind of loss. For a while they're not themselves. Believe me, I've seen it before."

They rode inland from Spindlestone, more quietly now. The men had been sobered by what they'd seen in the village, and were looking for a trail, some trace of the direction the raiders might have taken. Guy and Bors were out in front, scanning the track on both sides.

Lance watched, too. There had to be something—horse droppings, the print of a hoof in the mud. This was the only route out, and he didn't think they'd missed much on the way in. He struggled against a sense of crawling unease. The frosted hawthorns were blindingly white in the sun, the fields around them dancing with light, but it didn't feel like the same morning or the same world in which they'd set out.

Up ahead, Guy's horse suddenly baulked. She'd tucked her haunches low, and Guy was struggling to keep his seat while she danced and reared. When he could, he spared a hand from the reins and gestured to them to approach.

Lance's heart sank. This wasn't another slaughtered sheep or cow. The shape on the ground was too eloquent, too finely wrought. *Too bloody human*, Lance thought. It had been one thing to see a beast torn up so. He would have to brace up to look at such butchery inflicted on a man. And he wanted even less for Art to see. "I don't like this," he said. "Will you let me go ahead?"

"What? Why?"

"Just to make sure everything's—"

"Are you trying to shield me?" Art glanced round, but the others were out of earshot. "Do you have any idea of the war zones I've ridden through? I've walked across battlefields with a dagger in my hand, sorting out the living from the dead."

"I know all that. But..."

"But still you're trying." He gave Lance a long look, in which yearning, gratitude and resentment were potently mixed. "I wish I could let you," he said roughly. "But it's impossible. Come on."

Worse than the man's ruined corpse was the child weeping over it. Art dismounted, threw his reins at the nearest soldier and crouched beside the little boy. Coel's battle-hardened soldiers, his own seasoned men, stood around in silence, trying not to look. "I don't understand," Guy said unsteadily. "I never saw a man slain like this. What kind of people *are* they, these raiders?"

Arthur looked up, hollow-eyed. "The dead kind, when I find them. And I will do worse to them than this." He detached the child from its grip on the dead man's shirt, took the boy in his arms and rocked him while his howls tore the sunny day to rags. He gestured to Drustan, who for all his airs was a kindly man, with sons of his own back in Cerniw. "Take this child back to the village. See if he has anyone there. If not, he must go to Din

Guardi. Coel must take him in as a page—I'll see to his training and his keep."

He got up and handed the child bodily to Drustan, who made a face as bloodstained hands clenched in his fine woollen tunic, then tenderly embraced his burden. Art turned to look at the rest of them, and Lance saw with prickling horror that the man he knew had vanished, replaced by something as wild and inhuman as whatever had caused these deaths. "Divide into parties of three. Ride this country. Quarter it. Go into villages—if anyone's harbouring these bastards, kill them, too. Make an example. Meet me here at sunset. And God help you if one of you doesn't bring me back a head on a spike."

He rode off without a word. He hadn't assigned Lance or Guy to a place in his rough division of the troops, and so, after trading troubled glances, they set off at a gallop after him.

Lance wasn't sure Art knew they were there. He didn't look back, or even slow his pace until they reached the first hamlet on their route. Finding no signs of trouble, he clapped his heels to his stallion's flanks once more, and pounded on.

Village after village, all along the wide coastal plain. There were Anglians in the area, plenty of them, but they were settlers, putting down tentative roots in a new country. It was hard to tell their hamlets apart from those of the Britons and Celts. The men they passed on the road were armed with nothing more deadly than shovels and hoes, and cringed back wide-eyed into the hedgerows at their headlong approach. Arthur led onward, through woods and rough country, moorland and bog. By the time the light began to fail, the horses were trembling with weariness beneath them, and Lance, who had kept his distance and his silence, began to wonder if he should ride up hard and grab Art's reins.

He hesitated, but not out of fear or respect. He was painfully sorry for his friend, and would no more have hesitated to tackle the king of the Britons than he had the boy he'd met on the moors three years before. But Guy was here, and it was his place to appeal to his younger brother—or, if necessary, ride him off the road. Lance urged Balana closer to his snorting, panting mare. "It's getting dark, Guy. One of us should stop him."

"And you think it should be me," Guy said wearily. "And you're right, but... I've never seen him like this. All right, wait here. I'll catch him up."

Lance reined in and waited quietly, keeping a watchful eye on the darkening countryside around them. In the distance he heard a scuffle of hoofbeats—as if Guy had indeed ridden him down into the bushes at the side of the track—and then scraps of a brief argument, conducted in a mix of courtly Latin and very plain Kernewek.

After a while, they made their way back towards him. Art was expressionless, colourless under the dust and marks of a day's hard riding. He came to a stop before Lance, as if called to give an account of himself there. "My brother tells me," he said, not meeting Lance's eyes, "that I'm misusing my men in keeping them out so long on a fruitless mission. I agree, to the extent that I will ride back to the meeting place and send all of you home. But for myself, I reserve the right to stay out here and search."

Guy drew a breath to protest, but Arthur turned on him in anguish. "What use am I otherwise?" he cried. "How can I claim to be king of these people, to defend them from invasion, if I can't find one murderous raider?" And with that, he put his heels to the weary stallion's flanks and sped off once more into the dusk.

He was moving too fast to be caught. Lance, seized with a formless dread of letting him out of his sight, started after him,

Guy on his heels. "Lance!" Guy shouted, and he slowed up long enough to let him draw abreast. "Lance, distract him. Head him off."

"How am I supposed to do that?"

"Think of something. I'll meet up with the men back at Spindlestone. Can't let them see him like this."

"Why?" Lance demanded. "He's upset, that's all. And just a man himself."

"Ah, no. You're wrong, Lance. That's just what he can't be. Make him follow you. Go on!"

***

It was a neat piece of playacting, for a man unused to anything but truth. "Art!" Lance bellowed at the top of his lungs, turning Balana's head westward. "Art, I see them!"

He didn't look back to check if Art had heard him: no headstrong knight on the scent of his prey would have done so. Pelting into the fire of the dying sun, he almost convinced himself. And, just on the edge of a wild stretch of moorland, he heard behind him the rhythm of following hooves.

They rode on a little way, their pace slackening as the pretence dissolved. Lance kept his gaze fixed on some point between Balana's ears. Neither he nor Arthur spoke, and only the hiss of a night-wind off the sea, and the snorts of their winded horses, broke the silence.

"That was good, Lance," Art said at length. He was out of breath too, and he sounded more amused than otherwise. "You did it well. Have I made so very great a fool of myself?"

"No. But you're tired. We all are. Guy's gone to take the men home."

"Rather than let them see their king in a wild-eyed fury."

"Rather than let you run them and yourself into the ground."

"Lance, I know my brother. You needn't defend him. I love him, just as I did his father." Art reined up, and turned to Lance, smiling. "I *am* tired. I can hear a stream over there. Let's rest these poor horses before we go home."

The stream ran down past the ruins of a decaying Roman camp. Even half buried in turf, its lines were recognisable to Lance, who had grown up among just such order, such concise locking of wall to wall. He approved its position, too, on a small rise of land, commanding wide views over the moor. Defensible. Deciding it was safe to relax, he sat down at the foot of a wall and opened up his saddlebag.

Art returned from the stream, leading the two horses. "What is that? Not the food we packed up at the castle this morning?"

"You didn't give anyone time to eat it. Including yourself."

"Oh." Frowning, Art unfastened his own pack. "Of course. God, Lance—I really have been outside of myself."

"Well, get back in and eat."

They sat together in a silence that became easier as it extended, passing back and forth between them the flagons of wine and water, listening to the wind. The food seemed to restore Art to his mortal, loving self, and he suddenly let his weight rest against Lance's shoulder. "Do you think they'll forgive me for today?" he asked roughly. "The soldiers? My own knights?"

Lance shrugged. "From what I could see, they were impressed. Decisive action in enemy territory. Ruthless pursuit of your prey." He paused. "The only thing they wouldn't forgive is your premature death, Art. We have to keep you alive, you know—for your future wife and the kingdom."

The words were serious, but he'd let a faint gleam of laughter rise to touch his voice. Art shook his head. "My future wife, who's supposed to rise up out of the very earth to greet me? I'm starting to think that must be bollocks, Lance, Merlin or no Merlin."

"Do you ever hear from Ireland—from Modron, I mean, about your son?"

"Not a word. But I didn't expect to. I can't acknowledge him, not the way things are now, and Modron—my half-sister, after all—will have no small ideas about her own royal blood, and his. It's a mess."

It sounded very much as if it was going to be. "You said the boy was healthy, for all your blood and Modron's is close. Why shouldn't you bring him forward?"

"Most of my so-called kingdom is Christian now." He lifted a hand to his breastbone, as if seeking something there. "They'd never accept a bastard, especially not a halfling got at a Beltane fire."

"Then a lawful heir it must be."

"It must. And thanks to you, I stand a chance of begetting one."

The gleam of laughter became definite. "Not on your own."

"No. I swear to God, though, Lance, if I could lay you down here and do it with you, I would."

Tears stung Lance's eyes. He laid a hand on top of Art's. "Where is the sign you used to wear—the solar disk, with the moon on the reverse?"

"Torn off me in battle. The priest gave me a cross to wear in its stead, but there must have been an impurity in the gold. Brought me out in a rash."

"Impurity, my arse," Lance rasped. He set his flagon down and moved lithely to straddle Arthur's lap. The countryside was hushed around them, their refuge safe enough for now. "You're my pagan-hearted king. That's why a cross won't stay on your beautiful bloody hide."

"Oh, God. How can we do this?"

"Quickly, I'd suggest. It's getting dark."

"No, you dolt. How can I have nights with you—the kind of night we just passed—and be your king and your master by day?"

Once, long ago, it wouldn't have mattered. Art could have ridden out in front of his whole army with his warrior-lover, unhidden and respected, at his side. Lance didn't understand the differences now, except that they were connected to Medraut, the offspring of the starry May-tide, now a sin to be hidden away. "Listen," he said, kissing Art's brow. "I'm not another Modron, not a thing for you to worry about and fear. You can have your nights—and me—whenever you want. And by day I'll be your faithful friend. Whose business is it, after all?"

"No-one's. Just…"

"Just yours and mine."

"Doesn't it strike you as ironic—that you healed me last night, with your magic and your love, only for me to ride out today in search of blood?"

"Well, you didn't get any on your sword." Lance ran the heel of his hand down Art's chest and stomach, feeling the scratch of his chainmail, the tough leather cuirass he wore underneath. After that there was still the tunic to be negotiated, the crotch-string of his deerskin britches. It would be difficult, loving a soldier on the field. Lance felt joyously prepared to meet the challenge. "The goddess of healing and of warriors *is* one and the same. It's your work now, as king of this land, to bring this truth to your people."

"How can I? I don't understand it myself."

"It's not a thing to understand. It's a thing to be. Like this, my dear master. Like this." Lance got the string undone. This time he found a rich and ready cock-stand awaiting his touch, and Art arched up with a groan, pressing into his hand. Lance kissed the warm mouth seeking his. "There you are. There."

"I won't last long. Sorry."

"Didn't I say we'd have to work fast?"

"But what about you?"

"Just take hold of me over my clothes. Ah, yes—let me ride your strong hand."

"Ah, Lance, will you always do this—break my bloody ice, bring me back to life?"

"As long as there's life in me." Lance leaned down, kissed and gently bit the side of Art's neck. The hot shaft leapt in his hand, and he heard with the deepest delight of flesh and spirit the grinding moan of his lover's release. Enough for him—too much, and he thrust into Art's hard grasp, pleasure thudding into him like arrows. "Art! Ah, holy goddess, yes!"

Chapter Twelve

"We should start home. I don't fancy meeting your sheep-eating raiders in the dark."

Art yawned hugely. His head was comfortably pillowed on Lance's shoulder. Even though frost was beginning to crackle in the moss and fallen leaves around them, their tangle of entwined limbs remained warm. "No more talk of worms and dragons, then, Lance?"

"Hardly. Coel must have got to me with his phantasms. I should never be surprised, when men invent some novel way of slaying one another. Come on, before we go to sleep here and freeze to..." He fell silent. "Wait. Do you hear that?"

Art listened. "Hoofbeats. Damn. We'd better take cover."

"No, it's..."

The sounds intensified. Not the ordinary, blood-stirring rhythm of flying hooves, which to Lance was a sound of life even when it meant his enemy bearing down on him, the prelude to a good fight or a chase. This slowed his heart to a crawl of cold fear. And he'd heard it before—only last night, or in the small hours of this very morning, shaking the foundations of Din Guardi.

Art was scrambling to his feet, wide-eyed. "What in hell's name is that?"

"I don't know, but we need to get away from it. Grab your horse before he bolts."

Art made a dive for the stallion, closing a hand on the beast's bridle before he could uproot the sapling he'd been hitched to. Lance untied Balana and made ready to spring onto her back.

Too late. The rumble escalated to a roar. Off to the east, between earth and sky, somehow bigger than either, a shape stirred, so vast his mind refused to take it in. "Get down!" he yelled. "Art, get down!" He began a move to tackle him, drag him to the ground. Then there was no need—the earth heaved, knocking them both flat among the ruins.

On instinct Lance held fast to Balana's rein, though she almost tore his arm off in her struggle to escape. Distantly he saw that Art had done the same, that the stallion was snorting and rearing, eyes rolling in terror. Then he couldn't look anywhere but at the thing bearing down on them across the fields.

The worm. His mind tried to slip its moorings. His vision felt twisted, forced into a place where nothing made sense, where the angles were wrong and the veil had been torn between his familiar world and a dimension of shrieking insanity. The moon hadn't risen, yet everything was bathed in a pale sickly light. Through it moved—or coiled, or slithered; Lance didn't have a name inside himself for the way it covered the ground—a gleaming tube, tall as a horse, and God knew how long. It reached the foot of the hill where he and Art had taken refuge, and something—perhaps the rise of the ground—made it divert, begin a thunderous slide past, length after length with no end in sight. The earth shuddered beneath it, and a rank smell of rotten flesh and dying vegetation filled the air.

White, it was white. It had a luminescence of its own, a faint firefly green. In flashes, Lance saw that its body was segmented, marked here and there with things like giant scales, with flaps of skin like a bat's unfurled wings. No end in sight... Then it narrowed, and the last few yards of it rushed past, and it was gone as fast as it had come.

It left a trail of dead grass across the moor. Lance sat up. Art was picking himself up off the ground. They looked at one another in utter consternation. Then Lance, who had never seen anyone's face quite such a picture as Art's, began to laugh. After an astonished moment, Art joined in.

"My God," Lance said when he could. "What are we going to do?"

"Follow it, of course. Why didn't it eat us?"

"It was moving too fast. Don't think it noticed us." He coughed, and tried to catch his breath. "*Follow* it? What the hell would we do if we caught it up?"

"Kill the damn thing, before it gets to the villages. That's what's been causing all this slaughter and havoc. Come on!"

Lance felt no fear: didn't pause for an instant to question his king's command. They were two scraps of flesh and bone in pursuit of a fifty-foot nightmare, but he sprang onto Balana's back, and it felt like the beginning of a ride after a deer or a hare. He and Art set off to slay the worm.

The trail was easy to follow. The places where slime remained were faintly glowing, like phosphorescence on the inside of a cave. Where flat ground gave way to trees and gorse, the creature hadn't turned but smashed its way through, leaving a gap large enough for Art and Lance to gallop through abreast. Jagged branches stood out against the sky as if startled by their sudden maiming. Everywhere the birds were silent, a quiet deeper than sunset. The horses flew, catching their riders' intent, their fear suspended by it. "It's making for Spindlestone, that same poor hamlet where we started this morning," Art called, pointing ahead, and Lance saw the thing like a ghostly snake on the horizon. "Take its left flank. I'll take the right."

"How have we come back here? I thought we were miles away."

"Must've gone round in a circle."

"How are we gaining on it?"

Arthur shot him an unfathomable glance. "Do you *want* me to say I think it's waiting for us?"

Lance absorbed this chilling idea. He couldn't argue. The beast had effortlessly mounted the Spindlestone crags, and was coiling itself amongst the scrubby thorn trees that grew there, a constant movement like a dance, hard for his mind to grasp. Then a head the size of a horse emerged from the coils, and it was the most terrifying thing he had ever seen—a vast skull barely covered in glistening worm-skin, the bones contorted, spikes springing up and retreating all down the length and over the crown of it, rippling. "Art, pull up."

"Why? We're nearly on top of it."

"We're inside its striking range, is where we are."

"How can it strike? I don't even think it has a…"

A neck extended itself from nowhere. Two green eyes shone deep in ridged sockets. The thing seemed to scan them—one at a time, thoughtfully.

For the second time that day, Lance saw the pale mask of combat wipe out all trace of humanity from Arthur's face. Beast, Saxon, invading army—nothing mattered but his blind need to meet his foe headlong. Before Lance could draw breath to shout a warning, he'd turned his stallion's head and pointed him straight at the foot of the crags.

Lance had a blind need of his own. He'd felt it once before, up on the dragon's-spine ridge near Vindolanda. He'd have gladly galloped Balana off the edge of a cliff that day, if Art had leapt first. He'd been a boy then. The childish impulse of that day had become the deep will of a man, a compulsion he would carry unto death. He crouched low along Balana's neck and tore off after his king.

Too late to reach him, but he could give the beast a choice. Halfway up the crag, Balana slithering and jolting under him, he drew his sword and waved it wildly in the direction of one glowing eye. "Hoi!" he yelled, ignoring Art's cry of warning. "Here, you brute! Over here!"

The worm chose him. Its movement—from a coiling stillness to a pounce—was horribly swift. Only the rush of its proximity saved Lance: he and Balana were knocked aside by the shock it produced in the air. The mare went down on her flank, but somehow struggled up again, Lance clinging to her neck and her mane.

The beast was intelligent. Lance, mind cold and clear as White Lawns snow now, saw it turning, reassessing its prey, lurching round on one huge coil to strike at him again. Its breath snatched his own from his lungs with its foul heat, underlain by a tang like scorching, like the tinder-dry moment before a forest fire. One great green eye brought its eerie light to bear on him. Lance drove his sword up, but the tip glanced off the socket's bony ridge, striking sparks.

He had one more chance. The creature arching over him, he pulled his spear from its leather hoops. It was the same weapon he'd carried since he'd grown tall enough to lift it and hunt deer on the moors, Ban's spare army lance, the source of his own name. Drawing back with all his strength, he thrust it at the place where the beast's jugular ought to be.

The skin looked thin as silk. Beneath it he saw organs shifting, veins pulsing. His spear's bronze head struck true—impacted with the impossible clang of metal on its own substance, and snapped in two.

Lance was finished. Time dilated unnaturally around him, as the worm reared back to strike again, and he found he could reflect on this, and even feel an instant of relief. He'd been in Art's service for less than two days. Now, at least, he would never have a chance to fail him. *No chance to betray him*, something hissed inside his mind, and he cast around him, bewildered, for the source of the terrible voice, almost blind to the descent of the beast's gaping mouth…

It swung away from him, grazing Balana's ears, spattering the front of his chainmail with slime. The night cracked in half to a shriek which held a note of outrage and surprise, and he saw blood fly from a hole torn in the beast's neck. Not his own doing… Shocked at the human scarlet of the wound, he spun Balana around.

Art was so close to the worm that he had almost disappeared within one coil. If the creature was immune to ordinary blades, Excalibur could hurt it still. Art lunged again and again, using his stallion's terrified leaps for escape to carry him close and fast enough to strike. He wasn't doing much damage, but the creature was distracted.

He hadn't thought the matter through any further than that. His expression, when he threw a dismayed glance at Lance, was almost comical. The worm shot its great neck to its fullest extent, out of the reach of this small, biting nuisance, then arched like a hard-curbed charger and slowly, deliberately, brought its head down, down, to stare direct at Art. It pushed its nose forward until it was almost resting on the poor stallion's muzzle, and whether out of terror or the sheer force of its rider's will, the horse stayed motionless. Art gazed into the maw of the dragon, his face a blank of fascination, colourless in the beast's moonlight gleam. Then, very slowly, step by step, he began to back the stallion up. "Lance," he said, never taking his eyes off the beast. "Lance, what do I do?"

How should I know? But, inexplicably, Lance did. He looked to the top of the crag, where a single spire of rock was outlined against the sky. "Tell her to go to her stone."

"*Her?*"

"Of course. Can't you feel it?"

"All I can feel is her breath. She's got flames in her gullet. I think she can spit fire. What stone, for God's sake?"

"The spindle stone that gives this place its name—up there. You have to command her."

"What? She's about to devour us both."

"If she could kill you, you'd be smoking bones by now. She'd love to, but something's stopping her."

"What—my kingly authority?"

"No. I think it's the sword. Try!"

Art opened his mouth for another question, but it was too late. The worm was coiling herself up for a strike. Her horse-sized maw gaped wide, and Lance tensed to dodge a fireball, but what came forth was a shriek that shook the rooks from their roosts and sent surviving children in villages five miles around wailing to their parents' beds. His eardrums tried to burst beneath the strain of it. Art was closer. Surely the sound would paralyse him, drop him where he and his stallion stood...

But Arthur gave no sign of fear or pain. His face exalted, rapt with vision. He lifted the sword high above his head.

The shrieking stopped. Lance drew a deep, shuddering breath. What should Arthur fear? With Excalibur in his hand, was he not as strong as the earth on which he stood? Could he not, if he wished, stretch out and encompass the whole night sky, and was not the moon, now rising full to the southeast, his protection and guide, promised to him in the forbidden rites of his childhood?

Lance lost the sense of his own interior, the sense of himself as a spirit marooned on an island of flesh. When Arthur spoke, it was as if he'd drawn the words from Lance's own deepest soul. He spoke with the voice of the sea in the darkness to the east of him, the night-wind that stirred in the gorse. "Creature of earth," he cried, and the worm went still, arrested at the moment of her final rush. "Creature of earth, return to your stone. Trouble the people of these lands no more."

The worm raised her great head. She swayed it from side to side, as if considering obedience. Lance urged Balana forward. Whatever the outcome of this confrontation, he had to share Art's fate. The lantern eyes glowed fiercely. The swaying intensified, and then the creature gaped, issued a frustrated hiss, and darted off sharp to the left.

She wound herself sunwise three times round the hill, and clasped it so hard that the very stone cried out. She squeezed, and the hill would forever retain the spiral grooves of her form. She howled, but there was no resisting the sword's command—and anyway, now her rage was done, she wanted to obey. It was right to do so: she had somehow forgotten. She had been lost.

Unwinding herself from the hill, she shrank to half her size, and then a quarter, and then when there was just enough of her to fit, she slithered to the foot of the spindle of rock. Wearily she coiled her way up it, and rested her head on the top.

Lance and Arthur rode after her. They stopped the horses by the rock. Lance said uncertainly, "You could kill it now."

Back in his skin, shaking with reaction, Arthur looked at him. "I thought it was… You were calling it *she*."

"I know. That makes it harder to kill, though. I'll finish it off, if you don't want to."

"It's all right. I must, I suppose. Well, you murderous brute," he said without enthusiasm, "you deserve it, don't you?" Two green eyes, still full of uncanny light, fixed on him unfathomably. "Why, Lance, look—it's nothing but a snake!"

The snake shrank still further. The fires of its eyes went out. It became a worm indeed, a little turner of the soil no longer than Lance's finger. The worm found a hole in the rock: formed a small circle around it. Touched its nose to the tip of its tail as if in salute, vanished into the hole and was gone.

Chapter Thirteen

A mile or so from the castle, they met with the search party Guy had sent out for them. "You little sod," Guy yelled across the timber bridge, as soon as Art came within earshot. "I've been pacing the ramparts in this ball-shrinking gale for hours. Not to mention that I've had the ghost of poor Ector breathing hellfire down my neck all night for leaving you behind."

He met the party in the light of the torches down by the gates, and seized Art in a half-savage bearhug as soon as he was down off his horse. It was the first time Guy had dared speak his father's name to him. Art smiled in acknowledgement, pulling back to look into his brother's tired face. "Well, he shouldn't have. You did your best—you always have done. I'm hard to look after. It's not your job anymore."

Guy nodded. Eyes too bright, he turned to Lance. "Well, did you find your raiders?"

Lance looked at Arthur. A fledgling king couldn't afford to tell a story of a dragon-hunt. If Art wished him to invent a battle, Anglian heads knocked together or hewed off, he'd do it. He knew how badly Art had wanted such a simple answer for the woes of the land, how set he'd been on finding it.

But Arthur shook his head. "No, Guy," he said, and when the soldiers of the search party turned to stare and listen, went on unflinchingly, "It wasn't Saxons who did this. We found nothing. I was wrong."

***

Lance dismissed the groom who tried to take Balana from him. It was so much his habit to bed the horse down himself that he couldn't rest until the job was done.

Even more of an obligation, after the uses he'd put her to today. He checked her limbs while she ate her hot mash, smiling over the old scars on her knees. Ector had been so incandescently furious...

Movement from the stable's torchlit doorway caught his eye. Art must have taken the time to splash his face in the horse-trough, but other than that was just as their wild ride had left him, mud-spattered and weary and, to Lance, more beautiful than the dancing flames. "Ah," he said. "The prince of White Meadows, rubbing down his own mount with a handful of straw."

"I'm sure you've just done the same."

"Yes. For the first time in years."

"Why did you stop?"

"Injuries. Battle-fatigue. More than anything, half-arsed advice from counsellors who told me a king couldn't act like a stablehand. Ector liked me to do it, though."

Lance straightened up, leaning on Balana's shoulder. "You should name that horse, you know."

"I came to the same conclusion myself. I've called him Calonek, a name from the Cerniw and Breton tongues. It means *brave*."

"Ector would have liked that, too."

They stood in the warm hush of the stables, letting the words, with their load of pain and love, settle in the air. Art didn't flinch or turn away. "Well," Lance said eventually, "I'm glad you didn't tell Guy we'd been off fighting raiders. But didn't you want everyone to know you slew the dragon?"

"I want everyone to believe I'm safe outside of a madhouse, if it's not too late for that." He pushed the stable door open and came in, glancing behind him to check none of the grooms was within earshot. "Anyway, I'm far from sure I slew anything. What *did* we do out there tonight, Lance? How did you know the worm would go to the stone?"

They'd barely spoken on their ride back from Spindlestone Heughs. Partly their silence had been shock and exhaustion, partly the feeling that no words would be adequate. "I don't know," Lance said, in answer to both questions. "I... wonder if I remembered something Viviana told me. Sometimes I feel as if I *should* know, about many things, but something gets in my way. A dream speaks, and then it's gone."

"Well, your dream spoke timely out there, or we'd be dead." He went to lean on the wall by Balana's feedbox, idly pulling at her mane. "Look at this horse! I know you love her, but you have to let me get you something better now."

"Younger, maybe." Lance grinned. "You'll never do better. Though I think I knocked some stuffing out of her tonight."

"Let me retire her honourably. I'll send her back to Vindolanda if you like."

Lance shuddered. "No, please. She'll end up pulling a plough."

"Or on the table?"

"I don't think so. We still had hard winters, but things were never as bad with us again after you brought the spring back to the moors."

Art's expression softened. "All right. I'll dispatch her down to Cerniw with my next messenger, and she can eat her head off in Britannia's greenest fields for the rest of her life." He paused, rubbing the mare's soft nose as it came up to quest around his hands for food. "What do you think it all means, Lance? The worm, or the dragon, and the sword? She *did* obey it—Excalibur, not me."

Lance had no answers for him. For an instant, out on the windswept plain, he had seen with a dragon's green eyes, felt a presence as ancient and as female as the earth, felt waiting fire in his own gut. Now he was only a man. When he tried to recapture his brief, effortless grasp of the worm's universe, it hurt his head and filled him with a sense of baulked frustration, like a dream that faded even as he reached to grasp it. *I don't have the means*, he thought incoherently. *The women and the stones and the dragons are all dead...*

"Lance, are you all right?"

"Yes. Just tired." He sought to turn the subject. "You missed a conference today, didn't you?"

"Two of them, I'm afraid."

"I don't suppose they cancelled them."

"Oh, no. Put them off till tomorrow." Art sighed. "I'd rather face the worm again, you know."

"I know. Is it any comfort to you, that you're good at this diplomacy you hate so much?"

"Am I? It comforts me a little, if *you* think so." He made a bitter face. "I wasn't much good this morning, was I, riding out of here damning every foreigner ever born."

"Oh, you were much worse later, when you were demanding their heads on a spike." Lance carried on grooming while Art registered outrage then reluctant amusement. "On the whole, though…"

"Thank you. You're saying it's no good my preaching peace to Coel and the Hen Ogledd kings while I can't keep my temper with my own neighbours. It's fair enough. As for Garbonian and his plans for a joint Anglian defence force, I… just hated the idea, which wasn't a good reason for rejecting it. It didn't work in the south, but Garb's right—the people *are* more settled here. I could hardly tell the villages apart, riding around out there today."

Lance listened with affection while he reasoned between his instincts and his conscience. He had no political answers either, but was starting to understand that Art needed someone he could ask, someone who wouldn't perceive uncertainty as weakness. He brushed the last of the dried sweat out of Balana's coat. "Well, sleep on it," he said. He looked beyond Art's shoulder, to the starry half-circle of sky framed in the stable's arched door. "You'd better start soon, or it'll hardly be worth it."

"Will you attend the debates? I know you want to work, but there'll be time for that, I promise."

"I'll be there."

"And… will you come with me now?"

Lance shivered. He'd made no assumptions. One night didn't mean a shared bedchamber. "Yes," he said longingly. "Of course."

There was no-one in the stableyard or the cobbled lane beyond. Art slung an arm around Lance's waist. He smelled of leather and sweat and horse, a combined fragrance that made Lance's head spin with desire. He returned the embrace, and they entered the stronghold together, matching step for step and pulse for pulse.

A tang of ozone sharpened the air in the hall. Lance looked around, expecting to see lightning over the dark sea horizon behind them, a winter storm on the way. His ears popped. His vision flickered as if he'd blinked too hard, and suddenly instead of the empty staircase ahead, there was an old man standing upright and stark-faced on the seventh step. Reflexively Lance grabbed for his sword. "Where did he come from?"

Art dropped a warm, restraining hand onto his. "Easy. Don't kill my Merlin."

"Is that... Are you sure that's who this is? He doesn't look the same."

"Of course he is." To Lance's dismay, Art bowed deeply before the old man—and then, as if that wasn't enough, went down on one knee. "Greetings, Lord Merlin. I hope this cold night finds you well."

The Merlin pushed back the hood of his robe. Lance was certain that the narrow skull with its few strands of white hair was different to the one he'd seen in the debating hall, but he'd been a long way off. "Greetings, Lord Merlin," he echoed for Arthur's sake. He'd never knelt to anyone in his life, but he made a courteous bow of his own. "May I ask how you got here, sir? I didn't see you arrive."

"My means of travel are no business of skinny-shanked princes of moorland and mud, Lance o'Lough. Is the work done, King Arthur? Is the dragon slain?"

Lance stared. His ears tried to pop again, and his sinuses crackled as if he'd surfaced too fast from a dive. If he could only close a grip on the veil of illusion hanging between him and this old man, he was certain he'd see...

"Lance? Are you all right?"

Art, still kneeling, was gazing up at him in concern. "I'm fine," Lance said, and leaned to help him up. "Come on. No-one commands the king of the Britons this way—not even a Merlin. Isn't that right, my lord?"

Unreadably the Merlin held his gaze. "The king of the Britons has not yet answered my question."

Art seemed to pull himself out of a mild trance. "No, I haven't. Not slain, Merlin, but made harmless, I'm sure. The creature became a snake, and then a little earthworm. Then it vanished into a rock on Spindlestone Heughs."

"The spire on the top of the crags? The very spindle stone?"

"That's right. How did you know?"

The old man spread his arms. "How do I know that you must fight the Saxon enemy, not appease him? That your bride will soon arise like the dawn to honour and bless your realm, and until that time, the less you're seen wandering these halls in the arms of your new general, the better?"

Lance wanted to laugh. Worse, he wanted to reach out and pull the Merlin's long white beard—as if by so doing he could tug off a mask, and find beneath it… What? A familiar friend, playing an unfathomable practical joke? That was the feeling he had, but Art clearly didn't share it. His face had darkened with anger. "Come with me," Lance said, trying to ease him away. "It's late. Never mind the prophecies for now."

"I'm not concerned about those. Listen to me, Merlin—I'll wander in anyone's arms I choose. And you'll address my general with respect. He healed me, which was more than you could do with any of your potions and chants."

No point for Lance in reminding Art that he was nobody's general yet. And he wasn't about to discuss his dubious healing powers—or his methods—with this suddenly keen-eyed old man. "Arthur," he said, not concealing a rasp of authority. "Come away and get some sleep."

"Why?" Art demanded. "Does it bother *you* to be seen in my arms? Would *you* rather hide?"

"I'll hide it from anyone who has no business with my affairs or yours. But, for the needs of this moment—yours, your Merlin's, any walls with eyes or ears—I'm asking you to accompany me to my bedchamber, and heaven help anyone who disturbs us there before dawn."

Art's eyebrows flew up. He underwent a perfect sunrise of his own, with colours to match. For this moment at least, all thoughts of old men and prophecies were forgotten. Lance seized his opportunity and began to push him up the stairs.

The Merlin stepped aside for them. "Even as much as you love him," he said as they went past, and his voice had lost its caw and gained a resonant sadness that tugged on layers of Lance's memory, "even that much, to that very height and depth, you will betray him."

Art whipped round. Lance stopped him by main force, planting one hand on his chest, taking hold of his jaw and turning him so that they were nose to nose, sealed into a world that held only the two of them and was complete. "Arthur, *don't*."

"You heard him. I'll have him killed for you."

Lance risked a flicker of a smile. "We don't even know which of us he meant."

"Well, it can't be you. And it certainly can't be me, because…"

The scent of ozone rose again, copper and salt and blood. Lance didn't have to look to know that the old man was gone. He kept his grip on Art's jaw, leaned down—of the two, Lance was a little the taller now, though he couldn't have said when that had happened—and kissed him until he was quivering, eyes closed, a frozen river ready to burst into a torrent of springtime melt. "I'll love you until your throat's raw with saying my name," Lance promised. "And then I'll love you to sleep, because if I don't, Garbonian will make mincemeat of you in the debating chamber tomorrow. And those are all the prophecies you need."

Chapter Fourteen

"Your Majesty," a small voice said, so faint that it was almost lost in the debating hall's echoes. The speakers and audience had barely finished settling down after their arrival. A page boy approached Arthur with deferential step. "Your Majesty," he repeated. "I come from Prince Garbonian."

Lance leaned forward. He could have had a front-row seat today, but preferred the broad perspective of his former perch, from which all kinds of things could be seen. Briefly Arthur met his eyes, in wry acknowledgement that neither of them—nor Coel himself, to judge by his expression—had missed Prince Garb so far.

"Very well," Arthur said, gesturing the boy forward. "I trust the prince is in good health?"

"Yes, Your Majesty. He..." The boy stopped. Clearly it was one thing to be given a message, and quite another to deliver it. "He begs King Arthur and King Coel to allow him to enter Din Guardi with Oesa, a nobleman from the Anglian settlement near Alauna. Oesa has his wife and children with him to offer as hostages. He wishes to treat for peace."

Lance had fulfilled his prophecies. Art had slept well. It had only been for a few hours, but he had fallen into smiling dreams as easily as if his head had never borne a crown. He looked refreshed. His world and his beliefs had been turned upside down and shaken until they rattled since last he had stood in this hall. *Not Anglian raiders but a dragon, now become a worm again and sent harmlessly back to the earth…* He turned to Coel. "Your Highness, will you consider it?"

Coel grunted in astonishment. "No, of course not," he said reflexively. Then he looked into the face of this young king who was shedding the light of a new age around his gloomy home. "Why? Do you think we should?"

"Not on Garbonian's terms. We will ride out and see these Anglians of his on neutral ground." He met Coel's woebegone expression with a smile. "We'll have our best archers man the walls, sire, just in case."

But Garb's Anglian didn't look like a threat. Nor did they look especially noble. Riding across the windy plain at Arthur's side— aware of Guy, Bors and Drustan behind them along with Coel and his personal guard, all of them armed to the teeth—Lance wondered what the outcome would be of this strange meeting. He was startled that Arthur had agreed, and more surprised still that the Merlin had kept silence, not stirring from his seat in the shadows behind the throne.

The man called Oesa stood with his eyes downcast as they approached, his bearing meek, although he towered over Garbonian's soldiers around him. He was massive and fair, thick hair in a plait down his spine. He wore a finely worked torc around his throat, and a good leather sword belt from which the scabbard hung conspicuously empty. Otherwise he was dressed like a well-to-do farmer, in brightly coloured tunic and calfskin breeches, a red woollen cloak swept back across his shoulders. Looking past him, Lance saw a woman huddled by the flank of her pony. She and the two children clinging to her skirts were as fair as Oesa, but their posture indicated less respect than terror. Arthur drew his party to a halt a few yards away. "Garbonian," he said. "Who are these people?"

Garb was pale with nerves. He twitched as Oesa cut with a low-pitched growl across his attempt to reply. "He, er—he wishes to speak for himself, Your Majesty."

Lance felt a brief, reluctant sympathy for Oesa. One thing to decide on a diplomatic mission—quite another, to be brought to it under guard by a diminutive British prince he could have probably snapped over his knee. Lance exchanged a glance with Art, offering a small nod in answer to the question in his eyes. "Then let him," Art said. "Who are you, sir, and what do you want at Din Guardi?"

The Anglian nobleman looked up. When he did so, Lance understood why he had been told to keep his eyes on the ground: they were fearless, a blazing frosty blue. "I am Oesa of Alauna," he said in rough Latin. "I lead the people of my settlement—they call me their thegn. We came here five years ago from the kingdom the Romans call Anglia."

"Why did you come?"

Oesa shrugged. "We heard the land was undefended."

Garb went paler still. Watching, Lance thought that he might have liked to poke Oesa in the ribs to remind him of his manners. Art sounded half-amused, too. "And did you find it so?"

"Almost. We did not have to kill many to make our claim. But now we have farms of our own. Fields, homes, children. We don't want others of our kind to come and take them from us. Neither do you want more of us in your land. We have common cause."

"Doesn't dress it up, does he?" This from Guy, who had leaned forward on his horse's neck to listen. A ripple of laughter went through the assembled soldiers. Oesa stared brazenly back at them. "Better an honest enemy then a snake-tongued friend," he said, and gave Garb a nudge that made him stumble and the guards laugh more loudly still. "You need not fear me, King Artorius. My wife Aedilthryd will answer for it, if I behave ill."

"No, Thegn Oesa," Arthur told him politely. "*You* will answer for it. I don't take women and children hostage. But, with King Coel's agreement, I will welcome you and your family at Din Guardi as guests." He turned to the elder king. "What do you say, sire?"

The poor old man looked ready to slide off his horse and die of despair on the ground. "My father was a tribal chief," he announced unexpectedly. "He was in charge of a hillfort, twenty people and some goats. The Romans came, and they made me a king. I took their money and the title they gave me. Then they vanished, and they left me their gift as a curse in my hands, an unbearable burden. Now you, Artorius—the hope of Britannia, as the people claim, and as I truly believe you to be, with your wisdom and kindness—you, of all men, ask me to open my own castle doors to the invaders."

"Not if you don't wish it. Say the word." Art lowered his voice so that only Coel and the men closest to him would hear. "I know what it is that I'm asking you, my friend. I do understand."

"I feel ancient, Arthur. And lost."

"You're neither, I swear. I will stand by you, no matter what you decide."

"Will your general, too—good Sir Lancelot?" Coel's brow creased. "Odd name, isn't it?"

"Very," Lance agreed, as solemnly as he could. He supposed *Lance o'Lough* had been round the fortress a few times and come back to him like this. "But my king's allegiance is mine."

Coel turned back to Arthur. "Are you truly certain this is wise?"

"I'm not certain at all," Art said honestly. "Our grandchildren will judge us for it, one way or the other—as visionaries or fools. But I think we have to try."

***

So Anglians came within Din Guardi's walls, and the world went on. Oesa's wife sat among the women of Coel's household and sewed, and did not have much of a time of it until she learned a few words of Latin and the women learned how to pronounce her name. Her children, not subject to such constraints, rolled and played with the others in the dunes.

As for Oesa himself, he took a place of honour in the debating hall. For almost a week, he, Coel and Arthur thrashed out an agreement in principle by which the Anglian populations around Din Guardi would provide a militia in case of attack. Oesa knew what had happened in Vortigern's kingdom, and serenely accepted the restraints Arthur suggested to prevent a repeat of the disaster. The settlers' soldiers would act only in conjunction with equal numbers from among Coel's men. They would hold no meetings on their own, and no-one in their villages would send messages, food or other support to arriving immigrants. Coel himself would provide for the newcomers, if he saw fit and they came to him in peace.

God knew there was plenty of land. Bryneich was empty and vast—a realm for settlers, not invaders. Oesa assured Coel that he understood the difference. Good service in defence of Bryneich's shores would be richly rewarded: aware of Anglian practicality, Coel didn't leave this promise in the air but called for his scribes to mark down on parchment how much and what for. The Hen Ogledd kings, disgusted that their quarrel had been shelved but not quite daring to leave, hung about in the debating hall, and after a few days began to be a little ashamed of themselves, that this foreigner could talk peace while they remained at daggers drawn.

In the evenings, Oesa made himself comfortable in the dining hall. Lance, concerned that Aedilthryd was left disregarded in the women's quarters, suggested to Art that she join them, but soon learned that a thegn's wife did not partake of his rank or even shine with his reflected light, and Art, shrugging at Lance to indicate he'd done his best, settled to talk with their exotic visitor.

There was much to learn. The settlers were a mystery no-one had cared to unravel. They were unenlightened heathens, and the Christian priests hadn't dared enter their settlements to remedy that. They lived by blade and barter. Beyond attempts to stem the tide of their invasion, the Britons had taken no interest in them.

But for all their ferocity, once they had taken the lands they wanted, the villages they built there were extraordinarily peaceful. They didn't seem to fight amongst themselves. Oesa, leaning his elbows on Coel's table as if he owned it, told Arthur of the laws and customs the settlers had brought over with them from Anglia—a strange, simple, visceral set of societal restraints that bore no resemblance to the Roman legal system. They lived by the blood-feud. If one man killed another, the victim's family were honour-bound to avenge his death by slaying the killer in his turn.

At home in Anglia, these cycles of murder and vengeance could roll majestically around the large communities, gathering tales and songs about them. Out in the new world of Britannia, however, the small groups of immigrants had soon realised the impracticality of their old ways. The blood-feud tradition remained in place, but nobody was keen to start one. Extinction would soon swallow up a tiny town at war with itself, and so they behaved. Some forward-thinking souls, Oesa said, had even tried to find a substitute for blood-vengeance, one that wouldn't depopulate a settlement faster than children could be born into it. In a few places, the *wergild* had taken the place of the like-for-like killing. It literally meant *the price of a man*: you could pay with money, not with your life, for your crime.

Arthur was fascinated. There was no equivalent concept in the Celtic world, or even in the more prosaic Roman one which had swallowed it. He and Lance spent long hours discussing with Oesa the extraordinary idea of quantifying the value of a human life. Oesa was proud of the *wergild*, and didn't seem to realise that his companions were incredulous as well as intrigued, and more than anything repelled. He talked on, explaining how the man-price could be changed to deal with lesser offences, how each body part—an arm, a toe, a tooth—could be assigned its own value. If you blinded a man, why, you could pay for the price of an eye.

It made sense to him. In practical terms, Lance and Art agreed that they too could see the use of it. Better to pay up than be blinded yourself in your turn. But who decided the price? How was the sacred gift of vision, or of life in your lungs, reductible to a fixed amount of gold pieces, or of sheep or goats or cows, which could also be bartered? Misinterpreting the thrust of their questions, Oesa explained that these ideas were only in their infancy. But for now, the state of suspended blood-feud worked well as a deterrent.

Art had to agree that it kept the peace. Wouldn't the settlers be more inclined to do as they were told, for a price, if the Britons entered into their way of thinking, and rewarded and punished them as rigidly as they regulated themselves? Paid mercenaries…

Yes, it could work. Art could see that Vortigern's failure had largely been down to mismanagement.

His own army followed him from loyalty. He could be certain of that, he said, because although he paid them what he could afford, that sum was so tiny, they could have no other reason. He would trade glances with Coel, who was in his turn visibly remembering his own campaigns, his glory days beneath the golden standards of Rome, and the pair of them would look almost as grim as each other.

Nevertheless, Arthur summoned Garbonian, who had been keeping a discreet distance since his diplomatic triumph. Garb, delighted at his promotion from traitor to ambassador, eagerly set forth his plans to organise the militia. His father's gaze on him was heavy with reproof, but there was nothing the old man could do, not while Garb had Art's authority to speak. Garb tried, and failed, to conceal his enjoyment.

Lance watched it all, for the most part in silence. He spoke only when Arthur questioned him directly, or when he thought he saw flaws in Garb's ideas of tactics or defence. For all he'd tried to divert Art's blind rage against the settlers, he was uneasy about using them as soldiers on home turf. Perhaps, he reflected with shame, he was as bigoted as anyone else. He recalled his own childhood hatred for the whole race, his readiness to rush down a hill and kill the strangers approaching Vindolanda simply because they'd been fair-headed, not been Roman-Celtic dark.

Peace had to be a better way. During the week that followed, a deep winter cold set in. The shortest day was approaching, and the dragon was heard of no more. As soon as Lance could be spared from the debates, he went down and found for himself a place among Arthur's soldiers, glad to be away from the swirling political tides within the castle. The men were leery of him at first—this new favourite of the king's—but Art's favourites were renowned for being useful, and if Lance was a prince in his own land, he was also no more than a farmer's son. He proved himself on the archery field, knocked a few major players off their horses with a blunted spear, and at the end of the week had the ordinary number of friends and rivals amongst the troops.

He and Arthur slept in the bright eastern chamber that overlooked the sea. Art's quarters were better, but the king seemed to understand without words Lance's love for the place: that he felt at home there as he never had in his father's house, or even on the northern moors. As night after starry, entwined night went by, their exchanges in the sturdy wooden bed became less frantic, the passions of men arising like deep sea currents through the wild waters of boyhood. In after years, Lance would remember the breaking of light on tumbled bedclothes, the shape of his king's worn-out profile, as the dearest and best of scenes. If anyone—Guy, the Merlin, the ladies and lads of the court who might have fancied their chances with Art until his prophesied bride arrived—noticed that the king's rooms stood vacant, none of them spoke.

***

Lance slept profoundly after love. He was exhausted anyway, from drilling or sitting up at all hours round the fire while Art wrestled with some new twist of the peace process. He never knew what woke him, deep in the night of the dark moon. He'd been dreaming of the dragon—not the twisted worm of Spindlestone Heughs, but the dragon of the ridge, a creature huge as the sky, who danced among the stars. In this dream, her dance was urgent, and he opened his eyes on thick darkness, his mind resounding with her fear.

He turned back his blanket and slipped out of bed. The darkness seemed to press on his eyes. Still drenched in sleep, it took him a few seconds to realise the profound difference between this night and all his others within Din Guardi's walls: no torchlight painted the courtyard below him. The cressets were out. Heart pounding, he found his way by fingertip touch to the door, where he unhooked his shirt and breeches and Art's. Their sword belts and scabbards hung in their accustomed place by the bed. By the time he got back to Art's side, he was calm again, his pulse down to a cool steady throb.

Art was sleeping flat-out on his belly, pillow as usual impatiently cast to the floor. He rolled over, and Lance planted a hand on his mouth. "Trouble," he whispered, when Art's eyes focussed on his, and he smiled at the soldierly swiftness with which the king's dreams dissolved to bright purpose. Peace might be the way, but getting there could be a tremendous bore. "Here's your clothes. Get dressed!"

Chapter Fifteen

The lights were out all over Din Guardi. A guard lay slain in the corridor outside their room, corpse still warm. Taking the steps one at a time, cat's-whisker fingers extended in the pitch black, Art and Lance made their way down towards the courtyard. On their way they found other corpses, and kept between them a grim silent count. Six. The whole watch. Someone had come here and silently pulled the castle's teeth. Hard-trained soldiers - who could get close enough to them? Perhaps to come up to them, bid them good night and good watch, engage them in talk? Their throats had been slit or less expertly slashed, wounds meant to hush the first cry. The work of several hands. Only their friends could have done this...

Or Garbonian and his. Lance felt the thought flash between him and Arthur as surely as if he'd spoken it. He shot out a hand and grabbed Art's wrist, held him locked still until his first shock of rage and horror passed.

By now the smallest distinctions between light and dark were bright to them. They paused, poised and listening, beneath the tower's arch. The courtyard was full of the pale blue radiance of stars—and, down by the gate, the glow of a single lantern. The portcullis was raised. Coel's fortress had been breached.

Three dozen or so Anglians, filing in silence through the gate. The time for silence was past. Art's first yell, a full-blooded battle cry, would bring Coel's surviving soldiers and his own to startled waking in their beds around the castle. He and Lance ploughed into the stealthily moving line, using to its full extent their one brief advantage of surprise.

They would only have to hold on here for a minute before Guy had the guard out in force. Lance began his soldier's task, calmly dispatching his first man then the next. His mind cleared to the crystal lucidity of combat, and he swung round with a backhand thrust to bury his dagger in a third.

Then Oesa sprang at Arthur out of the crowd, face bestial in the lamplight, and Lance had all his work cut out to protect Art's back. The king and the Anglian met like the predestined foes they were. Uther Pendragon's blood-lust awoke in Art's veins, Excalibur's magic in his hands, with a roar Lance could almost hear. Lights were flaring in the tower and royal quarters. A horseman was flying out through the gates to alert the army. If Lance could only hold on…

Oesa fought bravely and well, and with every sign of enjoyment. "So much for your hostage wife," Art yelled at him over the clash of bronze on steel.

"Ah, but you don't take women hostage, do you?"

"I might bloody start, after you. What of your children?"

"Slay the brats. I've half a dozen more. As for my Aedilthryd—she did it well. Meek little mouse-wife! She was flashing her teats at the nightwatch while Garb's men killed the guards."

Lance glimpsed Art's nod of acknowledgment from the corner of his eye. This had been, in his way, a noble enemy.

Excalibur flashed, faster than hand or mind could account for, and Oesa, still grinning, crashed down.

Behind him were twenty more. Art turned his back to Lance. Lance mirrored his movement, and they stood spine to spine, swords ready, facing the oncoming horde.

***

Gaius and the guard arrived, not an instant too soon, and such a battle ensued as would echo down the ages at Din Guardi. The numbers stood more or less even until Art's soldiers began to pour in through the gate. Some of Coel's men had switched sides: the fight became sharper as their comrades discovered which. Excalibur moved like a scythe through harvest, and Lance continued his methodical dispatch of anyone who entered sword or dagger's reach.

Prince Garb was nowhere to be seen, but must have been watching from somewhere—when the army began to turn the tide, he appeared on the far edge of the melee, ducked down and started to run low along the courtyard wall. Catching sight of him, Art made a grab at Lance's shirt. "There he is, the weasel. Get him! I've got my hands full."

"Leave him to me," Lance said grimly, thinking of the butchered guards, and the poor old king whose heart would surely be broken by this. He dodged out of the fray and ran.

Garb was hard to follow. Born and raised within Din Guardi's walls, he knew its every bolt-hole, and terror had made him swift. Lance tailed him as he would have done a deer in a deep hungry winter—single-minded, remorseless, not dismayed at losing sight of him, every sense alert for the marks of his passage. A door left ajar, a dying patter of feet, a scrap of rich fabric left torn on a nail... Skidding into a wine vault, Lance cornered him, desperately trying to raise a trap-door by its iron ring.

As soon as he saw the game was up, he left off his efforts and straightened, backing away, both hands held in front of him. "Ah, it's you, Lance! Don't hurt me!"

Despite everything, Lance was reluctant to finish him off. Weasel or not, this was the heir to Bryneich, the last of Coel Hen's dynasty. Lance had never killed a surrendered man. "Why not?" he demanded. "You've betrayed your own kingdom. Your father!"

"I didn't mean it! I swear, Lance, right up until the last minute, I only meant to make peace. And then... Then yesterday, a boatload of pirates made it ashore a few miles south of here. They'd been raiding. They were dripping gold. They got a message to Oesa somehow, and he offered me so much money to open the gates..." Garb shook his head at the memory, eyes gleaming feverishly. "So much, I could barely imagine it. *You* could barely imagine it! We could go—we could find him. He needs men like you."

"Oesa is dead."

"Then... if you get me out of here, I'll take you down the coast with me to the pirates' camp. I'll speak for you, don't worry..." He tailed off. Lance of Vindolanda, so grave in the debating chamber, had leaned a shoulder against the wall and started to laugh. "What's wrong with you? Don't you want to be rewarded?"

"Was Oesa paying you from the beginning?"

"Oh, what do *you* think?" Garb dropped the pretence, and dared a couple of steps toward Lance. "You think I ran about for months between Coel and those Anglian brutes for nothing? For the sake of some idiot's dream of peace? I did it for gold. And then I got a better offer. I'm trying to share it with you."

"Shut your traitor mouth."

Garb's face twisted. "Ah, that's right," he snarled. "You do it all for the honour, don't you? Honour and love. What do you think your honour will buy you, when you've trailed your sacred king around the country for ten years, spilled out your life in his service? Will his love warm your bed for you then?"

Lance went still. Laughter ran out from him like grain from an upturned sack. He reached out and grabbed Garb by the arm. "You're not worth my blade," he said hoarsely. "Come on. Your father can choose your reward for this night's work."

Garb was a carrion bird, not a killer. He never should have got a blow past Lance's guard. But Lance was suddenly tired and sick. Garb writhed back and struck at him like a snake.

Lance felt the blade enter his side as a thud, a strange inner punch. Why had his grasp loosened on his prey? One leg folded beneath him and he seized at the rim of a barrel for support. Garb was retreating backwards, pale with disbelief. He took a few uncertain strides, then turned and ran for his life.

***

The kings of Bryneich and Britannia stumbled away from the end of their separate battles, and met in the courtyard, bloodstained and weary. Lance had made it back there too, but only as far as the shadows of a tumbled archway, where his legs had turned to water and he'd fallen to his knees among the stones. The strange thing was that he couldn't bring himself to care, or draw breath to call to Art, who was only a shout and a gesture away. A massive indifference was filling him. It almost felt like relief.

Coel looked more cheerful than Lance had ever seen him. Lance guessed the old king's world had been restored. Art's, as well: Briton versus Anglian, blood on the turf. Grinning, propping his hands on his knees to catch his breath, Art nodded to Coel. "We made a good try for peace, sire."

"Aye, and bloody tiresome it was. I'm almost grateful to my vermin son for ending it. I suppose I do have him to thank?"

"It looks that way. We saw him bolting when my army turned the fight. I'm sorry."

"Don't be. Best I know. Where is he now?"

"Lance went after him." Art straightened up and looked directly at him, but Lance was only part of the broken darkness now. Fires had started here and there, and Coel's servants were dashing around putting them out. "Our household priest used to say hell would look like this. And I was destined to go there, if I didn't leave off the girls and the boys and get myself to his church."

"Aye, ours said the same. Where do they get their ideas, these frock-clad fools from Rome? Fanciful, it seemed to me, the dreams you'd have after an over-rich feast. But you're a Christian king, Artorius. Don't you believe in hell?"

"Not the lurid tale of it that priest told. No man of common sense could swallow such fantasies. I got a second opinion from another priest."

"What did that one say?"

"He was more of a philosopher. He told me hell was the knowledge of being forever alone. And that *did* put the fear of God into me." He wiped blood and sweat from his eyes and scanned the flame-lit dust clouds anxiously. "Where's my Lance?"

"I'm here," Lance said, but the words had no sound, no force. He was less badly hurt than he'd thought. He was bleeding, but couldn't tell how much in the flickering light, not with so many other bloodstains daubing his shirt and hands. He was neatly punctured between two ribs, he thought, but that was all. He couldn't believe in the wound. His whole side was numb. Apart from that, he was fine.

Shame landed on him like a rockfall. Nothing short of death could have excused his letting Garbonian go. He got his legs under him. Walking felt odd, as if his feet were skimming an inch or so over the red-pooled flagstones, barely in touch with them. Arthur and Coel had seen him now, were turning to him open-mouthed. His heart tried to crawl to a halt in his chest. The only way out was immediate confession of his fault. "Art," he gasped. "Coel, Your Majesty... I've failed you. I let the traitor go."

The courtyard lurched: knocked him sideways onto his arse. His disgrace was complete. But Art didn't seem to care. He dashed across to crouch at his side, and his warm strength, lifting and propping, was the only thing left in the world Lance cared to have. Gratefully he leaned against his chest. When he breathed Art's scent through the open neck of his shirt, he could read every minute of the night his king had passed, the hot reek of battle and beneath it the traces, deep and fresh, of their long, loving struggle for release in the wooden bed. Art rocked him. "What are you talking about?"

"Didn't you hear me? Garb got away."

"For the love of Tamar, Lance, you had to leave *one* alive tonight. You fought like a demon—didn't he, Coel?"

"A very demon," Coel agreed, thudding down beside them. "It was *my* job to stop Prince Garb, not yours—and I should have done it twenty years ago. Ah, it was a grand fight! I haven't seen the like in years."

All three sat in silence, taking in the devastation. It didn't seem strange to Lance, to be sitting in the midst of scattered corpses with the two high kings. Had Arthur reached over and handed him bread and a flagon, that would have felt natural too, as if they'd stopped their horses in the dunes to rest and eat. Art didn't think much of Lance's injury, if he'd noticed it at all: was holding him as if he'd stumbled out of a fistfight and just needed steadying until the world stopped spinning round.

All was well. And if Art and Coel didn't care about Garbonian, why should he? For Lance, whose sense of responsibility was acute, the sudden rush of freedom came as something wild and new. Mirth shook him, and Art, who had scarcely ever heard him laugh without restraint, looked down at him strangely. "What ails you?"

"Nothing, love. Nothing at all."

Coel grinned at them, as if they met his satisfaction too. "You'll have to take care, lads," he said. "These damned Roman priests want bodies and souls for their church, and if you're not getting children—in lawful wedlock, at that—by your passions, they'll tell you you're hellbound for that, as well. For myself, I think it does a man good to love a fellow soldier. Teaches him responsibility—the bonds of combat, not this titupping courtly love we hear of from the travelling players." He regarded them, smiling, a merry old soul indeed. "I'll tell you what. I wish you two had been my sons. Bryneich would have *been* a kingdom then." He held up his sword, considered its bloodstained blade thoughtfully in the firelight. "I believe that I shall leave this place. I believe that I shall go and take up the work I abandoned in the northwest, against the Scots and the Picts."

Art shook his head. "That's a lost cause, Coel, and you know it."

"I do. However, it is *my* cause. It always has been. I am an old man, Artorius, and I don't expect to return from such a campaign." He nodded at them contentedly. "I have not been happy here, trying to fill the boots the Romans measured for me. I will be glad to take my last journey. And that leaves my fortress here empty, with no heir."

"Your Majesty, Garb may still be alive."

"Not to me. No, not to me. I'd hand it to you, Artorius, did I not know that soon you'll have more strongholds than you can deal with. You, Lance, however… I knew your father a long time ago, and old Ban, though he can die and make a king of you, will never leave you a castle. And that's a bad state of affairs. A king should have one—a grand rock like this, from which he can hold the whole north for Arthur of the Britons." He flashed a triumphant smile at Lance, reached out a bloodstained paw to pat his face. "You it was who lifted the curse, who took the worm out from my heart. Din Guardi shall be yours, the Castle Dolorous no more. From now on it shall be Joyous Gard. What do you say?"

Lance couldn't say anything. He was numb now from his throat to the pit of his stomach. He heard Art observe, "I think he's a bit overwhelmed," and watched as if from a great distance as his friend released him, stood up, took him by both cold numb hands and tried to hoist him to his feet. "Come on, then, Lance of Joyous Gard. You've earned your rest. Coel, I'm sure he'll thank you in the morning."

Coel stared. His old eyes were still sharp—the sharper, for his night wielding a sword. "Never mind that now. He's bleeding, Artorius. Look to him!"

Chapter Sixteen

Garb's knife had been tainted. For several days afterwards, Lance lay desperately ill. When his delirium ebbed, his chief impression was of Arthur, shouting: at Coel's herbalists and physicians, at his brother, when Guy had come and tried to prise him away from the bedside to get some rest, and then at Lance himself when he showed signs of giving up.

Hearing him did Lance more good than any amount of poultices or the herbal draughts being poured down his unresisting throat. His deepest instinct was to obey his king, and so he lived.

He surfaced in sunlight, in the chamber that overlooked the sea, to the scent of a driftwood fire. Arthur was sleeping uncomfortably, propped on a stool against the wall. When Lance said his name, he woke with a jolt that almost knocked him to the floor. It took him a moment to regain his poise, but as soon as he saw that Lance was smiling and clear-eyed, he straightened up, pushed his hair back and came to sit on the edge of the bed as though nothing had happened.

Lance surveyed him. He was unshaven, his eyes red-rimmed with exhaustion, and he looked ten years older. "Well," he said. "Are you done scaring the wits out of me?"

"I... think so, yes." Lance tried to push upright, but his muscles were water. "How long did I take over it?"

"Almost a week. It's been quite inconvenient."

"Yes, I can see that. I'm sorry."

Art leaned over him. In frowning silence, he folded back the bedclothes. Someone had dressed Lance in a short winter tunic of the softest wool, thick enough to keep him warm but easy to manage in a sickroom. Lance didn't own such a garment, but he'd seen one like it among Art's things. Art eased the hem up, lifted the bandages beneath with a practiced, cool-fingered touch. "You're almost healed. Your wound wasn't deep, but there was some kind of poison on the blade."

"You've nursed me with your own hands."

"Least I could do, after the healing you brought me." He glanced up. "I did try it, you know—asking Excalibur to give me that power. But for me she's just a sword."

"Such a sword as never was seen. You and she swept like fire through that fight."

"But is that all there is to it, Lance—the fight, and the fire?"

Lance didn't know. He'd thought there would be more, with Excalibur in this man's hands...

Better to take the baffled pain out of his eyes. Art had clearly had time to think during the long watches of the night, and too much of that wasn't good for him. "Remember," Lance said, laying a hand to his tired face, "we were loving each other when I healed you. Maybe it takes that too, and I've hardly been in any fit state. I am now, though."

Art chuckled. "Really, Sir Lancelot? You've just barely woken up."

"Still. Touch me and see."

The capable warrior's hand pulled the tunic hem down, moved warmly into the front of the woollen britches in which Lance had also been tenderly encased. "Oh. You weren't kidding."

"Course not. Think about it. I've had you seven ways to sunset every night since I got here, until the fight. I've just done without for a week. No wonder I'm up for it now."

Art shook his head. The shadows around him had vanished. "Incorrigible," he whispered, smiling. "Wait while I go and wedge this stool against the door. Half the castle's got used to barging in here to see how you are, especially Coel. Don't want *him* to see you with your britches down and your cock down my throat, do you?"

Glad Art hadn't suggested anything more strenuous—his arousal was real but fragile—Lance watched him seal them in. He let go a long, shuddering breath and arched his back as Art knelt over him. No healing miracles here: when he tried to thrust up, an unmanning weakness seized him, threatening the hopeful lift of his shaft. "It's all right," Art told him quickly, pressing hot kisses to his belly just above the place where the vigorous sable hair began. "It's all right, dear love." He pushed his hands under Lance's backside and lifted, not far enough to hurt, just to give him the motion his flesh craved, the rhythmic, writhing push he'd have made for himself if he'd been able, up and into his lover's waiting mouth.

Lance turned his head aside on the pillow, closing his eyes. He snatched up the edge of a blanket and pressed it to his lips. A cry would bring doctors, Coel and probably the Merlin in here, stool or no stool. A storm of anguished joy was building in the cauldron between his hips. Art closed his mouth hard around his cock— held him back for a few seconds with a restraining squeeze of finger and thumb around his root—then plunged down, opening

278

his throat. The storm found passageway. After a floating, flailing instant when Lance thought deliverance would tear him apart, he went rigid, every muscle clenching.

Art held him in place until he was done. He swallowed, coughed, let Lance's spent shaft ease out of his mouth, and knelt grinning in delight at his work. Then he folded, bright-eyed and feverish, into the bed beside him. "Better?"

"Let me show you how much."

"Oh, that fine beast of yours has spilled all its fire for now."

"I still have a hand."

"Better put it on me, then. Ah, like that. Harder. Tighter. Oh, God."

***

"You can tell me who did this to you now."

Lance frowned. In the wake of passion, his mind clear, his shame was undiminished. "It was Garbonian."

"What, that little rat?"

"Yes. It was how he got away from me." He shifted in Art's embrace. The temptation was enormous, to bury his face in the warm, rough silk of his hair and hide away. "He said something to me... I can't remember. Anyway, I let him go. I was distracted. It was unforgivable."

"Oh, Lance, as if anyone cares. You're Coel's favourite son now, in case you don't recall. The heir to Din Guardi."

"I do recall. And I can't accept it."

"I told him you'd say that. He said I must persuade you. And I knew you wouldn't be swayed by how useful you'd be to me personally, holding a stronghold up here, so I thought I'd try a dirty trick." He kissed Lance's brow, his left cheek, his right, and finally his chin, a Celtic cross of love, more ancient and sacred than he could know. "Vindolanda's very fine, but that long winter hurt the place. The soil's exhausted. How would it be if you brought your people here?"

"My White Meadows villagers?" Lance broke into laughter. "We'd rattle like peas in a barrel."

"What, all those little princes and princesses Ban's no doubt already conceived? You said he was a terror among the milkmaids."

"My mother said it kept him occupied during her pregnancies. And she didn't mind if the milkmaids didn't, and the bairns were strong and well cared for. You're right—I doubt he's changed."

Arthur sobered. "This would be a chance for you to restore his honour, if you still care for that."

Lance lay and watched him in silence. This view of things hadn't occurred. As for Ban's honour, that was Ban's own to win again or lose, but the idea of lifting the whole struggling community he'd fought so hard to protect away from their poverty and into this safe refuge… That was almost intoxicating, the kind of sweeping miracle only a king could perform. A king with a castle as well as a name. He smiled.

Arthur nodded at him, aware he'd scored the point. An urgent rapping at the door broke their silent communion. "Here they come—the doctors and the sorcerers. The butcher, the baker, old King Coel and his fiddlers three." He sprang out of the bed, pausing to see that Lance and his clothing were decent before he turned away. "Think about it. I'll leave you to the mercies of your medical men. You should get some rest." He stretched, yawned till his jaw cracked. "God knows I have to."

He was halfway to the door when Lance asked, "What happened to Aedilthryd, by the way?"

"Who?"

"Oesa's woman. The mouse-wife."

Art looked at the ground. "I had her killed." Then he sighed, shoulders sagging, and shoved the stool more firmly into place. "Wait a damn second, out there! Look, Lance, I know how you feel about women. You set them aside, away from our mess and our blood. But she was man enough to help Garb and Oesa crack this castle wide open, and I gave her a man's death for it. A soldier's. I don't know, love. Which of us really treats them according to their deserts?"

He tugged the stool away. Immediately the door swung wide, admitting a torrent of servants and physicians. Arthur entered the stream like a salmon, flashed Lance a last grin over his shoulder, and disappeared.

When the kind souls of Din Guardi had finished with him, Lance lay tucked up in his clean bedding, wound dressed, poultices and witch hazel applied. He was lost in thought. Art needn't have run away from him. Lance had no easy answers, and was in no more of a hurry to pass judgement now than he had ever been.

That there was ice in Art's nature, acquired since their brief spring at Vindolanda, Lance knew. He wasn't sorry for it. It would keep Art alive longer than his boyish readiness to compassion, which Lance thought had probably been interred along with poor Sir Ector. And as for how Lance felt about women, he wasn't sure he knew. Art had been wrong. He didn't think them fragile and pure, to be set aside for those reasons. Nor were they less than men - impure, untrustworthy, and therefore also to be set aside.

Yet he was cold with shock, that Aedilthryd had been put to the sword. The kingdom of Britannia belonged to men. The scales had tipped, he believed, in his mother's time. Something had died with her passing, though he couldn't define the loss. What was gone? *Sanctity*, his mind told him. *Sacred strength. The dragon...*

He shivered: perhaps Garb's poisons were at work in him still. He was anyway too tired to think for long about anything. Arthur hadn't tended *him* with coldness, hadn't spent a sleepless week cajoling him back into life out of a ruthless heart. Right or wrong, that was enough for Lance. Art loved his friends blindly, and God help his enemies.

Sleep tugged at him, strong as spring tides. Curling onto his side, he let his eyes close in the bright sun that gilded Din Guardi, the Joyous Gard which was and always had been his own.

Chapter Seventeen

Battles breed legends—of cowardice and heroism, and things in between, small in themselves, growing large with the retelling. As well as the warriors' tales, the battle for Din Guardi generated a short-lived ghost story.

It was Guy who first said that he and the men had heard children's voices coming through the walls. From anyone else, Art might have dismissed such a story, but Guy was completely and comfortably without imagination, and so he set out with his brother and Lance to investigate.

They made their way along the seaward terrace, listening to the wind and the surf. It was Lance's first venture outside in ten days, and the world seemed impossibly bright to him, the salty air intoxicating. He paused to lean on the parapet. Guy and Art stopped too, and took up their places—a pair of ill-matched, considerate bookends—on either side of him. "A little more to the left, Guy," Lance said.

"What?"

"A little to the left. Then you'll be shielding me properly from the wind."

"Insolent," Guy said happily, shifting to do as he was told. "It's good to have you up and about again, Lance. Still, if you weren't the heir to this place, I'd chuck you off this wall to feed the fish."

Down on the plain far below, feverish activity was taking place. A dozen or so Anglian farmers in crimson tunics were sawing the branches and roots off an enormous trunk of oak. "What are they up to?" Lance asked dubiously. "Is that their new battering ram?"

"Oh, not a bit of it," Arthur said, resting his elbows on the wall to watch. "Guy and I were busy while you were lazing about. We took a deputation into the nearest villages—on foot this time, so we wouldn't look so Roman and stuck up. Even Coel came with us. We talked to some of the elders."

"Wasn't that a bit risky?"

"Oesa's rebellion didn't go far. Most of the people down there are happy enough with the treaties and trade arrangements we set up. We talked to the fellow who's taken Oesa's place asked about their daily lives and customs—and that, my dear Lance, is a *Jol* log. They all seem to call it different names depending on where they come from, but the idea is that they haul it with oxen right into their chieftain's hut, place one end in the hearth, light it from the remains of last year's log and burn it with great feasting and rejoicing over the next few days, to help bring back the sun."

"Sounds like a good time. Perhaps we should get one."

"You underestimate me. In Coel's great hall right now—the sweetest fruits of my diplomacy so far, I think—is a trunk even bigger than that one, ceremoniously delivered last night with good wishes from the new chieftain himself. Coel wanted to saw it open and check no Anglians were hiding inside, but he accepted graciously, on the whole. He wants to leave you a peaceful kingdom."

Lance made a sidelong study of his king. Strands of hair were escaping his braid and catching scarlet in the low sun. A smile was curling the corner of his mouth, and he looked much happier with his Jol log than with the results of all the hacking and slaying he'd done. "That was noble," Lance said quietly. "To go down to them like that and talk."

Art cleared his throat in embarrassment. "I thought it would please you. There's something catching about their festivities, isn't there, Guy? Even old Coel's been infected. He wants us to have our own Jol-tide feast tomorrow night, which is the longest one, according to the cunning-women in the villages."

"They're right." Lance didn't question the deep conviction in his bones. "We used to celebrate that night too, with a great fire and feasting and an exchange of gifts."

Arthur's eyes kindled. "Gifts? What kind?"

"Modest ones," Lance said hastily, afraid of what his generous lover might do. "Remember I'm already getting a castle this year."

"If you live to inherit. You're still looking peaked—we should get you indoors out of this blistering cold." He straightened up, smiling. "As for you, brother, I think you and your soldiers have been at that barley rotgut you brew up in the camp. I can't hear any children, inside the walls or out of them."

They were turning away when the faint, eerie laughter rang out. Guy's mouth fell open. "I told you," he said. "It came from that direction. Come on!"

They searched all along the eastern wall, went inside and followed the line of it through the granary and store rooms. The sounds came again and again—laughter, and a wild, high chatter, somewhere between teasing and terror. But all they saw was an occasional rat, efficiently pursued through the barrels and bales by one of Coel's brindled cats. Lance was glad to emerge into the sun. He still couldn't quite catch his breath with ease, and hiding this from Art's quick perceptions was taking him all his time.

At least he wasn't alone in breathless pallor. Even Guy was looking around him, clearly unnerved. He said, faintly, "It's surely just the village brats, playing tricks."

"Must be," Art agreed, and they stood disconcerted in the crystalline sea light, unwillingly hearing the inhuman babble continue.

Lance hesitated. Then, because it was a question he had to ask, he looked squarely at his king. "Art, what happened to Oesa's children?"

"I don't know. I thought they'd just run off during the battle." Suddenly he too went white, in a mix of denial and anger. "I never laid a hand on them, Lance. And nor would any of my men."

"I know that," Lance returned quietly. He waited, meeting Art's eyes without challenge, until Art gave a shamefaced nod and looked away.

The high-pitched chatter faded off into the sound of the wind. Guy shrugged. "We're all imagining things, if you ask me."

Lance reached out a hand to still him. "Wait. Look!"

Two small ragged children had darted out of the granary's far door. They were filthy and skeletally thin. They froze for an instant in the sunshine, staring directly at Art, Lance and Guy, and then before any of them could move or draw breath, melted like fish into shadowy water and disappeared.

Despite seeing them, Lance wondered if he was chasing ghosts. By the time he and the others had found the gap in the parapet wall, there was no sign of them, only a trace in the air—a fading whisper, the patter of bare soles on stone. There was barely space for a grown man to fit into the moss-lined hole. Art managed it, at the cost of some grazing. Lance, stripped down by illness, followed more easily, but burly Guy, who had never liked tight spaces, shook his head. "You must be joking."

"All right." Arthur grinned up at him. "We'd never get you out, and then there'd be another ghost in Din Guardi's walls. Go and fetch Coel. He might know where this passage leads."

Lance made his way a few yards down into the dark. "Come on," he called. "We'll lose them if we don't go now. They looked like they were starving."

"You should stay here. You're still not well."

"Oh, you want to go down there alone?"

"I'd rather stick pins under my nails." His pupils were wide with fear. *You're made for the sun,* Lance thought fervently. *Sun and air.* "All right, come with me, but I'm sending you back if you get tired. We'll need torches. Guy, run and grab us a couple from the granary."

Glad to do anything that didn't involve squeezing into that dark hole, Guy ducked under the granary's arch and took two cressets from the basket. He struck them into flaring light with a flint and passed them down into Art's hands. "I could get some of my lads to do this, you know. You don't have to pull the brats out with your own royal hands."

"There's no time."

"Well, they're only that traitor Anglian's brood. Is this because you had the mother killed?"

Arthur winced and looked back over his shoulder at Lance. "No. Well, maybe. Go and fetch some men just in case, and some ropes and more cressets. I'll see you soon—I hope."

Lance was waiting at the first turn of the passage. "They went this way," he said, taking the torch Arthur passed him. "I can still hear them. We have to move quietly, or we'll scare them deeper still."

By the flaring light, they began to scramble downwards into Din Guardi's foundations. The hard rock had been roughly carved into steps at some distant time, and not used often since, to judge from the lichen and mosses growing where the last light filtered down. Between brief pauses to listen, Lance set a rapid pace, trying to ignore the ache of unused muscle in his legs, the breathless tugging in his chest. The children's sounds were changing: there was no laughter now, only ragged panting, the odd high-pitched rasp like sobbing or bitten-back fear. "Here," he called out, unconsciously dropping back into Elena's tongue, the language of the mother, summoning her brood home from the dark. "Wait. We're not going to hurt you."

"That heathen babble won't help," Art said, a smile in his voice, slithering to a halt behind him. "They might know some Latin from Oesa, but that exhausts your shared languages."

Lance shook his head at the lapse and tried again. "*Manete, parvuli. Non vos nocebimus.*" There was a listening silence, but then the receding slither of small feet came again. "We could get lost down here, you know," he said, glancing back. Art's face was composed, but Lance by now knew him well. "Why don't you go and fetch someone who knows this place? It might make more sense."

Art grimaced at the kindly offered get-out. "Thanks," he said, "but I don't think I'm to be allowed easy escapes in this life. Let's go."

Deeper and deeper, into the roots of the rock. How had the passages here been carved? Their glistening black walls felt the same as the rock of the breaking-wave crests to the north of Vindolanda, the whin-stone the Romans had used to pave their roads. It was backbreakingly hard to quarry or shape... Maybe they were following a natural fault, a split in Din Guardi's foundation, but Lance thought he could still see remnants of steps, and the jagged arcs above his head had a regularity that suggested the work of men. "Watch out," he said, grabbing Art's wrist. "It's getting steeper."

"I know. I'm less worried now about getting lost than getting back up. I'm torn between telling you to turn round and begging you not to leave me alone down here."

"I'm not going anywhere. You try calling them." He smiled. "You might sound more commanding."

Art shuddered. "Wonderful," he said. "Kindly Lance has failed, so let's make the bullying king have a try. I'm not an absolute savage, you know, no matter what you might..."

But whatever his defence might have been, the truth caught up with him, a hungry wolf. Cowering in the crevice a few feet below them, a tiny boy, so filthy and ragged he had blended into the rockface, suddenly scrambled upright, pointed a finger straight at him and whimpered, "Him! The king who killed my mother!"

"Lance," Art said faintly, putting a hand to the wall. "What is that—some kind of hobgoblin?"

"Of course not. Just a little boy." Lance scrambled down the rockface far enough to grab the child and haul it into his arms. He carried it into the torchlight, rat's tails of dirty fair hair swinging into its eyes. "Poor thing. He's skin and bone. Did he see the woman slain?"

"I don't know what came over me. I'd just seen you carried off the battlefield, and... I thought you were dying. I only remember my rage. It was so pure and bright... The woman was with the other prisoners. She was laughing. She broke away from Guy and ran at me."

"You did it with your own hand?"

"Yes. I didn't even think."

Lance glanced up at him quietly. "Where did it happen?"

"In the storage rooms to the north of the keep."

Lance put a hand to the back of the child's bowed head. "Is that where you were hiding, after the fight? With your sister?" He waited until the little skull moved in a nod. "Did you see it happen?"

Another nod. Arthur drew a ragged breath. "I wouldn't have… I didn't know they were there."

Lance hefted the little boy in his arms. Suddenly he missed his family. In his anxiety to be away from Vindolanda, he had distanced himself from the good things about it—the ordinary rhythm of its days, the presence of unfrightened children. But he'd chosen a life of warfare at Arthur's side. He had chosen. "Listen," he said. "On the night of the battle, if I'd seen you as you saw me—if Oesa had killed you, and I'd found *your* corpse—I'd have done as you did with the woman, or worse."

Art stared at him. Then his eyes filled with tears, and he put out a tentative hand to stroke the little boy's hair. "I can't believe he's survived down here for so long," he said. "And the girl, too. I'll see they're both provided for."

"Good." Detaching the child's wiry clench from round his neck, Lance sat him down in a niche in the rock. He took off his cloak and bundled him into it. "Stay here, boy. Do you hear me? We're going to find your sister."

A large promise, given more in courage than hope. The chasm yawned beneath them—to infinity, for all Lance or Arthur knew. They picked their way down a rocky scree that threatened to crumble beneath them at every step. "Guy will send people after us," Art said confidently, and Lance held fast to the assurance. He didn't share Art's fear of the dark, but he had no wish to be entombed down here. Carefully, slowly, down they went, trying to balance out caution against the life left in the torches.

Then the ground beneath them shook. The voice of the worm they had conquered rose up through the dark, huge as the night sky, shaking the marrow of their bones. Her green light shone up at them like midwinter dawn, or like the spectral glow that sometimes touched the face of the dark moon. And underneath the terrible voice was a human one—a child's, a girl's, screaming as if her heart was being ripped from her breast.

Lance fell. In the flashing green-lit dark he felt Art near him: the helpless grab he'd made to pull Lance back, then a thud against his shoulder as Art too lost his grip. Lance grabbed at a handhold: let it go along with the torch, the price of a rescue. The rock turned to glass and ran out, and he dropped for a heartbeat through empty air.

He hit wet sand. The girl's shrieks entered him like blades, and he flipped onto his front, then his hands and knees. He'd landed in a high-roofed cavern. By the weird light filling it, he saw Art pushing up onto his backside, intact but clutching one ankle. Lance crawled over to him. "Are you all right?"

"What in unholy damnation do *you* think?"

"Don't worry. Stay here."

"Lance, no! That... That's the worm."

"I know."

"You can't fight it alone. Anyway, it's my task. I killed the mother."

"Redress it some other time. I have to go." Reluctantly Lance pulled free of Art's grasp, the circle of human warmth enclosing his arm. He didn't want to run alone into the alien light, toward that terrible screaming. If he didn't do it instantly, his blood would curdle cold in his veins. "Wait for me here, love! Don't be afraid. Guy will be down soon."

Chapter Eighteen

Lance ran through curving chambers and passages of rock. With every flying step, his fears blew off him like cobwebs. He should have known: always *had* known, in some recess of his heart's memory, that the core of Din Guardi was hollow. Din Guardi was the dragon's home. He couldn't become lost down here. The tunnels were a spiral, a labyrinth: one route in, one route out, the journey from life into death and back, which he could make in safety if he were only willing. The dragon's roar became a song, and the child's screams blended with it and turned to music too.

Lance rounded the last curve, and there they were—the dragon, twice the size of the creature he'd encountered on the Spindlestone crags, and a thin little girl, no more than ten years old, standing serenely before her. He had reached the centre.

No need for him to be afraid, not when the child was waiting so calmly, looking up into the dragon's face. He didn't even need his sword. He sheathed it, and the girl said calmly, "You see, my lady. I have brought him to you, as you wished."

Lance approached in silence. The girl was surrounded by a coil of the creature's tail, which he had to step over to reach her.

He did it without hesitation, even when a bony spike brushed his knee. He lifted the child into his arms. She smiled, but hardly seemed to notice him. "Raise me higher," she said.

"What are you going to do?"

"I want to give my lady the dragon a kiss."

"Won't she eat you?"

"Don't be silly."

"Well, if she does, she'll no doubt swallow me too. So neither of us will have long to worry about it." He did as the child had bidden him, hoisting her up by the armpits.

She put up her arms in a gesture of yearning and welcome. And the beast bowed its abysmal face, that great skeletal shape as big as a horse, down and down until the child could touch it. Lance watched as she put her two hands on its muzzle, brushed them over the gaping nostrils. He remembered the fire, and he shuddered. But more and more it seemed to him that he was looking at a mask. The great eyes with their cold light that filled the chamber were only lanterns in a window now, a sea-widow's last hope.

A terrible sadness took hold of Lance. Dragon to worm to harmless snake—all this he'd seen, but Excalibur had only changed the beast, not slain her. She had been able to change back. This would be the end of it—this, when he followed the movement the child was showing him, and put his own hand on the dragon, and leaning forward, pressed his lips to her face.

He set the child down, and lifted the mask away. It was light as dried bone now, easy as taking the shield from the corpse of a fallen foe. When he put it aside, it crumbled to powdery dust.

A woman was kneeling where the dragon had been. She was curled up so tight that her brow was pressed to the wet sand of the chamber floor, her hands locked behind her skull as if expecting the roof to fall in. Her skin and her black hair were soaked, gleaming with the same weird liquid that had painted the track of the dragon all over King Coel's lands. Her bony spine, like a dragon's crests, looked ready to burst through her scant flesh. Her raw newborn nakedness was terrible to Lance. When she unclasped her hands and slowly raised her head, he stepped back from her as he had not done from the beast. But the green glow swiftly faded, and she looked at him with brown eyes like his own.

Just like his own. He stared at her. What transmuting mirror, polished Roman copper or ancient obsidian, could show him his own face thus transformed? "Who… Who are you?"

"I am the white wave," she said, and he realised he'd asked in his own language. She had replied with the same—a sweet, strange voice, rough with newness, reaching awkwardly for each syllable—and it sounded like *guen yvre*. "Your kind call me so, who've seen me dancing the rock crests, or rolling in the breakers to the shore."

"My kind… Aren't *you* my kind?"

She knelt up a little. He wanted to cry out in warning: the raw bones were retracting somehow under the surface of her skin, which looked more like silk than like scales now, stripped of its power to break spears and swords. How would she live? She lifted her hands and examined them. "It seems that I am. Has it happened? Is it time?"

Lance had no idea. It didn't matter. A great calm descended on him, a silence as deep as the earth. Fear and wonder left him. There were no more choices to be made. No more fighting, no more burned villages, no scared children, no man or woman riven through the heart of their own nature by the sun god, by the Son of God, who carved flesh away from spirit, life from death, creator from created. He would touch her, raise her to her feet.

The two halves of their separated worlds would join, and all would be well.

"Yes," she said, as if he'd spoken. "All will be well. You will bring the land to life through me. Through me, you'll hold the kingdom in your hands. I am the *graal*, the holy cup of life. I'll give you an heir to make war and sorrow a memory, the heir of the sword and the stone." The words had come from her with passion, but as if they had been something learned, a message she had to deliver. Now she stopped, and her formality dropped away. She gave Lance his own wry, half-hitched smile of relief and joy, and held out her hands to him. "Ah, but I'm so glad it's you, my brother!"

"Lance?"

He spun round. Art was there in the entrance to the chamber, leaning heavily on the wall. "I heard the thing howling," he said. "My ankle was twisted, that's all, so I ran to find you. I..." He fell silent, and stared beyond Lance at the woman kneeling on the sand. "My God," he whispered dryly. "Who's that?"

Lance answered with helpless truth. "She's the dragon."

"The dragon?" Arthur glanced back at him in concern. "You had a pretty hard fall. Did you hit your head?"

"No. She's the dragon, Art. I took off her mask and she changed."

"All right. We'll have you both out of here soon. Guy's setting up some ropes in the chamber back there." He limped over, unfastening his cloak. "Why on earth is she naked? And... Lance, did you somehow find your long-lost sister here?"

"What?"

"Well..." Art looked between Lance and the woman, frowning and smiling at once, his face a picture of bewilderment. "If you were a beautiful maiden instead of the handsome fellow you are, that's how you'd look. Just like her."

"Art, I tell you, she—"

"My lady Guenyvre!" The child's clear voice cut through the cavern like a blade. Oesa's little daughter, who had moved into the shadows, now stepped forward, her spine straight, her small face serene. She lifted one hand and pointed straight at Arthur. "Look! The sword you sing of. The sword *ex calce liberatus.*"

The woman fell back on her haunches. She twisted round to stare at Lance. In the depths of her dark gaze, he saw a flash of denial—and then her lights went out, one by one, candles in the Vindolanda church snuffed out by the shuffling priest. She said, faintly, "Are *you* not the bearer of this sword, my brother?"

"Of Excalibur? No." A hard lump rose in Lance's throat. He held out one hand, and she took it, and her grasp was cold as stone. With the other he gestured to Art. "My lady, this is my king—the king of Britannia, Arthur Pendragon. The sword Excalibur is his."

Art stumbled forward. He could barely walk, but he took Guenyvre's free hand and helped Lance lift her upright. "You must be chilled to the bone," he said, and wrapped his cloak around her.

She stood between them, clutching their hands, and she lowered her head, a gesture of hopeless surrender that almost tore a cry from Lance. She said, softly, "Yes. Artorius, my foretold king. I remember now. You will bring the land to life through me. Through me, you'll hold the kingdom in your hands. I am the *graal*, the holy cup of life. I will give you an heir…" Her voice faltered. "An heir to make war and sorrow a memory, my lord. The heir of the sword and the stone."

She tried to fall to her knees once more, but Art prevented her. "Stop that," he said, gently. "Get up." He took her pale face in his sun-browned hand and looked at her, frowning. "How long have you been down here? Did you hide with the children after the fight?"

Lance made one last attempt. "Art, I told you—she came from the dragon."

Arthur shook his head. "You need some air and daylight. I can hear Guy and the others shouting for us. Come with me, both of you, and bring that child."

***

In the sunlit world above, the strangest silence reigned. Lance couldn't read it. The hush was profound yet vibrant. The buzzing pressure of it hurt his ears, made the ground lurch beneath his feet.

He was tired, that was all. Guy and the others had widened the gap in the wall, knocked masonry out of the top and propped the arch with a wooden scaffold. He'd gone in like a snake but was able to walk out like a man, only ducking his head. Guy, who had practically carried him up the last twists of the stairs, gave him an anxious look. "I'm all right," Lance told him. "Go and help Art with Guen."

"With who?"

"With..." Lance rubbed his brow. There was no *Guen*, no familiar shape in his memory to fit the short, loving name. "With Guenyvre, the woman from the cave. That's what she's called."

"There's no need. Look, my Ardana's come to look after her—Coel's wife, too. And that little Anglian brat is stronger than she looks."

The child was helping Guenyvre over the rubble. Ardana reached out a steadying hand and drew her into the light, where the elder woman was waiting, a length of richly figured fabric in her hands. The golden embroidered beasts and knotwork drifted hypnotically in the wind from the sea. "Come here, dear," the old lady called. "You have to put this on."

"Hold on a moment." Arthur emerged from the darkness. He'd kept to the rear of the procession back from the cave, uncharacteristically slow to return to the light. "Isn't that the gown you and your women made when we first arrived here, and the Merlin prophesied my wedding?"

She dropped him a nervous curtsey. "It is, Your Majesty. Yes."

"Well, the girl's welcome to it—but don't you have anything warmer?"

"Yes, Your Majesty. For now, though, she has to wear this."

Arthur sighed in impatience. "Guy, you're supposed to keep me informed about local customs. I don't want to tread on anyone's toes. Is this something to do with the solstice?"

"Not that I know of." Guy turned on him gruffly. "Since when was I your cultural advisor? What do we keep a Merlin for, if not to—"

"Do shut up, Guy."

"Why, you little…"

A long, thin shadow bisected the scene. It fell like a blade across the gathered women: the elderly queen lifting up the ragged girl, Guenyvre puzzling over the magnificent garment in her hands. Night would come hard and fast on this raw solstice eve: already the sun was dying beyond Traprain Law to the west. The Merlin stood outlined in its light. "Artorius," he called, voice carrying like a raven's windblown caw. "Cover the woman's nakedness. Invest her in her robes."

Nobody seemed to know what to do. Art drew a breath as if he would argue, even with a Merlin's command, but then let it go and stood swaying, buffeted by the cold gale. For some reason tears were spilling down the old lady's cheeks. As for poor Guen, if she knew the hem of the robe from its beautiful sable-trimmed neck, she was giving no sign. At last it was Lance who stepped forward. "Here," he said kindly. "It goes like this, Guenyvre." He took the robe from her hands and shook it out. "My lady Coel, will you stand just here to shield her? That's right."

He unfastened the cloak Art had tied at her throat. The cloak had billowed out like clouds behind her, like wings, and she hadn't been naked at all: only her pale breasts and belly exposed, her dark pubic patch. Who cared if such things were seen? They were part of the glory of the world. "It's all right," he said, because she was staring at him in depthless bewilderment. "Let the cloak drop. Now I put this over your head. It goes on like so, and your arms in here and here."

She obeyed him like a child. God, she was comely! All trace of the dragon was gone. The robe settled as if it had been made for her. Lance, smiling at her in spite of himself, raised the sable-trimmed hood as a frame for her rosy face. "Well, there you are, Lady Guen."

"I like that name. Not the lady part—just Guen. You must always call me so."

"If I can. My name is Lance."

"What do they want of me, Lance—these people?"

"I don't know. Arthur will, though." He held out a hand. "Art, come here."

Slowly Arthur approached. He let Lance take hold of his hand and put it into Guenyvre's. Once more he glanced between them, taking in their sameness and their difference. Nobody could resist Guen's bright face for long, and he tightened his grip. "All right, you two. I don't know what the Merlin's cooking up, but it's better we meet it head-on. Old man! Whatever you're up to, get on with it, please, before this lass dies of the cold."

The Merlin swung his blackthorn staff out to the right. Between the rod and his own gaunt frame, the gesture was akin to the opening of a door. "Come, Artorius and Guenyvre," he called, loudly enough to scare up the ravens from their perches on the tower. "The white wave has risen from the earth, the queen the prophecy foretold. Come and be sanctified—man to woman, sun to earth, sword to grail. Come forth in holy union!"

Art looked at Lance in alarm. "What is all this? Do you know?"

"Not a clue, but we'll sort it out later. Humour him."

"A grail, though—isn't that what you said *you* were, Guenyvre?"

"A *graal*, yes." She put a hand to her brow. "I don't know what it means anymore. I'm forgetting."

"The prophecy was that I was meant to find one," Art said. "A graal, I mean, after I'd found the sword. That was drummed into me when I was a boy, and I don't know what it's all about, either. So don't be afraid—take my arm. We'll find out together."

Lance stood aside to let them pass. Guy appeared beside him and clapped him on the shoulder as if to tell him to buck up, and he raised his head, grateful for the reminder. The two fell into place behind Art and Guenyvre, Ardana and the others clustering behind. Only the little girl seemed unaffected by the occasion's sudden deep solemnity. She rushed around the group in a wide orbit, emitting high-pitched cries, a little foreign seagull in a world of her own. The Merlin led on. He strode around the outer wall of the keep, then through the tunnel beneath the tower.

And now at last Lance understood why the silence had felt like a pressure in his head. The courtyard was full. Every soldier, servant and stable boy—the Hen Ogledd kings in their separate huddles of bodyguards and hangers-on, the women of Coel's household from their secluded quarters, Arthur's knights, Coel himself, frowning tremendously—all were gathered, and some power or command of the Merlin's had held them mute.

Certainly it wasn't by Coel's priest's authority. He was trembling in the archway, staring as if he'd been expecting the dragon herself from the fort's foundations. He was no more than a boy, hollows beneath his eyes from poring over parchment by candlelight. The Merlin gestured to him curtly. "Well, bless the union, then! Since it must be so these days."

The priest raised his staff. It was topped with a golden cross, and looked puny beside the blackthorn rod. Arthur and Guen emerged from the tunnel and stood like dazed children in front of the crowd. "In the sight of God," the priest quavered out, "let the joining of this man and this woman be sanctified." He dropped his voice to a whisper directed at the Merlin. "They'll still have to be married, you know—in the church."

"Yes, yes. Get on with the rest of it."

"In the name of our saviour, may it be so. This is the bride the Merlin foretold. They will be wed when the proper preparations have been made." A few cheers arose from the crowd. Encouraged, he ploughed on more boldly. "Welcome them, good souls of Din Guardi—King Artorius and the lady Guenyvre, soon to be his queen."

Chaos erupted like beer from a fermented cask. Whatever magic Merlin had worked to hush this many people, the enchantment wore off in a flash. Winters were long on this northern coast, the days cold and short, festive times few and far between. The maids and stable lads flung up their hands, laughter and shouts ringing out. Art's soldiers, normally stolid fellows, caught the infection and began to cheer too, and that blew the top off the barrel entirely. The women launched into a rich-toned chant, their children joining hands around them and starting a wild, spinning run of a dance.

Coel pushed his way to the front. Of the Din Guardi people, only he still looked sombre. Ignoring the priest and the Merlin, he stumped up to stand in front of Arthur. "This is all very fine, lad," he said, just loudly enough to be heard over the racket. "But are you sure it's what you want?"

It took Arthur a long time to respond. Guenyvre had huddled against him, recoiling from the noise. He'd put an arm around her, but to Lance it looked like the action of a man lost in a dream. "What I want?" he echoed. "I don't know. It's what the Merlin prophesied."

"This is my castle still. I can have your Merlin thrown off its ramparts. What about Lance?"

So strange to hear his own name! Lance had begun to forget that he was here. If Art was dreaming, so was he. Perhaps they'd wake up in the sea-lit chamber, limbs entwined. "I'm fine," he said dazedly. "Guen has to marry the king."

"I don't understand. You found this woman… in the caves beneath the fort, the place where the worm used to dwell?"

"That's right. The worm won't ever come back now, Your Majesty." Lance held out a hand to Arthur, who was gazing back over his shoulder at him in desperation. "Everything will be all right, Art! It's Guenyvre, your white wave. She's meant for you. All will be well."

Chapter Nineteen

Lance was up early on the shortest day. He dressed in silence, and kissed Art's sleeping face before padding barefoot out of the room. He put on his boots in the corridor outside, shivering in the icy blast from the stairwell. He and Art had spent their first chaste night—not talking, not loving, barely even breathing as the wakeful stars had wheeled by. They'd clung to each other like frightened children, badger cubs in dried leaves, dependent on silence for survival. A cold grey light had been painting the sky before Art had gone heavy and still in his arms.

Let him sleep. Today would be a day for celebrations—Coel's midwinter festivities, and a banquet to welcome Guenyvre as Art's chosen bride. Everything was unfolding as it should—and yet, if Art felt within himself the plunging weariness that was still dogging Lance, he'd need all the rest he could get. Pausing in the open doorway to the courtyard—empty now, only wisps of straw from the stables being whipped about on the wind—he drew deep lungfuls of the air that had done him so much good since his arrival.

Not today. His wound was almost healed, but poisons must still be chilling and darkening his blood. He leaned on the sandstone pillar by the door, distractedly admiring the feathery swirls the weather was beating out of its construction. Winter after winter, scouring off layer after layer…

"My lord Lancelot!"

He jerked his head up. That bloody name! But it was too late to put it right now, and here came the blacksmith trotting through the gateway, red in the face with exertion, saving Lance a walk into the village he wasn't sure he'd have been strong enough to make. "Good morning, Aedan."

"It's finished, my lord. And since I was coming up here, I thought I'd bring it to you. Here—see what you think."

He thrust out a small leather pouch at Lance. A chain was dangling brightly from the open end. Lance caught hold of it and gently withdrew the heavy pendant inside. He turned it over in his palm: held it up to the weak sunlight making its way through the clouds. "Beautiful," he said. "Very fine workmanship."

"I'm glad. I had to watch out over my shoulder while I was hammering out the shape of it. That priest of Coel's taken to snooping round the smithy."

"What on earth for?"

"Forbidden images like this, I suppose, my lord."

"Here, then. I know we agreed on less than this, but you did well, and it's worth it to me."

The blacksmith flipped the coin Lance had given him in delight. It was a gold piece from the emperor Diocletian's time, still good currency in these parts. "Thank you, my lord! *God Jol* to you, and a blessing on the fruit of your loins."

Lance wasn't sure he'd ever muster any up, if he continued to feel this way. "Thank you. Er…God what?"

"God Jol, my lord. It's what the Anglians say to one another at this time of year. We're having a few of them over to feast with us tonight."

"Really?"

"Yes, sire. Whyever not? They're good enough fellows when you get to know them."

"I'm sure of it. God Jol to you, too."

Lance went back inside. The fort was beginning to wake up, servant lads and girls dashing about with hot water, the warlords and knights who'd overdone it at Coel's generous dinner table making their yawning way down the stairs. In the dining hall, a small team of men who were probably tired of their task by now were engaged in hefting the great Jol log another foot or so into the heath, where it was burning merrily. Gratefully Lance went to meet the heat halfway: he couldn't seem to get warmed through, although he'd put on his new woollen tunic and best coney-lined winter cloak.

Both of them gifts from Art. Wearily Lance sank onto the bench at the far end of the banqueting table. Coel had ordered great swathes of holly and ivy to be brought in and hung from hooks on either side of the hearth. The foliage cast deep shadows in the flickering light from the fire, maybe enough to keep him out of sight of talkative incomers. Even in Coel's generous household, the first meal of the day was a simple one, but there was plenty of dark rye bread, cheese and small ale set out.

He took a chunk of the bread. Ardana was responsible for the brewing of the morning ale, though she never got to sit down and partake of it herself. Perhaps her recipe was a kind of vengeance: she had it sent from the kitchens hot, sludgy and the colour of porridge. Still, Lance knew from experience that if he could keep the stuff down, it put a good lining on the guts, and perhaps the malty heat of it would drive out the crawling unease from his bones.

He paused, one hand on the jug. Sounds were issuing from within the thicket of leaves. Someone had burrowed even deeper into this hiding place than he had done—was, if possible, even less anxious to be found. Normally Lance would have respected such a wish and moved away.

But this was Guenyvre, sobbing in monotonous despair. Lance got up. He looked around. No-one was paying attention, so he pushed back a tangled curtain of ivy and ducked underneath it. He spoke without thinking. "Guen, dear. What on earth's wrong?"

She looked up wildly. She was hunched up on a footstool as close to the fire as she could get without singeing the strands of her unbrushed hair. A billowing nightgown—it looked like one of Queen Coel's—concealed her from neck to toes, and on top of that she was clutching a blanket. "Oh, Lance! They wanted me to sit in the solar and… and *embroider*!"

He wanted to laugh. Then tears of pity stung to his eyes. "May I sit with you?"

She nodded mutely, and he found a second footstool and pulled it round so that he could crouch in front of her. "It doesn't sound like much fun," he said, "but is it as bad as all that? Are they unkind to you—the other women, I mean?"

"Oh, no. Ardana and the queen are kindness itself. But there's *blood*, Lance—I have blood running from between my legs. I wish to go outside and bleed onto the earth, and to roll around on the earth, and let the earth take the ache from my belly and my back. But when I told this to the queen, she put a hand on my mouth and begged me to stop. She gave me a sorry little cloth to use, which chafes me. And she said… she said I should come and sit with the other women, and tend to my needlework, and the less I spoke about my sickness, the sooner it would go."

"It's your moon blood, Guen. It'll stop after a few days."

"How would *you* know? You don't have a hole that bleeds!"

"No, but I did have a mother. She would boil up dried mugwort leaves and drink the potion hot, and the rest of the water she'd put into a stone flask, and lay it to her stomach."

"Did that help?"

"Better than silence and sewing, I should think."

"And... may I have these things?"

"Of course. I'll fetch them for you myself."

"No, no. Clap your hands. My handmaiden will come."

Somehow she was queenly despite her matted hair and running nose. Lance passed her a square of linen from the tabletop. "You have a handmaiden?"

"Of course. I'm a bloody princess, I am. That's what Ardana told me to say, if anyone asked—a princess from a tribe in the far north, selected to be Arthur's bride. Go on—clap."

Wonderingly, Lance did as he was told. Promptly the ivy rustled and parted to admit the little Anglian girl from the dragon's cave. Unlike her mistress, she was impeccably turned out in neat linen tunic and apron. Something in her pale blue gaze unnerved Lance to the core. "What's your name, child?"

"Aedilthryd, sire. Like my mother."

"Go to the kitchens, please. Have a tisane made up of mugwort—artemisia, they might call it here, or wormwood. The root or the leaves will do. And have them fill a stone bottle with hot water, and bring these things here as soon as you can."

The child dropped him a curtsey, mechanical and perfect as if she'd been in service all her life. She whisked around and pattered off. Lance watched her go, frowning. "She seems helpful. Did Arthur give her to you?"

"Not exactly. He wanted me to have one of the girls Ardana offered. But I already knew the Anglian child, you see."

"Did you? Do you remember?"

"I think I used to dream of her. She was hungry and lost, deep in the coils of my cave. I would bring her whatever I'd caught that day—a cow, or a sheep, or… or a man, and when I'd satisfied my hunger, I'd blow fire from my mouth to cook the remains for her. She and her brother would sit at my feet and gobble up the scraps. They weren't afraid of me. It *was* a dream, wasn't it? It must have been."

She began to weep again. The lonely sound of it pierced Lance to the quick. Gently he laid a hand on her head. "Dream or no dream, the girl's provided for now. Her brother, too—Art promised."

"Is he a good man, Lance?"

"The best of men. You'll be all right."

Suddenly she sat up. She pushed her hair back from her face and fastened upon him a direct brown-eyed stare. "You love him."

Truth. There would never be room for anything but truth between Lance and this woman. "With all my heart. My life's his for the asking."

"Then… what is *my* place here? Why was I pulled out of the earth?"

"To do what you said, Guen. To give him an heir, and bring life back to the land."

"Those words were just a dream too."

"In that case… In that case, all you can do is learn to love him." Lance shivered, tried for a smile. "You won't find it hard."

"If I'm to marry him, he must sleep in my bed, not yours."

"I believe that's the usual arrangement, yes."

"Oh, Lance! What are we going to do?"

Did she mean herself and Art? All three of them, perhaps, caught as they were in this sudden thicket of magic and fate. "I don't know. Right or wrong, though, this marriage has been sanctified by the Merlin and the priest, in the sight of all Art's knights and soldiers. As he is dear to me, so is his honour, Guen. It's my whole duty to preserve and guard it."

She put out her hand. Lance took it, and because it was painfully cold, he folded it between both of his. A stillness came over him. The chatter and bustle from the hall faded out. Time began to slip past, only the shift of the leaf-shadowed firelight to pick out one moment from the next. He closed his eyes, and even that demarcation was gone.

Guen began to speak, low and soft. Her voice seemed to come from inside his head. If he opened his mouth, her words would form on his own tongue. "Listen, Lance. Soon these memories too will fade, and I'll be mortal flesh, a leaf on the stream just like you. When you took my power, slew the dragon with your kiss, you took the force of the ocean and poured it into a narrow little glass." Her grip tightened on his hand. "This body is weak. It sways and changes with the moon. Insatiable hungers go through it like fire. The dragon understands what she must do, but Guenyvre—all Guen feels is the force of her own desire. Take her back, Lance! Let her be part of the earth and the dragon again."

"How can I?"

"You and she are one."

"I don't understand."

"Oh, God. You must. Feel her hand. You don't even know which of the fingers are yours and which are hers."

It was true. He opened his eyes. She had slithered off her stool and was kneeling in front of him. An eerie green glow was fading from her irises. She was just a distraught girl. She tore her hand free, flung her arms around his neck and began to kiss him fiercely, almost biting, as if she were trying to gnaw her way into his skin or out of her own. He gave a cry of fear: grabbed the hair at the back of her neck to pull her away, but to do her violence was beyond him.

The curtain of ivy swept back. Guenyvre froze in his arms. There stood the child Aedilthryd, a goblet of steaming liquid on a bronze tray in her hands, a stone water bottle hitched to her leather belt. Her face was devoid of expression. Her pale eyes glittered like frost. Behind her—so close that she must have summoned them, brought them, lured them here with God only knew what words—stood Drustan, Bors, and all three of the brothers from the Northern Isles. And stumbling up in their wake, pale with horror, only an instant but fatally too late, Guy and Coel.

Guy shoved his way to the front. He turned on the others like an enraged bear. "Get out of this, all of you! Get away." He swung round to stare at Lance and Guen. Tears were streaming down his face. "Ah, no, Lance. Not *you*."

Chapter Twenty

Two guards stopped Lance at the door with crossed staves. He stepped back, the momentum of his run recoiling upon him. He knew the men. They part of Coel's household: kindly, efficient, ordinary. They were looking at his feet, the air over his head, anything rather than meet his gaze. "Please," Lance said. "I have to see him."

"He's in conference with the Merlin, sire. No-one is to disturb him." The guard made another inspection of Lance's boots. "I'm sorry."

The passageway outside the debating hall was draughty. Two alcoves had been set into the walls to allow the night-watch some shelter. Lance made his way to the nearest and sank down on the bench. He could have dispatched Coel's guards with one hand tied behind his back, but first he had to recoup his strength. Tremors were running through him, as if he and not poor Guen had been poured out of a vast dragon form and into a weak, cracked vessel. He drew one knee up to his chest. If he opened his mouth, nothing would come out of it except the name of his king—in rage, love, supplication, louder and louder until he brought the house down. He pressed his lips to the back of his hand.

"He'd do better to consult with me than that heathen sorcerer."

The niche across the way was occupied. Lance hadn't seen the priest huddled there. He blended with the stonework in his grey-brown robes. Lance had nothing against the lad, who looked as if he had the weight of the world on his shoulders and no friendly earth on which to set it down. Suddenly, vividly, Lance remembered Father Tomas from Vindolanda, the human warmth that had underlain the old man's bitterness. "Good morning," he said, as civilly as he could. "The Merlin has always guided the king. But Arthur will listen to anyone who comes in good faith to advise him."

The priest stared. Unlike the guards, he had no difficulty in meeting Lance's eyes, and he did so coldly. "Good faith? Those words should burn your mouth."

Lance uncurled. His hand was on the hilt of his sword before he could collect himself. "Your cloth protects you," he growled. "If a man spoke to me so, he'd repent his words at the tip of this blade."

"I am but a poor soldier of Christ, Sir Lancelot. I need no sword. You, however, are in sore want of repentance. Make your confession to me now, on this morning which is the day of our saviour's birth! Your weak flesh has betrayed you, but your soul may yet be saved."

Lance subsided onto the bench. The priest's words were like a lead-weighted mesh. He'd thrown them well. Lance owed his confession to no-one but Art, but how easily the will could be drained from the weary and the sorrowful by such promises! *Tell me, and in the name of God I'll absolve you. I'll take your crime away.*

Nothing could do that. An old, bloody-minded instinct stirred in Lance, born of all the debates with Tomas by the Vindolanda fireside at night. "My soul and my weak, damned flesh are one and the same thing, priest. You can't pull me out like a winkle from a shell. It's not that easy—for either of us. And..." He paused, pushing a hand through his hair. "Since when did the solstice mark the birth of your god? I grew up with a Christian priest, and he'd come to our bonfires because he liked the warmth and all the food. But he never made such a claim."

"You come from the wild moors. Your priest can have been little more than a farmhand."

"On the contrary, he'd served at the shrine at Brocolitia, after Emperor Theodosius ordered the temple of Mithras there destroyed. As he constantly reminded us."

"He was right to keep such honourable service in your minds. But he cannot have received the teaching from Rome that Christ was conceived at spring equinox, which fixes his birth at..."

"Winter solstice. Yes, I see. My father was a Roman soldier, and he and his comrades welcomed back the unconquered sun at this time, once the darkest night was done."

"My teachers have warned me against such comparisons. Mithras, *Sol Invictus*—these are ancient demons, sent from the past to tempt men into their former bad ways. *Christos* is the only true child of the light reborn."

Lance considered this. He was miserable enough that an argument—with anyone, about anything—felt like a blessed distraction. And poor Tomas had long ago thrown away his chances of creating a blind follower by teaching him—however reluctantly—to read. "I know a tale," he said quietly, settling back onto the bench, "of a god who came to the earth in the form of a human child. The prophets who'd expected him called him the word-made-flesh, the son of man."

"Be careful what you say, sire. Take care not to blaspheme."

"The child taught in the temple when he was twelve summers old, and his elders listened. He was baptized in the river Iarutana, which the Hebrews call Jordan, by a helper named Anup—Iochanan in their language, John in ours. And this Anup the baptist was slain, beheaded by their enemies. This god-child grew up—was put to death, and reborn at the equinox of spring."

"You will tell me this is the story of one of your father's demon gods, Ahura Mazda, Mithras or—"

"Neither. It's the story of Osiris, who was ancient in the land of Egypt before Persian Mithras ever thought to slay his bull. Osiris was called *the anointed one*, and his story came to us through the Greeks, who translate that title as *Christos*." He sat up, words coming to him with unaccustomed ease, as if Viviana herself had found her way inside him, or the ancient dragon's fire. "Listen to me, priest. All faiths borrow and build upon what went before. Teach the people what you like. Lead whoever will follow you. But don't steal their gods and their legends, *then* turn upon them with cries of blasphemy for worshipping in their own old ways."

The priest drew breath to reply. Lance wanted to close his eyes. This new faith would never allow the elder ones the last word. The day was lost, he knew, the lamps of learning being pinched out, snuffed or suffocated all over the dragon's isle. And now that his burst of energy was past, he no longer cared.

The priest was staring at the doors to the hall. They had drifted open silently, as if pushed wide by the breeze. The guards, staves crossed again on the off-chance, were gazing anxiously inside. Lance picked up a trace of ozone in the air. One of the guards leaned into the hall, listening. After a moment he turned. "You're to go in, Lancelot, sire. His Majesty is waiting."

***

Had the veil been parted to the future? Lance stood in the great vacant hall, its benches bare, its echoes returning with the distant flutter of the doves taking refuge in its rafters from the cruel sea wind. Arthur was alone. He was seated in the throne Coel had placed centrally to honour him, and he looked like a war-weary chieftain of forty summers or more. In decades to come, when battles and loss had worn out the youth from him, this was the face the men and women who loved him would see—hollowed beneath the eyes and cheekbones, pared down to unbearable beauty. After rage and sorrow had passed, and only gentleness remained... "Lance," he said. "I knew you'd be there."

"How did you know?"

"Where else would you be on a day of upheaval like this? I hope you'll always come and find me at such times."

"I'd have come sooner, but the guard said you were with the Merlin. Where is he?"

"Gone. Completely, in the same way he did when we met him on the stairs that night—with that popping sound, and the smell of copper and the sea—and I pretended not to notice. I think you were right, Lance—I don't think this one *was* the same as the one in my visions and dreams, or even the one Ector thought he remembered. He was dying, and he wanted me to go on having a father. Any old man who'd turned up then would've probably got the job."

"Oh, Art. Whoever he was—did he say anything to help you before he disappeared?"

"He said he'd done all that he could. That things hadn't turned out as he'd planned, but events had been set in motion, and I had to make the best of it." He shrugged tiredly. "I never did understand him. Come and sit with me, please—here at my right hand, where you've always belonged."

315

Lance approached him slowly. He'd have given anything to obey—to take what Art was offering, as blindly as it was being given. But there was only one place where Lance belonged now. He came to a halt in front of the throne. Then he sank to his knees at Arthur's feet. He buried his face in Art's robe, and for the first time since his childhood, began to weep.

Arthur leaned over him. He stroked Lance's hair: swept it aside, and the warmth of his mouth descended on his nape. "Dear Lance. Please don't."

"Send me away, my liege lord!" Lance made a massive effort for control. "Send me to where I can serve you. Or, if I can't— weak and useless as I am—I will go back to Vindolanda."

"You *are* wanting in health, love. Who knows what poison was on Garbonian's blade? That's why you're prey to… to morbid fancies."

"Fancies?" Lance didn't want to let Art draw his face up, but the tender, lifting fingertips were irresistible. "My waking world is sorrow enough to me. I have no fancies, morbid or otherwise."

"Yes, you do. The whole court is distempered. Otherwise, the things they've seen—the things they've come rushing like children to tell me—couldn't be."

"Oh, God. Don't. None of it happened for the reasons they believe, but… I have to leave here, for your sake and for hers."

"The next soul who breathes a shadow upon either of your names, I'll put to the sword. I've told them so." He gave Lance the ghost of a smile. "They can't say they weren't warned."

"What will happen to Guen?"

"She'll be honoured as befits my future queen. And, in the fullness of time, if she consents… she'll marry me, as the Merlin foretold." He stopped Lance's protest with a cobweb touch to his mouth. "I *will* send you away, if that's what you truly want. You'll go down to Camelet, where it's warmer, and my people can take care of you. You'll get better."

"No, Art."

"And… when the spring comes, I will join you there."

They sat in stillness. Through the windows to the east, the first light of the newborn sun began to disperse the clouds. At last Arthur shifted, just enough to let Lance huddle more closely between his knees. "I'm glad," he said, "that I decided to ignore you when you said our Jol gifts should be modest."

"What've you done?"

"She's in the stable next to Balana's—Roman-bred, used to combat, fast and strong. She'll be a fine ride for your journey to Cam. You'll have armed guards to protect you, and a groom to lead Balana on a rein."

Lance eased back onto his heels. His head was pounding, his vision blurred. He took out the leather pouch from the pocket of his jerkin. "My gift to you seems a poor thing now."

"Nothing from you could be poor. Let me see."

The blacksmith had followed Lance's instructions well. He'd fashioned a piece of rich raw gold into the shape of a sun, rays flaring brightly. On the other side of the solar disc, he'd hammered a crescent of silver, so that—as on clear summer twilights at White Meadows—the new moon seemed to lie in the arms of the old. "The chain is strong," Lance said hoarsely, as Art took the pendant from him and turned it over in the light. "But one link is meant to break if anyone pulls on it hard. Because…"

Art nodded. "Because there's nothing worse than being throttled in a fight by your own jewellery. Fasten it on me, Lance. No-one—not priest, not prophet—will take it from me, not until you do it with your own hands."

"When you come to join me in spring."

"Yes."

Tenderly Lance reached up and hooked the bronze catch into place. Arthur picked up the disc and pressed his mouth to it—the sun and then the moon, and then Lance's upturned face. "Don't grieve anymore," he said, as his tears splashed onto Lance's hands and the ancient flagstones of Joyous Gard. "Don't grieve. Spring will come."

Epilogue

As for Prince Garb: he survived. He didn't take up with the Anglian pirates. They would have laughed, he knew, at so puny a creature as he, and despised him for his treachery even while they profited by it. Instead he ran deep into the moorlands of Bryneich. His mother had relatives in the villages who would harbour him.

He hid, and he watched and he waited. He saw his father march off north to his last war, taking with him the standing army of Din Guardi. A well-drilled regiment of King Arthur's troops took their place, and went efficiently about their business. After a month or so, in the coldest part of the year, he saw a weary crowd of travellers arrive from the west—women, children, carts piled high with household goods, as if somewhere a whole town had been emptied and transplanted here. A fair-haired man rode at their head, his bearing noble despite his ragged clothes. They gathered outside the Din Guardi walls, and then the gates opened, and they all were taken in.

Shortly after that, when the days were beginning to lengthen, festivities shook the grim old fortress, and Garbonian heard from a source among the kitchen staff that a great wedding had happened there.

Then news came from the south of terrible Saxon incursions, and Arthur's army marched. Garbonian had no doubt that his father's new heir, Lance of Vindolanda, would find whatever battlefield it was and meet them there.

Arthur left the fort amply garrisoned, but Garb watched, and bided his time. Men like Lance, who rode bravely, flags flying, never lasted long. Down among the grasses like a snake, like a toad beneath a stone, Garb could endure indefinitely, passive and unnoticed. Din Guardi would be his again. He knew he could outlive King Arthur's one good lance.

About the Author

Harper Fox is the author of many critically acclaimed M/M Romance novels, including Stonewall Book Award-nominated *Scrap Metal.* To find out more about Harper and see updates on her current writing projects, please visit www.harperfox.net